A Garland Series

Foundations of the Novel

Representative Early

Eighteenth-Century Fiction

A collection of 100 rare titles
reprinted in photo-facsimile in 71 volumes

Foundations of the Novel

compiled and edited by

Michael F. Shugrue
Secretary for English for the M.L.A.

with New Introductions for each volume by

Michael Shugrue, *City College of C.U.N.Y.*
Malcolm J. Bosse, *City College of C.U.N.Y.*
William Graves, *N.Y. Institute of Technology*

The
Consolidator

or Memoirs
of Sundry Transactions
from the
World in the Moon

by

Daniel Defoe

with a new introduction
for the Garland Edition by
Malcolm J. Bosse

Garland Publishing, Inc., New York & London

1972

The new introduction for the

Garland *Foundations of the Novel* Edition

is Copyright © 1972, by

Garland Publishing, Inc., New York & London

All Rights Reserved

Bibliographical note:
*This facsimile has been made from a copy in the
Beinecke Library of Yale University*
(IK D362 705i)

Library of Congress Cataloging in Publication Data

Defoe, Daniel, 1661?-1731.
  The consolidator.

  (Foundations of the novel)
  Reprint of the 1705 ed.
  I. Title. II. Series.
PZ3.D362Co6 [PR3404]   823'.5   75-170513
ISBN 0-8240-0521-X

Printed in the United States of America

Introduction

The title page of The Consolidator *announces that this work is by "the Author of the* True-born English Man." *Defoe calls attention to the long poem he had written in 1701 during the public outcry against King William's foreign policy and preference for his Dutch compatriots. The poem in defense of racial and religious tolerance had brought Defoe the king's friendship and plunged the writer even more deeply into the political life of the day. In* The Consolidator *Defoe continues his defense of a strong anti-French policy, discusses at length the War of the Spanish Succession, describes the religious and political controversy that landed him in the pillory, and boldly outlines a plan for the harassed Dissenters to gain economic power that will protect them against their enemies. All of these matters are placed in the fictional framework of an imaginary voyage to the moon, whose customs and politics clearly reflect those of England.*

The unidentified narrator is an inquisitive traveler who wastes no time telling us who he is; his account begins with a short travelog through Russia, then through China, whose people he calls "Ancient, Wise, Polite, and most Ingenious" (p.4). Among them he meets a learned projector who has built a machine for flying to the moon. This contraption, made of feathers,

5

INTRODUCTION

is described in great detail by the narrator, who, as a forerunner of Robinson Crusoe, is a meticulous gatherer of facts. Soon it is apparent that the consolidating machine corresponds to the English House of Commons:

> *Nor are these common Feathers, but they are pickt and cull'd out of all parts of the Lunar Country, by the Command of the Prince; and every Province sends up the best they can find,* or ought to do so at least. . . *(p. 38).*

Once the allegory begins, Defoe concedes little to the demands of storytelling. The voyage to the moon is uneventful; indeed, the traveler sleeps all the way there and soon finds lunar life much as it is on earth. He meets the Man in the Moon who gives him a spyglass through which he views "the State of the War among Nations" (p. 76). In the succeeding polemic Defoe blames King William's arch-enemy Louis XIV for Europe's troubles and castigates those princes who, like the Duke of Savoy, shift their allegiance according to the fortunes of war. The moon-visitor then discovers the Cogitator, a thinking machine, into which men are strapped so they may think clearly. Defoe enumerates a number of mistakes that would have been avoided in recent European history had great personages been given a chance to sit in this "Chair of Reflection." Yet another lunar machine, the Elevator, enables the narrator's mind to range far and wide in its fancy. Helped by this device to see clearly, he turns to the affairs of Ireland, Scotland, and England. Defoe's prose

INTRODUCTION

takes on a biting eloquence as he admonishes England for crippling the trade of Ireland and sapping the economic strength of an entire people. The major problem of Scotland in Defoe's opinion is religious; he deplores the conflict within the protestant movement that keeps England and Scotland apart. The allegory then focuses on English church affairs, particularly on the Occasional Conformity Bill which had the Solunarians (Anglicans) and the Crolians (Dissenters) locked in furious debate during the year of 1702. Defoe describes vividly the fever of the time, when Sacheverell's zealous High Church sermons lashed the Tories into a mood of fear and anger against the Dissenters. He gives an explicit account of his own part in the controversy when his satiric pamphlet, The Shortest Way with the Dissenters *(1702), which ironically called for violent suppression of the Dissenters, drew an outcry from both High Tory and Dissenter. Sought for libel by the Earl of Nottingham, a High Tory called "the Great Scribe of the Country" (p. 212) in this account, the fugitive Defoe was finally caught and severely questioned. His harsh sentence of three days in the pillory was modified by the people themselves, who strewed flowers in his way and drank his health. Although the bill he fought against was defeated in the House of Lords, Defoe expatiates ruefully on the misinterpretation of his satire by people of his own persuasion. As if to insure that such a mistake will never reoccur, Defoe lectures his readers on the meaning of satire:*

INTRODUCTION

The Discovery being made, People ever since understand him that when he talks of the Dissenters Associations, Murthers, Persecutions, and the like, he means that his Readers should look back to the Murthers, Oppressions and Persecutions they had suffered for several past years, and the Associations that were now forming to bring them into the same Condition again (p. 224).

Defoe continues his treatment of the religious problem with the bold suggestion that Dissenters of the trading class can effect changes in their situation by uniting economically. By pooling resources, by creating their own banks and systems of credit, they can virtually control the nation's economy and thereby win concessions from the government. In Defoe *(1937), James Sutherland points out, "It was this sort of suggestion, so full of alarming possibilities, that made Defoe something of a bogey to his political and religious opponents" (p. 143).*

Once again in the narrative Defoe turns to the War of the Spanish Succession, tracing its inception from the partition treaties through the death of Charles II and his will that left Spain to Philip of Anjou, grandson of Louis XIV. With apparent relish Defoe handles the claims and counterclaims that characterized the jockeying for power between France and the coalition of England, Austria, Holland, Denmark, and Portugal. Defoe's readers, who were still living through the war, would scarcely have needed a key to recognize the following people involved in the conflict:

8

INTRODUCTION

Louis XIV of France — King of Gallunaria
Charles II of Spain — Late King of Ebronia
Leopold I, Holy Roman Emperor — The Eagle
Joseph I, King of Hungary — Eldest Son of the Eagle
Archduke Charles — Second Son of the Eagle
Philip of Anjou — Grandson of the Gallunarian Monarch
The Hapsburg Family — Men of the Great Lip
The English — Solunarians
The Dutch — Mogenites

Displaying that practical turn of mind which in fiction would have its fullest exercise in the portrayal of Robinson Crusoe, Defoe concludes that for England and Holland the war is essentially a fight for trade routes.

After a look at parliamentary politics, his own views coinciding with those of the moderate Tories led by Robert Harley, Defoe makes a half-hearted return to the concept of a moon voyage. The main thrust of The Consolidator, *however, is political, and after the opening pages in which a rudimentary sort of narrative framework has been established, Defoe devotes his energies to opinions which he strongly held on vital issues of the day. The writer of the later novels is seen intermittently here in flashes of vigorous prose, in mastery of detail, and in a clear-eyed respect for the realities of life lived in trade and for God.*

Malcolm J. Bosse

9

THE
CONSOLIDATOR:
OR,
MEMOIRS
OF
Sundry Transactions

FROM THE

World in the Moon.

Translated from the Lunar
LANGUAGE,

By the AUTHOR of
The True-born English Man.

LONDON:
Printed, and are to be Sold by *Benj. Bragg*
at the *Blue Ball* in *Ave-mary-lane,* 1705.

THE

Confolidator, &c.

IT Cannot be unknown to any that have travell'd into the Dominions of the Czar of *Mufcovy*, that this famous rifing Monarch, having ftudied all Methods for the Encreafe of his Power, and the Enriching as well as Polifhing his Subjects, has travell'd through moft part of *Europe*, and vifited the Courts of the greateft Princes; from whence, by his own Obfervation, as well as by carrying with him Artifts in moft ufeful Knowledge, he has tranfmitted moft of our General Practice, efpecially in War and Trade, to his own Unpolite People; and the Effects of this Curiofity of his are exceeding vifible in his prefent Proceedings; for by the Improvements he obtained in his *European* Travels, he has Modell'd his Armies, form'd new Fleets, fettled Foreign Negoce in feveral remote Parts of the World; and we now fee

B   his

his Forces befieging ftrong Towns, with
regular Approaches ; and his Engineers
raifing Batteries, throwing Bombs, &c.
like other Nations ; whereas before, they
had nothing of Order among them, but
carried all by *Ouflaught* and *Scalado*,
wherein they either prevailed by the
Force of Irrefiftible Multitude, or were
Slaughter'd by heaps, and left the Ditches
of their Enemies fill'd with their Dead
Bodies.

We fee their Armies now form'd into
regular Battalions ; and their *Strelitz Muf-
queteers*, a People equivalent to the *Turks
Janizaries* , cloath'd like our Guards ,
firing in Platoons, and behaving themfelves wirh extraordinary Bravery and
Order.

We fee their Ships now compleatly
fitted, built and furnifh'd, by the *Englifh*
and *Dutch* Artifts, and their Men of War
Cruize in the *Baltick*. Their New City
of *Petersburgh* built by the prefent Czar,
begins now to look like our *Portfmouth*,
fitted with Wet and Dry Docks, Store-
houfes, and Magazines of Naval Preparations,. vaft and Incredible ; which may
serve

ferve to remind us, how we once taught
the *French* to build Ships, till they are
grown able to teach us how to ufe
them.

As to Trade, our large Fleets to *Arch-
Angel* may fpeak for it, where we now
fend 100 Sail yearly, inftead of 8 or 9,
which were the greateft number we ever
fent before ; and the Importation of To-
baccoes from *England* into his Dominions,
would ftill increafe the Trade thither, was
not the Covetoufnefs of our own Merchants the Obftruction of their Advantages. But all this by the by.

As this great Monarch has Improved
his Country, by introducing the Manners
and Cuftoms of the Politer Nations of *Europe* ; fo, with Indefatigable Induftry, he
has fettled a new, but conftant Trade,
between his Country and *China*, by Land ;
where his Carravans go twice or thrice a
Year, as Numerous almoft, and as ftrong,
as thofe from *Egypt* to *Perfia :* Nor is the
Way fhorter, or the Defarts they pafs
over lefs wild and uninhabitable, only
that they are not fo fubject to Flouds of
Sand, *if that Term be proper,* or to Troops

of *Arabs*, to deſtroy them by the way ;
for this powerful Prince, to make this
terrible Journey feazible to his Subjeċts,
has built Forts, planted Collonies and
Gariſons at proper Diſtances ; where,
though they are ſeated in Countries intirely Barren, and among uninhabited
Rocks and Sands ; yet, by his continual
furniſhing them from his own Stores, the
Merchants travelling are reliev'd on good
Terms, and meet both with Convoy and
Refreſhment.

More might be ſaid of the admirable
Decorations of this Journey, and how ſo
prodigious an Attempt is made eaſy ; ſo
that now they have an exaċt Correſpondence, and drive a prodigious Trade between *Muſcow* and *Tonquin* ; but having
a longer Voyage in Hand, I ſhall not de-
tain the Reader, nor keep him till he
grows too big with Expeċtation.

Now, as all Men know the *Chineſes*
are an Ancient, Wiſe, Polite, and moſt
Ingenious People ; ſo the *Muſcovites* begun to reap the Benefit of this open
Trade ; and not only to grow exceeding
Rich by the bartering for all the Wealth
of

of thofe Eaftern Countries ; but to polifh
and refine their Cuftoms and Manners, as
much on that fide as they have from their
European Improvements on this.

And as the *Chinefes* have many forts
of Learning which thefe Parts of the
World never heard of, fo all thofe ufeful
Inventions which we admire our felves fo
much for, are vulgar and common with
them, and were in ufe long before our
Parts of the World were Inhabited. Thus
Gun-powder, *Printing*, and the ufe of the
Magnet and *Compafs*, which we call Modern Inventions, are not only far from
being Inventions, but fall fo far fhort of
the Perfection of Art they have attained
to, that it is hardly Credible, what wonderful things we are told of from thence,
and all the Voyages the Author has made
thither being imploy'd another way, have
not yet furnifh'd him with the Particulars
fully enough to tranfmit them to view ; net
but that he is preparing a Scheme of all
thofe excellent Arts thofe Nations are
Mafters of, for puhlick View, by way of
Detection of the monftrous Ignorance
and Deficiencies of *European* Science ;
which may ferve as a *Lexicon Technicum*

for

for this prefent Age, with ufeful Diagrams for that purpofe ; wherein I fhall
not fail to acqaint the World, 1. With
the Art of *Gunnery*, as Practis'd in *China*
long before the War of the *Giants*, and
by which thofe Prefumptuous Animals
fired Red-hot Bullets right up into Heaven, and made a Breach fufficient to encourage them to a General Storm ; but
being Repulfed with great Slaughter, they
gave over the Siege for that time. This
memorable part of Hiftory fhall be a
faithful Abridgement of *Ibra chizra-le-*
peglizar, *Hiftoriagrapher-Royal* to the Emperor of *China*, who wrote *Anno Mundi*
114. his Volumes extant, in the Publick
Library at *Tonquin*, Printed in Leaves of
Vitrify'd Diamond, by an admirable
Dexterity, ftruck all at an oblique Motion, the Engine remaining intire, and
ftill fit for ufe, in the Chamber of the
Emperor's Rarities.

And here I fhall give you a Draft of
the Engine it felf, and a Plan of its Operation, and the wonderful Dexterity of
its Performance.

If

If thefe Labours of mine fhall prove
fuccefsful, I may in my next Journey that
way, take an Abftract of their moft admirable Tracts in Navigation, and the
Myfteries of *Chinefe* Mathematicks ; which
out-do all Modern Invention at that
Rate, that 'tis Inconceivable : In this E-
laborate Work I muft run thro' the 365
Volumes of *Augro-wachi-lanquaro zi*, the
moft ancient Mathematician in all *China* :
From thence I fhall give a Defcription
of a Fleet of Ships of 100000 Sail, built
at the Expence of the Emperor *Tangro*
the 15th ; who having Notice of the General Deluge, prepar'd thefe Veffels, to
every City and Town in his Dominions
One, and in Bulk proportion'd to the
number of its Inhabitants ; into which
Veffel all the People, with fuch Movea-
bles as they thought fit to fave, and with
120 Days Provifions, were receiv'd at the
time of the Floud ; and the reft of their
Goods being put into great Veffels made
of *China* Ware, and faft luted down on
the top, were preferv'd unhurt by the
Water : Thefe Ships they furnifh'd with
600 Fathom of Chain inftead of Cables ;
which being faftned by wonderful Arts

B 4   to

to the Earth, every Veffel rid out the
Deluge juft at the Town's end ; fo that
when the Waters abated, the People had
nothing to do, but to open the Doors
made in the Ship-fides, and come out,
repair their Houfes, open the great *China*
Pots their Goods were in, and fo put
themfelves in *Statu Quo.*

The Draft of one of thefe Ships I may
perhaps obtain by my Intereft in the prefent Emperor's Court, as it has been preferv'd ever fince, and conftantly repair'd,
riding at Anchor in a great Lake, about
100 Miles from *Tonquin* ; in which all
the People of that City were preferv'd,
amounting by their Computation to about
a Million and half.

And as thefe things muft be very ufeful
in thefe Parts, to abate the Pride and
Arrogance of our Modern Undertakers of
great Enterprizes, Authors of ftrange Foreign Accounts, Philofophical Tranfactions, and the like ; if Time and Opportunity permit, I may let them know, how
Infinitely we are out-done by thofe refi-
ned Nations, in all manner of Mechanick
Improvements and Arts ; and in difcour-
fing

sing of this, it will necessarily come in
my way to speak of a most Noble Invention, being an Engine I would recommend to all People to whom *'tis necessary
to have a good Memory* ; and which I design, if possible, to obtain a Draft of,
that it may be Erected in our Royal Societies Laboratory : It has the wonder-
fullest Operations in the World : One
part of it furnishes a Man of Business to
dispatch his Affairs strangely ; for if he
be a Merchant, he shall write his Letters
with one Hand, and Copy them with the
other ; if he is posting his Books, he
shall post the Debtor side with one Hand,
and the Creditor with the other; if he be
a Lawyer, he draws his Drafts with one
Hand, and Ingrosses them with the other.

Another part of it furnishes him with
such an Expeditious way of Writing, or
Transcribing, that a Man cannot speak
so fast, but he that hears shall have it
down in Writing before 'tis spoken ;
and a Preacher shall deliver himself to his
Auditory, and having this Engine before
him, shall put down every thing he says
in Writing at the same time; and so exactly is this Engine squar'd by Lines and
Rules,

Rules, that it does not require him that
Writes to keep his Eye upon it.

I am told, in some Parts of *China*, they
had arriv'd to such a Perfection of Knowledge, as to underſtand one anothers
Thoughts ; and that it was found to be
an excellent Preſervative to humane Society, againſt all ſorts of Frauds, Cheats,
Sharping, and many Thouſand *European*
Inventions of that Nature, *at which only
we can be ſaid to out-do thoſe Nations.*

I confeſs, I have not yet had leiſure to
travel thoſe Parts, having been diverted by an accidental Opportunity of a
new Voyage I had occaſion to make for
farther Diſcoveries, and which the Plea-
ſure and Uſefulneſs thereof having been
very great, I have omitted the other for
the preſent, but ſhall not fail to make a
Viſit to thoſe Parts the firſt Opportunity,
and ſhall give my Country-men the beſt
Account I can of thoſe things ; for I
doubt not in Time to bring our Nation,
ſo fam'd for improving other People's
Diſcoveries, to be as wiſe as any of thoſe
Heathen Nations ; I wiſh I had the ſame
Proſpect of making them half ſo honeſt.

I

I had fpent but a few Months in this
Country, but my fearch after the Prodigy
of humane Knowledge the People a-
bounds with, led me into Acquaintance
with fome of their principal Artifts, Engineers, and Men of Letters ; and I was
aftonifh'd at every Day's Difcovery of
new and of unheard-of Worlds of Learning ; but I Improv'd in the Superficial
Knowledge of their General, by no body
fo much as by my Converfation with the
Library-keeper of *Tonquin*, by whom I
had Admiffion into the vaft Collection of
Books, which the Emperors of that Country have treafur'd up.

It would be endlefs to give you a Ca-
talogue, and they admit of no Strangers
to write any thing down, but what the
Memory can retain, you are welcome to
carry away with you ; and amongft the
wonderful Volumes of Antient and Modern Learning, I could not but take Notice of a few ; which, befides thofe I
mentioned before, I faw, when I lookt
over this vaft Collection ; and a larger
Account may be given in our next.

It

It would be needlefs to Tranfcribe the *Chinefe* Charaĉter, or to put their Alphabet into our Letters, becaufe the Words would be both Unintelligible, and very hard to Pronounce ; and therefore, to avoid hard Words, and Hyroglyphicks, I'll tranflate them as well as I can.

The firft Clafs I came to of Books, was the Conftitutions of the Empire`; thefe are vaft great Volumes, and have a fort of Engine like our *Magna Charta*, to remove 'em, and with placing them in a Frame, by turning a Screw, open'd the Leaves, and folded them this way, or that, as the Reader defires. It was prefent Death for the Library-keeper to refufe the meaneft *Chinefe* Subjeĉt to come in and read them; for 'tis their Maxim, *That all People ought to know the Laws by which they are to be govern'd* ; and as above all People, we find no Fools in this Country, fo the Emperors, though they feem to be Arbitrary, enjoy the greateft Authority in the World, by always obferving, with the greateft Exaĉtnefs, the *Paĉta Conventa* of their Government : From thefe Principles it is impoffible we fhould ever hear, either

of

of the Tyranny of Princes, or Rebellion of Subjects, in all their Histories.

At the Entrance into this Class, you find some Ancient Comments, upon the Constitution of the Empire, written many Ages before we pretend the World began; but above all, One I took particular notice of, which might bear this Title, *Natural Right prov'd Superior to Temporal Power*; wherein the old Author proves, the *Chinese* Emperors were Originally made so, by Nature's directing the People, to place the Power of Government in the most worthy Person they could find; and the Author giving a most exact History of 2000 Emperors, brings them into about 35 or 36 Periods of Lines when the Race ended; and when a Collective Assembly of the Nobles, Cities, and People, Nominated a new Family to the Goverment.

This being an heretical Book as to *European* Politicks, and our Learned Authors having long since exploded this Doctrine, and prov'd that Kings and Emperors came down from Heaven with Crowns on their Heads, and all their Subjects

jeƈts were born with Saddles on their
Backs; I thought fit to leave it where I
found it, leaſt our excellent Traƈts of Sir
Robert Filmer, Dr. *Hammond*, L...y, S....l,
and Others, who have ſo learnedly treated of the more uſeful Doƈtrine of Paſſive
Obedience, Divine Right, *&c.* ſhould be
blaſphem'd by the Mob, grow into Contempt of the People; and they ſhould
take upon them to queſtion their Supe-
riors for the Blood of *Algernon Sidney*,
and *Argyle*.

For I take the Doƈtrines of Paſſive O-
bedience, *&c.* among the States-men, to
be like the Copernican Syſtem of the
Earths Motion among Philoſophers;
which, though it be contrary to all antient Knowledge, and not capable of
Demonſtration, yet is adher'd to in general, becauſe by this they can better ſolve,
and give a more rational Account of ſeveral dark Phænomena in Nature, than
they could before.

Thus our Modern States-men approve
of this Scheme of Government; not that
it admits of any rational Defence, much
leſs of Demonſtration, but becauſe by
this

this Method they can the better explain, as well as defend, all Coertion in
Cafes invafive of Natural Right, than they
could before.

Here I found two famous Volumes in
Chyrurgery, being an exact Defcription of
the Circulation of the Blood, difcovered
long before King *Solomon*'s Allegory of
the Bucket's going to the Well ; with feveral curious Methods by which the Demonftration was to be made fo plain, as
would make even the worthy Doctor
B----- himfelf become a Convert to his
own Eye-fight, make him damn his own
Elaborate Book, and think it worfe Nonfence than ever the Town had the Freedom to Imagine.

All our Philofophers are Fools, and
their Tranfactions a parcel of empty Stuff,
to the Experiments of the Royal Societies
in this Country. Here I came to a Learned Tract of Winds, which outdoes even
the Sacred Text, and would make us believe it was not wrote to thofe People ;
for they tell Folks whence it comes, and
whither it goes. There you have an
Account how to make Glaffes of Hogs
Eyes,

Eyes, that can fee the Wind; and they give ftrange Accounts both of its regular and irregular Motions, its Compofitions and Quantities; from whence, by a fort of Algebra, they can caft up its Duration, Violence, and Extent : In thefe Calculations, fome fay, thofe Authors have been fo exact, that they can, as our Philofophers fay of Comets, ftate their Revolutions, and tell us how many Storms there fhall happen to any Period of time, and when; and perhaps this may be with much about the fame Truth.

It was a certain Sign *Ariftotle* had never been at *China*; for, had he feen the 216th Volume of the *Chinefe* Navigation, in the Library I am fpeaking of, a large Book in Double Folio, wrote by the Famous *Mira-cho-cho-lafmo*, Vice-Admiral of *China*, and faid to be printed there about 2000 Years before the Deluge, in the Chapter of Tides he would have feen the Reafon of all the certain and uncertain Fluxes and Refluxes of that Element, how the exact Pace is kept between the Moon and the Tides, with a moft elaborate Difcourfe there, of the Power of Sympa-

Sympathy, and the manner how the heavenly Bodies Influence the Earthly : Had he feen this, the *Stagyrite* would never have Drowned himfelf, becaufe he could not comprehend this Myftery.

'Tis farther related of this Famous Author, that he was no Native of this World, but was Born in the *Moon*, and coming hither to make Difcoveries, by a ftrange Invention arrived to by the *Virtuofoes* of that habitable World, the Emperor of *China* prevailed with him to ftay and improve his Subjects, in the moft exquifite Accomplifhments of thofe *Lunar* Regions ; and no wonder the *Chinefe* are fuch exquifite Artifts, and Mafters of fuch fublime Knowledge, when this Famous Author has bleft them with fuch unaccountable Methods of Improvement.

There was abundance of vaft Claffes full of the Works of this wonderful Philofopher : He gave the *how*, the *modus* of all the fecret Operations of Nature ; and told us, how Senfation is convey'd to and from the Brain ; why Refpiration preferves Life ; and how Locomotion is directed to, as well as perform'd by the

C   Parts,

Parts. There are fome Anatomical Dif-
fections of Thought, and a Mathematical
Defcription of Nature's ftrong Box, the
Memory, with all its Locks and Keys.

There you have that part of the Head
turn'd in-fide outward, in which Nature
has placed the Materials of reflecting ;
and like a *Glafs Bee-hive*, reprefents to
you all the feveral Cells in which are
lodg'd things paft, even back to Infancy
and Conception. There you have the
Repofitory, with all its Cells, Claffically,
Annually, Numerically, and Alphabeti-
cally Difpos'd. There you may fee how,
when the perplext Animal, on the lofs
of a Thought or Word, *fcratches his Pole :*
Every Attack of his Invading Fingers
knocks at Nature's Door, allarms all the
Regifter-keepers, and away they run,
unlock all the Claffes, fearch diligently
for what he calls for, and immediately
deliver it up to the Brain ; if it cannot
be found, they intreat a *little Patience,*
till they ftep into the *Revolvary*, where
they run over little Catalogues of the mi-
nuteft Paffages of Life, and fo in time never fail to hand on the thing; if not juft
when he calls for it, yet at fome other
time.   And

And thus, when a thing lyes very Abftrufe, and all the rumaging of the whole Houfe cannot find it ; nay, when all the People in the Houfe have given it over, they very often find one thing when they are looking for another.

Next you have the *Retentive* in the remoteft part of the Place, which, like the Records in the Tower, takes Poffeffion of all Matters, as they are removed from the Claffes in the Repofitory, for want of room. Thefe are carefully Lockt, and kept fafe, never to be open'd but upon folemn Occafions, and have fwinging great Bars and Bolts upon them ; fo that what is kept here, is feldom loft. Here *Confcience* has one large Ware-houfe, and the *Devil* another ; the firft is very feldom open'd, but has a Chink or Till, where all the Follies and Crimes of Life being minuted are dropt in ; but as the Man feldom cares to look in, the Locks are very Rufty, and not open'd but with great Difficulty, and on extraordinary Occafions, as Sicknefs, Afflictions, Jails, Cafualties, and Death ; and then the Bars all give way at once ; and being

preft

preft from within with a more than ordinary Weight, burft as a Cask of Wine
upon the Fret, which for want of Vent,
makes all the Hoops fly.

As for the *Devil's* Ware-houfe, he has
two conftant Warehoufe-keepers, *Pride*
and *Conceit*, and thefe are always at the
Door, fhowing their Wares, and expo-
fing the pretended Vertues and Accomplifhments of the Man, by way of Often-
tation.

In the middle of this curious part of
Nature, there is a clear Thorough-fare,
reprefenting the World, through which
fo many Thoufand People pafs fo eafily,
and do fo little worth taking notice of,
that 'tis for no manner of Signification to
leave Word they have been here. Thro'
this *Opening* pafs Millions of things not
worth remembring, and which the Regifter-Keepers, who ftand at the Doors
of the Claffes, as they go by, take no
notice of ; fuch as Friendfhips, helps in
Diftrefs, Kindneffes in Affliction, Volun-
tary Services, and all forts of Importu-
nate Merit ; things which being but Trifles in their own Nature, are made to be
forgotten.   **In**

In another Angle is to be feen the *Memory's Garden*, in which her moft pleafant things are not only Depofited, but Planted, Tranfplanted, Grafted, Inoculated, and obtain all poffible Propagation and Encreafe ; thefe are the moft pleafant, delightful, and agreeable things, call'd Envy, Slander, Revenge, Strife and Malice, with the Additions of Ill-turns, Reproaches, and all manner of Wrong ; thefe are careffed in the Cabinet of the *Memory*, with a World of Pleafure never let pafs, and carefully Cultivated with all imaginable Art.

There are multitudes of Weeds, Toys, Chat, Story, Fiction, and Lying, which in the great throng of paffant Affairs, ftop by the way, and crowding up the Place, leave no room for their Betters that come behind, which makes many a good Guefs be put by, and left to go clear thro' for want of Entertainment.

There are a multitude of things very curious and obfervable, concerning this little, but very accurate thing, called *Memory* ; but above all, I fee nothing fo

C 3   very

very curious, as the wonderful Art of *Wilful Forgetfulness* ; and as 'tis a thing, indeed, I never could find any Perſon compleatly Maſter of, it pleaſed me very much, to find this Author has made a large Eſſay, to prove there is really no ſuch Power in Nature ; and that the Pretenders to it are all Impoſtors, and put a Banter upon the World ; for that it is impoſſible for any Man to oblige himſelf to forget a thing, ſince he that can remember to forget, and at the ſame time forget to remember, has an Art above the Devil.

In his Laboratory you ſee *a Fancy* preſerv'd *a la Mummy*, ſeveral Thouſand Years old ; by examining which you may perfectly diſcern, how Nature makes a Poet : Another you have taken from a meer Natural, which diſcovers the Reaſons of Nature's Negative in the Caſe of humane Underſtanding ; what Deprivation of Parts She ſuffers, in the Compoſition of a Coxcomb ; and with what wonderful Art She prepares a Man to be a Fool.

Here

Here being the product of this Author's wonderful Skill, you have the *Skeleton of a Wit*, with all the Readings of Philofophy and Chyrurgery upon the Parts : Here you fee all the Lines Nature has drawn to form *a Genius*, how it performs, and from what Principles.

Alfo you are Inftructed to know the true reafon of the Affinity between Poetry and Poverty ; and that it is equally derived from what's Natural and Intrinfick, as from Accident and Circumftance ; how the World being always full of Fools and Knaves, Wit is fure to mifs of a good Market ; efpecially, if Wit and Truth happen to come in Company ; for the Fools don't underftand it, and the Knaves can't bear it.

But ftill 'tis own'd, and is moft apparent, there is fomething alfo Natural in the Cafe too, fince there are fome particular Veffels Nature thinks neceffary, to the more exact Compofition of this nice thing call'd *a Wit*, which as they are, or are not Interrupted in the peculiar Offices for which they are appointed, are fubject to various Diftempers, and more

parti-

particularly to Effluxions and Vapours, *Diliriums* Giddinefs of the Brain, and *Lapfæ*, or *Loofenefs of the Tongue* ; and as thefe Diftempers, occafion'd by the exceeding quantity of Volatiles, Nature is obliged to make ufe of in the Compofition, are hardly to be avoided, the Difafters which generally they pufh the Animal into, are as neceffarily confequent to them as Night is to the Setting of the *Sun* ; and thefe are very many, as difobliging Parents, who have frequently in this Country whipt their *Sons* for making Verfes ; and here I could not but reflect how ufeful a Difcipline early Correction muft be to a Poet ; and how eafy the Town had been had *N - - - t, E - - - w, T. B - - - P - - - s, D - - S - - D - - - fy,* and an Hundred more of the jingling Train of our modern Rhymers, been Whipt young, *very young*, for Poetafting, they had never perhaps fuckt in that Venome of Ribaldry, which all the Satyr of the Age has never been able to fcourge out of them to this Day.

The further fatal Confequences of thefe unhappy Defects in Nature, where fhe has damn'd a Man to Wit and Rhyme, has

has been lofs of Inheritance, Parents being aggravated by the obftinate young
Beaus, refolving to be Wits in fpight of
Nature, the wifer Head has been obliged to Confederate with Nature, and
with-hold the Birth-right of Brains, which
otherwife the young Gentleman might
have enjoy'd, to the great fupport of his
Family and Pofterity.   Thus the famous
Waller, *Denham*, *Dryden*, and fundry O-
thers, were oblig'd to condemn their Race
to Lunacy and Blockheadifm, only to prevent the fatal Deftruction of their Families, and entailing the Plague of Wit
and Weathercocks upon their Pofterity.

The yet farther Extravagancics which
naturally attend the Mifchief of *Wit*, are
Beau-ifm, *Dogmaticality*, *Whimfification*,
Impudenfity, and various kinds of *Foppe-
rofities* (according to Mr. *Boyl*,) which
iffuing out of the Brain, defcend into all
the Faculties, and branch themfelves by
infinite Variety, into all the Actions of
Life.

Thefe by Confeqence, Beggar the Head,
the Tail, the Purfe, and the whole Man,
till he becomes as poor and defpicable as
Negative

Negative Nature can leave him, abandon'd
of his Senfe, his Manners, his Modefty,
and what's worfe, his Money, having
nothing left but his Poetry, dies in a
Ditch, or a Garret, *A-la-mode de Tom
Brown*, uttering Rhymes and Nonfence
to the laft Moment.

In Pity to all my unhappy Brethren,
who fuffer under thefe Inconveniencies,
I cannot but leave it on Record, that
they may not be reproached with being
Agents of their own Misfortunes, fince
I affure them, Nature has form'd them
with the very Neceffity of acting like
Coxcombs, fixt upon them by the force
of Organick Confequences, and placed
down at the very Original Effufion of
that fatal thing call'd *Wit*.

Nor is the Difcovery lefs wonderful
than edifying, and no humane Art on
our fide the World ever found out fuch a
Sympathetick Influence, between the Extreams of *Wit* and *Folly*, till this great
Lunarian Naturalift furnifht us with fuch
unheard-of Demonftrations.

Nor

Nor is this all I learnt from him, tho'
I cannot part with this, till I have publifht a *Memento Mori*, and told 'em what
I had difcovered of Nature in thefe remote. Parts of the World, from whence I
take the Freedom to tell thefe Gentlemen,
That if they pleafe to Travel to thefe diftant Parts, and examine this great Mafter of Nature's Secrets, they may every
Man fee what crofs Strokes Nature has
ftruck, to finifh and form every extravagant Species of that Heterogenious Kind
we call *Wit*.

There C--- S--- may be inform'd how
he comes to be very Witty, and a Mad-
man all at once ; and P---r may fee,
That with lefs Brains and more P--x he
is more a Wit and more a Mad-man than
the Coll. *Ad---fon* may tell his Mafter
my Lord ---- the reafon from Nature,
why he would not take the Court's Word,
nor write the Poem call'd, *The Campaign*,
till he had 200 *l. per Annum* fecur'd to
him; fince 'tis known they have but one
Author in the Nation that writes for 'em
for nothing, and he is labouring very
hard to obtain the Title of Blockhead,
and

and not be paid for it : Here *D.* might underftand, how he came to be able to banter all Mankind, and yet all Mankind be able to banter him ; at the fame time our numerous throng of *Parnaffians* may fee Reafons for the variety of the Negative and Pofitive Bleffings they enjoy ; fome for having Wit and no Verfe, fome Verfe and no Wit, fome Mirth without Jeft, fome Jeft without Fore-caft, fome Rhyme and no Jingle, fome all Jingle and no Rhyme, fome Language without meafure ; fome all Quantity and no Cudence, fome all Wit and no Sence, fome all Sence and no Flame, fome Preach in Rhyme, fome fing when they Preach, fome all Song and no Tune, fome all Tune and no Song; all thefe Unaccountables have their Originals, and can be anfwer'd for in unerring Nature, tho' in our out-fide Gueffes we can fay little to it. Here is to be feen, why fome are all Nature, fome all Art ; fome beat Verfe out of the Twenty-four rough Letters, with Ten Hammers and Anvils to every Line, and maul the Language as a *Swede* beats Stock-Fifh ; Others *huff* Nature, and bully her out of whole Stanza's of ready-made Lines at a time, carry all before them, and rumble like diftant Thunder

der in a black Cloud : Thus Degrees and
Capacities are fitted by Nature, according
to Organick Efficacy ; and the Reason
and Nature of Things are found in them-.
felves : Had *D---y* feen his own Draft
by this Light of *Chinefe* Knowledge, he
might have known he fhould be a Coxcomb without writing Twenty-two Plays,
to ftand as fo many Records againft him.
Dryden might have told his Fate, that
having his extraordinary Genius flung and
pitcht upon a Swivle, it would certainly
turn round as faft as the Times, and inftruct him how to write Elegies to *O. C.*
and King *C.* the Second, with all the Coherence imaginable ; how to write *Reli-
gio Laicy*, and the *Hind* and *Panther*, and
yet be the fame Man, every Day to
change his Principle, change his Religion, change his Coat, change his Mafter,
and yet never change his Nature.

There are abundance of other Secrets
in Nature difcover'd in relation to thefe
things, too many to repeat, and yet too
ufeful to omit, as the reafon why Phifici-
ans are generally Atheifts ; and why A-
theifts are univerfally Fools, and generally live to know it themfelves, the real
Obftruct-

Obstructions, which prevent Fools being mad, all the Natural Causes of Love, abundance of Demonstrations of the Synonimous Nature of Love and Leachery, especially consider'd *a la Modern*, with an absolute Specifick for the Frenzy of Love, found out in the Constitution, Anglice, *a Halter*.

It would be endless to reckon up the numerous Improvements, and wonderful Discoveries this extraordinary Person has brought down, and which are to be seen in his curious Chamber of Rarities.

Particularly a Map of *Parnassus*, with an exact Delineation of all the Cells, Apartments, Palaces and Dungeons, of that most famous Mountain ; with a Description of its Heighth, and a learned Dissertation, proving it to be the properest Place next to the P---e House to take a Rise at, for a flight to the World in the *Moon*.

Also some Enquiries, whether *Noah's* Ark did not first rest upon it ; and this might be one of the Summits of *Ararat*, with some Confutations of the gross and palpable Errors, which place this extraordinary

nary Skill among the Mountains of the
Moon in *Africa.*

Also you have here *a Muse calcin'd,* a
little of the Powder of which given to a
Woman big with Child, if it be a Boy it
will be a Poet, if a Girl she'll be a Whore,
if an Hermaphrodite it will be Lunatick.

Strange things, they tell us, have been
done with this calcin'd Womb of Imagination ; if the Body it came from was a
Lyrick Poet, the Child will be a Beau, or
a Beauty ; if an Heroick Poet, he will be
a Bulley ; if his Talent was Satyr, he'll
be a Philosopher.

Another Muse they tell us, they have
dissolv'd into a Liquid, and kept with
wondrous Art, the Vertues of which are
Soveraign against Ideotism, Dullness, and
all sorts of Lethargick Diseases ; but if
given in too great a quantity, creates Poe-
sy, Poverty, Lunacy, and the Devil in
the Head ever after.

I confess, I always thought these Mu-
ses strange intoxicating things, and have
heard much talk of their Original, but
never

never was acquainted with their Vertue *a la Simple* before ; however, I would always advife People againft too large a Dofe of Wit, and think the Phyfician muft be a Mad-man that will venture to prefcribe it.

As all thefe noble Acquirements came down with this wonderful Man from the World in the *Moon*, it furnifht me with thefe ufeful Obfervations.

1. That Country muft needs be a Place of ftrange Perfection, in all parts of extraordinary Knowledge.

2. How ufeful a thing it would be for moft forts of our People, efpecially Statefmen, P ---- t-men, Convocationmen, Phylofophers, Phyficians, Quacks, Mountebanks, Stock-jobbers, and all the Mob of the Nation's Civil or Ecclefiaftical *Bone-fetters*, together with fome Men of the Law, fome of the Sword, and all of the Pen : I fay, how ufeful and improving a thing it muft be to them, to take a Journey up to the World in the *Moon* ; but above all, how much more beneficial it would be to them that ftay'd behind.

3. That

3. That it is not to be wonder'd at, why the *Chinese* excell so much all these Parts of the World, since but for that Knowledge which comes down to them from the World in the *Moon*, they would be like other People.

4. No Man need to Wonder at my exceeding desire to go up to the World in the *Moon*, having heard of such extraordinary Knowledge to be obtained there, since in the search of Knowledge and Truth, wiser Men than I have taken as unwarrantable Flights, and gone a great deal higher than the *Moon*, into a strange Abbyss of dark *Phænomena*, which they neither could make other People understand, nor ever rightly understood themselves, witness *Malbranch*, Mr. *Lock*, *Hobbs*, the Honourable *Boyle* and a great many others, besides Messieurs *Norris*, *Asgil*, *Coward*, and the *Tale of a Tub*.

This great Searcher into Nature has, besides all this, left wonderful Discoveries and Experiments behind him ; but I was with nothing more exceedingly diverted, than with his various Engines, and curi-

D   ous

ous Contrivances, to go to and from his own Native Country the *Moon*. All our Mechanick Motions of Bifhop *Wilkins*, or the artificial Wings of the Learned *Spaniard*, who could have taught God Almighty how to have mended the Creation, are Fools to this Gentleman ; and becaufe no Man in *China* has made more Voyages up into the *Moon* than my felf, I cannot but give you fome Account of the eafynefs of the Paffage, as well as of the Country.

Nor are his wonderful Tellefcopes of a mean Quality, by which fuch plain Difcoveries are made, of the Lands and Seas in the *Moon*, and in all the habitable Planets, that one may as plainly fee what a Clock it is by one of the Dials in the *Moon*, as if it were no farther off than *Windfor-Caftle* ; and had he liv'd to finifh the Speaking-trumpet which he had contriv'd to convey Sound thither, *Harlequin's Mock-Trumpet* had been a Fool to it ; and it had no doubt been an admirable Experiment, to have given us a general Advantage from all their acquir'd Knowledge in thofe Regions, where no doubt feveral ufeful Difcoveries are daily made by the Men of

of Thought for the Improvement of all
forts of humane Underftanding, and to
have difcourfed with them on thofe
things, muft have been very pleafant, befides, its being very much to our paritcu-
lar Advantage.

I confefs, I have thought it might have
been very ufeful to this Nation, to have
brought fo wonderful an Invention hither,
and I was once very defirous to have
fet up my reft here, and for the Benefit
of my Native Country, have made my
felf Mafter of thefe Engines, that I might
in due time have convey'd them to our
Royal Society, that once in 40 Years they
might have been faid to do fomething
for Publick Good ; and that the Reputation and Ufefulnefs of the *fo fo's* might
be recover'd in *England* ; but being told
that in the Moon there were many of
thefe Glaffes to be had very cheap, and I
having declar'd my Refolution of undertaking a Voyage thither, I deferred my
Defign, and fhall defer my treating of
them, till I give fome Account of my
Arrival there.

D 2   But

But above all his Inventions for making this Voyage, I faw none more pleafant or profitable, than a certain Engine formed in the fhape of a Chariot, on the Backs of two vaft Bodies with extended Wings, which fpread about 50 Yards in Breadth, compos'd of Feathers fo nicely put together, that no Air could pafs ; and as the Bodies were made of *Lunar Earth* which would bear the Fire, the Cavities were fill'd with an Ambient Flame, which fed on a certain Spirit depofited in a proper quantity, to laft out the Voyage; and this Fire fo order'd as to move about fuch Springs and Wheels as kept the Wings in a moft exact and regular Motion, always afcendant ; thus the Perfon being placed in this airy Chariot, drinks a certain dozing Draught, that throws him into a gentle Slumber, and Dreaming all the way, never wakes till he comes to his Journey's end.

Of the Confolidator.

THefe Engines are call'd in their Country Language, *Dupekaffes* ; and according to the Ancient *Chinefe*, or *Tartarian*,

Tartarian, Apezolanthukanistes ; in *English*, a *Consolidator.*

The Compofition of this Engine is very admirable ; for, as is before noted, 'tis all made up of Feathers, and the quality of the Feathers, is no lefs wonderful than their Compofition ; and therefore, I hope the Reader will bear with the Defcription for the fake of the Novelty, fince I affure him fuch things as thefe are not to be feen in every Country.

The number of Feathers are juft 513, they are all of a length and breadth exactly, which is abfolutely neceffary to the *floating Figure*, or elfe one fide or any one part being wider or longer than the reft, it would interrupt the motion of the whole Engine ; only there is one extraordinary Feather which, as there is an odd one in the number, is placed in the Center, and is the Handle, or rather Rudder to the whole Machine : This Feather is every way larger than its Fellows, 'tis almoft as long and broad again ; but above all, its Quill or Head is much larger, and it has *as it were* feveral fmall bufhing Feathers round the bottom of it,

which

which all make but one prefiding or fu-
perintendent Feather, to guide, regulate,
and pilot the whole Body.

Nor are thefe common Feathers, but
they are pickt and cull'd out of all parts
of the Lunar Country, by the Command
of the Prince ; and every Province fends
up the beft they can find, *or ought to do
fo at leaft*, or elfe they are very much to
blame ; for the Employment they are put
to being of fo great ufe to the Publick,
and the Voyage or Flight fo exceeding
high, it would be very ill done if, when
the King fends his Letters about the Nation, to pick him up the beft Feathers
they can lay their Hands on, they fhould
fend weak, decay'd, or half-grown Feathers, and yet fometimes it happens fo ;
and once there was fuch rotten Feathers
collected, whether it was a bad Year for
Feathers, or whether the People that gather'd them had a mind to abufe their
King ; but the Feathers were fo bad, the
Engine was good for nothing, but broke
before it was got half way ; and by a
double Misfortune, this happen'd to be
at an unlucky time, when the King himfelf had refolv'd on a Voyage, or Flight
to

to the *Moon* ; but being deceiv'd, by the unhappy Miſcarriage of the deficient Feathers, he fell down from ſo great a height, that he ſtruck himſelf againſt his own Palace, and beat his Head off.

Nor had the Sons of this Prince much better Succeſs, tho' the firſt of them was a Prince mightily belov'd by his Subjects ; but his Misfortunes chiefly proceeded from his having made uſe of one of the Engines ſo very long, that the Feathers were quite worn out, and good for nothing : He uſed to make a great many Voyages and Flights into the *Moon,* and then would make his Subjects give him great Sums of Money to come down to them again ; and yet they were ſo fond of him, That they always complyed with him, and would give him every thing he askt, rather than to be without him : *But they grew wiſer ſince.*

At laſt, this Prince uſed his Engine ſo long, it could hold together no longer ; and being obliged to write to his Subjects to pick him out ſome new Feathers, *they did ſo* ; but withall ſent him ſuch *ſtrong* Feathers, and ſo *ſtiff,* that when he had placed

'em

'em in their proper places, and made a very beautiful Engine, it was *too heavy for him to manage :* He made a great many Effays at it, and had it placed on the top of an old Idol Chappel, dedicated to an old *Bramyn* Saint of thofe Countries, called, *Phantofteinafchap* ; in *Latin, chap. de Saint Stephano* ; or in *Englifh,* St. *Stephen's* : Here the Prince try'd all poffible Contrivances, and a vaft deal of Money it coft him ; but the Feathers were *fo ftiff* they would not work, and *the Fire within* was fo choaked and fmother'd with its *own Smoak,* for want of due Vent and Circulation, that it *would not burn* ; fo he was oblig'd to take it down again ; and from thence he carried it to his College of *Bramyn* Priefts, and fet it up in one of their Publick Buildings : There he drew Circles of Ethicks and Politicks, and fell to cafting of Figures and Conjuring, but all would not do, *the Feathers* could not be brought to move ; and, indeed, I have obferv'd, That thefe Engines are feldom helpt by Art and Contrivance ; there is no way with them, but to have the People fpoke to, to get *good Feathers* ; and they are eafily placed, and perform all the feveral Motions with the greateft Eafe

and

and Accuracy imaginable ; *but it must be all Nature* ; any thing of Force diftorts and diflocates them, and the whole Order is fpoiled ; and if there be but one Feather out of place, or pincht, or ftands wrong, *the D---l would not ride in the Chariot.*

The Prince thus finding his Labour in vain, broke the Engine to pieces, and fent his Subjects Word what bad Feathers they had fent him : But the People, who knew it was his own want of Management, and that the Feathers were good enough, only a little ftiff at firft, and with good Ufage would have been brought to be fit for ufe, took it ill, and never would fend him any other as long as he liv'd : However, it had this good effect upon him, That he never made any more Voyages to the *Moon* as long as he reign'd.

His Brother fucceeded him ; and truly he was refoved upon a Voyage to the *Moon*, as foon as ever he came to the Crown. He had met with fome unkind Ufage from the Religious *Luneffes* of his ownCountry; and he tnrn'd *Abogratziarian*, a zealous fiery Sect fomething like our *Anti-*

every-

every-body-arians in *England*. 'Tis confeſt,
ſome of the *Bramyns* of his Country were
very falſe to him, put him upon ſeveral
Ways of extending his Power over his
Subjects, contrary to the Cuſtoms of the
People, and contrary to his own Intereſt ; and when the People expreſſed
their Diſlike of it, he thought to have
been ſupported by thoſe Clergy-men ; but
they failed him, and made good that Old
Engliſh Verſe ;

That Prieſts of all Religions are the ſame.

He took this ſo hainouſly, that he conceiv'd a juſt Hatred againſt thoſe that had
deceiv'd him ; and as Reſentments ſeldom
keep Rules, unhappily entertain'd Prejudices againſt all the reſt ; and not finding
it eaſy to bring all his Deſigns to paſs
better, he reſolved upon a Voyage to the
Moon.

Accordingly, he ſends a Summons to
all his People according to Cuſtom, to
collect the uſual quantity of Feathers for
that purpoſe ; and becauſe he would be
ſure not be uſed as his Brother and Father had been, he took care to ſend certain

tain Cunning-men Exprefs, all over the
Country, to befpeak the People's Care,
in collecting, picking and culling them out,
thefe were call'd in their Language, *Tfo-
pablesdetoo* ; which being Tranflated may
fignify in *Englifh*, *Men of Zeal*, or *Booted
Apoftles* : Nor was this the only Caution
this Prince ufed ; for he took care, as the
Feathers were fent up to him, to fearch
and examine them one by one in his own
Clofet, to fee if they were fit for his purpofe ; but, alas ! he found himfelf in his
Brother's Cafe exactly ; and perceived,
That his Subjects were generally difgufted
at his former Conduct, about *Abrogratzianifm*, and fuch things, and particularly fet in a Flame by fome of their
Priefts, call'd, *Dullobardians*, or *Paffive-
Obedience-men*, who had lately turn'd their
Tale, and their Tail too upon their own
Princes ; and upon this, he laid afide any
more Thoughts of the Engine, but took
up a defperate and implacable Refolution,
viz. to fly up to the Moon without it; in
order to this, abundance of his Cunning-
men were fummon'd together to affift
him, ftrange Engines contriv'd, and Methods prpos'd ; and a great many came
from all Parts, to furnifh him with Inventions

ventions and equivalent for their Journey ; but all were so preposterous and ridiculous, that his Subjects seeing him going on to ruin himself, and by Consequence them too, unanimously took Arms ; and if their Prince had not made his Escape into a foreign Country, 'tis thought they would have secur'd him *for a Mad-man.*

And here 'tis observable, That as it is in most such Cases, the mad Councellors of this Prince, when the People begun to gather about him, fled ; and every one shifted for themselves ; nay, and some of them plunder'd him first of his Jewels and Treasure, and never were heard of since.

From this Prince none of the Kings or Government of that Country have ever seem'd to incline to the hazardous Attempt of the Voyage to the *Moon,* at least not in such a hair-brain'd manner.

However, the Engine has been very accurately Re-built and finish'd ; and the People are now oblig'd by a Law, to send up new Feathers every three Years, to prevent the Mischiefs which happen'd by
that

that Prince aforesaid, keeping one Set so long that it was dangerous to venture with them ; and thus the Engine is preserved fit for use.

And yet has not this Engine been without its continual Disasters, and often out of repair ; for though the Kings of the Country, as has been Noted, have done riding on the back of it, yet the *restless* Courtiers and Ministers of State have frequently obtained the Management of it, from the too easy Goodness of their Masters, or the Evils of the Times.

To Cure this, the Princes frequently chang'd Hands, turn'd one Set of Men out and put another in : But this made things still worse ; for it divided the People into Parties and Factions in the State, and still the Strife was, who should ride in this Engine ; and no sooner were these *Skaet-Riders* got into it, but they were for *driving all the Nation up to the* Moon : But of this by it self.

Authors differ concerning the Original of these Feathers, and by what most exact Hand they were first appointed to this

particular

particular ufe ; and as their Original is
hard to be found, fo it feems a Difficulty
to refolve from what fort of Bird thefe
Feathers are obtained : Some have nam'd
one, fome another ; but the moft Learned in thofe Climates call it by a hard
Word, which the Printer having no Letters to exprefs, and being in that place
Hierogliphical, I can tranflate no better,
than by the Name of a *Collective :* This
muft be a ftrange Bird without doubt ; it
has Heads, Claws, Eyes and Teeth innumerable ; and if I fhould go about to defcribe it to you, the Hiftory would be fo
Romantick, it would fpoil the Credit of
thefe more Authentick Relations which
are yet behind.

'Tis fufficient, therefore, for the prefent, only to leave you this fhort Abridgement of the Story, as follows : This great
Monftrous Bird, call'd the *Collective*, is
very feldom feen, and indeed never, but
upon *Great Revolutions,* and portending
terrible Defolations and Deftructions to
a Country.

But he frequently fheds his Feathers ;
and they are carefully pickt up, by the
Proprietors

Proprietors of thofe Lands where they fall ; for *none but thofe Proprietors may* meddle with them ; and they no fooner pick them up but they are fent to Court, where they obtain a new Name, and are called in a Word equally difficult to pronounce as the other, but very like our *Englifh* Word, *Reprefentative* ; and being placed in their proper Rows, with the *Great Feather* in the Center, and fitted for ufe, they lately obtained the Venerable Title of, *The Confolidators* ; and the Machine it felf, the *Confolidator* ; and by that Name the Reader is defir'd for the future to let it be dignified and diftinguifh'd.

I cannot, however, forbear to defcant a little here, on the Dignity and Beauty of thefe Feathers, being fuch as are hardly to be feen in any part of the World, but juft in thefe remote Climates.

And Firft, Every Feather has various Colours, and according to the Variety of the Weather, are apt to look brighter and clearer, or paler and fainter, as the *Sun* happens to look on them with a ftronger or weaker Afpect. The Quill or Head of every Feather is *or ought to be* full of a

vigorous

vigorous Subftance, which gives Spirit, and fupports the brightnefs and colour of the Feather ; and as this is more or lefs in quantity, the bright Colour of the Feather is increafed, or turns languid and pale.

'Tis true, fome of thofe Quills are exceeding empty and dry ; and the Humid being totally exhal'd, thofe Feathers grow very ufelefs and infignificant in a fhort time.

Some again are fo full of Wind, and puft up with the Vapour of the Climate, that there's not Humid enough to Condence the Steam ; and thefe are fo fleet, fo light, and fo continually fluttering and troublefome, that they greatly ferve to difturb and keep the Motion unfteddy.

Others either placed too near the inward concealed Fire, or the Head of the Quill being thin, the Fire caufes too great a Fermentation ; and the Confequence of this is fo fatal, that fometimes it mounts the Engine up too faft, and indangers Precipitation : But 'tis happily obferved, That thefe ill Feathers are but a very few, compar'd to the whole number ;

ber ; at the moſt, I never heard they
were above 134 of the whole number:
As for the empty ones, they are not very
dangerous, but a ſort of *Good-for-nothing
Feathers*, that will fly when the greateſt
number of the reſt fly, or ſtand ſtill when
they ſtand ſtill. The fluttering hot-headed Feathers are the moſt dangerous, and
frequently ſtruggle hard to mount the Engine to extravagant heights ; but ſtill the
greater number of the Feathers being
ſtanch, and well fixt, as well as well furniſht, they always prevail, and check the
Diſorders the other would bring upon the
Motion ; ſo that upon the whole Matter,
tho' there has ſometims been oblique Motions, Variations, and ſometimes great
Wandrings out of the way, which may
make the Paſſage tedious, yet it has always
been a certain and ſafe Voyage ; and no
Engine was ever known to miſcarry or
overthrow, but that one mentioned before,
and that was very much owing to the precipitate Methods the Prince took in gui-
ding it ; and tho' all the fault was laid in
the Feathers, *and they were to blame e-
nough*, yet I never heard any Wiſe Man,
but what blam'd his Diſcretion, and particularly, a certain great Man has wrote

E   three

three large Tracts of thofe Affairs, and
call'd them,*TheHiftory of the Oppofition of the
Feathers* ; wherein, tho' it was expected
he would have curft the Engine it felf
and all the Feathers to the Devil, on the
contrary, he lays equal blame on the
Prince, who guided the Chariot with fo
unfteddy a Hand, now as much too flack,
as then too hard, turning them this way
and that fo haftily,that the Feathers could
not move in their proper order ; and this
at laft put the Fire in the Center quite
out, and fo the Engine over-fet at once.
This Impartiality has done great Juftice
to the Feathers, and fet things in a clearer
light : But of this I fhall fay more, when
I come to treat of the *Works of the Learned* in this Lunar World.

This is hinted here only to inform the
Reader, That this Engine is the fafeft
Paffage that ever was found out ; and
that faving that one time, it never mif-
carried ; nor if the common Order of
things be obferved, cannot Mifcarry ; for
the good Feathers are always *Negatives*,
when any precipitant Motion is felt, and
immediately fupprefs it by their number ;
and thefe *Negative Feathers* are indeed the
Travellers

Travellers safety ; the other are always
upon the flutter, and upon every occasion
hey for the Moon, up in the Clouds presently ; but these *Negative Feathers* are
never for going up, but when there is
occasion for it ; and from hence these
fluttering fermented Feathers were called
by the Antients *High-flying Feathers*, and
the blustering things seem'd proud of the
Name.

But to come to their general Character,
the Feathers, speaking of them all together, are generally very Comely, Strong,
Large, Beautiful things, their Quills or
Heads well fixt, and the Cavities fill'd
with a solid substantial Matter, which
tho' it is full of Spirit, has a great deal of
Temperament, and full of suitable well-
dispos'd Powers, to the Operation for
which they are design'd.

These placed, as I Noted before, in an
extended Form like two great Wings, and
operated by that sublime Flame ; which
being concealed in proper Receptacles,
obtains its vent at the Cavities appointed,
are supplied from thence with Life and
Motion ; and as Fire it self, in the Opi-

nion

nion of some Learned Men, is nothing but
Motion, and Motion tends to Fire : It
can no more be a Wonder, if exalted in
the Center of this famous Engine, a whole
Nation should be carried up to the World
in the *Moon.*

'Tis true, this Engine is frequently af-
faulted with fierce Winds, and furious
Storms, which fometimes drive it a great
way out of its way ; and indeed, confidering the length of the Paffage, and the
various Regions it goes through, it would
be ftrange if it should meet with no Ob-
ftructions : Thefe are oblique Gales, and
cannot be faid to blow from any of the
Thirty-two Points, bnt Retrograde and
Thwart : Some of thefe are call'd in their
Language, *Penfionazima*, which is as much
as to fay, being Interpreted, a *Court-breeze*;
another fort of Wind, which generally
blows directly contrary to the *Penfionazima*, is the *Clamorio*, or in *Englifh*, a *Country Gale* ; this is generally Tempeftuous,
full of Gufts and Difgufts, Squauls and
fudden Blafts, not without claps of Thunder, and not a little flafhing of Heat and
Party-fires.

There

There are a great many other Internal Blafts, which proceed from the Fire within, which fometimes not circulating right, breaks out in little Gufts of Wind and Heat, and is apt to indanger fetting Fire to the Feathers, and this is more or lefs dangerous, according as among which of the Feathers it happens ; for fome of the Feathers are more apt to take Fire than others, as their Quills or Heads are more or lefs full of that folid Matter mention'd before.

The Engine fuffers frequent Convulfions and Diforders from thefe feveral Winds ; and which if they chance to overblow very much, hinder the Paffage : but the Negative Feathers always apply Temper and Moderation ; and this brings all to rights again.

For a Body like this, what can it not do ? what cannot fuch an Extenfion perform in the Air ? And when one thing is tackt to another, and properly *Cofolidated* into one mighty *Confolidator*, no queftion but whoever fhall go up to the *Moon*, will find himfelf fo improv'd in this wonder-

F 3   ful

ful Experiment, that not a Man ever perform'd that wonderful Flight, but he certainly came back again as wise as he
went.

Well, Gentlemen, and what if we are
call'd *High-flyers* now, and an Hundred
Names of Contempt and Distinction,
what is this to the purpose? who would
not be a *High-flyer*, to be Tackt and *Consolidated* in an Engine of such sublime
Elevation, and which lifts Men, Monarchs,
Members, yea, and whole Nations, up
into the Clouds; and performs with such
wondrous Art, the long expected Experiment of a Voyage to the *Moon?* And
thus much for the Description of the *Consolidator.*

The first Voyage I ever made to this
Country, was in one of these Engines;
and I can safely affirm, I never wak'd all
the way; and now having been as often
there as most that have us'd that Trade,
it may be expected I should give some
Account of the Country; for it appears,
I can give but little of the Road.

Only this I understand, That when this
Engine, by help of these Artificial Wings,
has raised it self up to a certain height,
the

the Wings are as ufeful to keep it from falling into the *Moon*, as they were before to raife it, and keep it from falling back into this Region again.

This may happen from an Alteration of Centers, and Gravity having paft a certain Line, the Equipoife changes its Tendency, the Magnetick Quality being beyond it, it inclines of Courfe, and purfues a Center, which it finds in the *Lunar World*, and lands us fafe upon the Surface.

I was told, I need take no Bills of Exchange with me, nor Letters of Credit ; for that upon my firft Arrival, the Inhabitants would be very civil to me : That they never fuffered any of *Our World* to want any thing when they came there : That they were very free to fhow them any thing, and inform them in all needful Cafes ; and that whatever Rarities the Country afforded, fhould be expos'd immediately.

I fhall not enter into the Cuftoms, Geography, or Hiftory of the Place, only acquaint the Reader, That I found no

E 4   manner

manner of Difference in any thing Natural, except as hereafter excepted, but all was exactly as is here, an Elementary World, peopled with Folks, *as like us* as if they were only Inhabitants of the same Continent, but in a remote Climate.

The Inhabitants were *Men, Women, Beasts, Birds, Fishes,* and *Insects,* of the same individual Species as Ours, the latter excepted : The *Men* no wiser, better, nor bigger than here ; the *Women* no handsomer or honester than Ours: There were Knaves and honest Men, honest Women and Whores of all Sorts, Countries, Nations and Kindreds, as on this side the Skies.

They had the same Sun to shine, the Planets were equally visible *as to us,* and *their Astrologers* were as busily Impertinent as Ours, only that those wonderful Glasses hinted before made strange Discoveries that we were unacquainted with ; by them they could plainly discover, That *this* World was *their* Moon, and *their* World *our* Moon ; and when I came first among them, the People that flockt about me, distinguisht me by the Name of, *the Man that came out of the Moon.*

I

I cannot, however, but acquaint the Reader, with some Remarks I made in this new World, before I come to any thing Historical.

I have heard, that among the Generality of our People, who being not much addicted to Revelation, have much concern'd themselves about Demonstrations, a Generation have risen up, who to solve the Difficulties of Supernatural Systems, imagine *a mighty vast Something*, who has no Form but what represents him to them as one *Great Eye :* This infinite Optick they imagine to be *Natura Naturans*, or Power-forming ; and that as we pretend the Soul of Man has a Similitude in quality to its Original, according to a Notion some People have, who read that so much ridicul'd Old Legend, call'd *Bible*, That *Man was made in the Image of his Maker :* The Soul of Man, therefore, in the Opinion of these Naturallists, is *one vast Optick Power* diffus'd through him into all his Parts, but seated principally in his Head.

From hence they resolve all Beings to *Eyes,* some more capable of Sight and receptive

ceptive of Objects than others ; and as to
things Invisible, they reckon nothing so,
only so far as our Sight is deficient, contracted or darkened by Accidents from
without, as Distance of Place, Interposi-
tion of Vapours, Clouds, liquid Air, Exhalations, *&c.* or from within, as *wandring Errors, wild Notions, cloudy Under-
standings,* and *empty Fancies,* with a Thousand other interposing Obstacles to the
Sight, which darken it, and prevent its
Operation ; and particularly obstruct the
perceptive Faculties, weaken the Head,
and bring Mankind in General to stand in
need of the *Spectacles of Education* as soon
as ever they are born : Nay, and as soon
as they have made use of these Artificial
Eyes, all they can do is but to clear the
Sight so far as *to see* that *they can't see* ; the
utmost Wisdom of Mankind, and the
highest Improvement a Man ought to wish
for, being but to be able to see that *he was
Born blind* ; this pushes him upon search
after Mediums for the Recovery of his
Sight, and *away he runs to School* to Art
and Science, and there he is furnisht with
*Hocoscopes, Microscopes, Tellescopes, Cælis-
copes, Money-scopes,* and the D---l and
and all of Glasses, to help and assist his

Moon-

Moon-blind Understanding ; these with wonderful Skill and Ages of Application, after wandring thro' Bogs and Wildernesses of *Guess, Conjectures, Supposes, Calculations*, and he knows not what, which he meets with in *Physicks, Politicks, Ethicks, Astronomy, Mathematicks*, and such sort of bewildring Things, bring him with vast Difficulty to a little Minute-spot, call'd *Demonstration* ; and as not one in Ten Thousand ever finds the way thither, but are lost in the tiresome uncouth Journey, so they *that do*, 'tis so long before they come there, that they are grown Old and good for little in the Journey ; and no sooner have they obtained a glimering of this Universal *Eye-sight*, this *Eclaircissment General*, but they *Die*, and have hardly time to show the way to those that come after.

Now, as the earnest search after this thing call'd *Demonstration* fill'd me with Desires of seeing every thing, so my Observations of the strange multitude of Mysteries I met with in all Men's Actions here, spurr'd my Curiosity to examine, if *the Great Eye* of the World had no People to whom he had given a clearer Eye-sight,

or

or at leaft, that made a better ufe of it
than we had here.

If purfuing this fearch I was much delighted at my Arrival into *China*, it cannot be thought ftrange, fince there we
find Knowledge as much advanc'd beyond
our common Pitch, as it was pretended
to be deriv'd from a more Ancient Original.

We are told, that in the early Age of
the World, the Strength of Invention exceeded all that ever has been arrived to
fince : That we in thefe latter Ages, having loft all that priftine Strength of Reafon and Invention, which died with the
Ancients in the Flood, and receiving no
helps from that Age, have by long Search
arriv'd at feveral remote Parts of Knowledge, by the helps of reading Converfation and Experience ; but that all amounts
to no more than faint Imitations, Apings,
and Refemblances of what was known in
thofe mafterly Ages.

Now, if it be true as is hinted before,
That the *Chinefe* Empire was Peopled long
before the Flood ; and that they were
not

not deftroyed in the General Deluge in
the Days of *Noah* ; 'tis no fuch ftrange
thing, that they fhould fo much out-do us
in this fort of *Eye-fight* wc call *General
Knowledge,* fince the Perfections beftow'd
on Nature, when in her Youth and Prime
met with no General Suffocation by that
Calamity.

But if I was extreamly delighted with
the extraordinary things I faw in thofe
Countries, you cannot but imagine I was
exceedingly mov'd, when I heard of a
Lunar World ; and that the way was
paffable from thefe Parts.

I had heard of a *World in the Moon*
among fome of our Learned Philofophers,
and *Moor,* as I have been told, had *a Moon*
in his Head ; but none of the fine Pretenders, no not Bifhop *Wilkins,* ever found
Mechanick Engines, whofe Motion was
fufficient to attempt the Paffage. A late
happy Author indeed, among his Mechanick Operations of the Spirit, had found
out an Enthufiafm, which if he could have
purfued to its proper Extream, without
doubt might, *either in the Body or out of
the Body,* have Landed him fomewhere
here-

hereabout ; but that he form'd his System
wholly upon the miſtaken Notion of *Wind*,
which Learned Hypotheſis being directly
contrary to the Nature of things in this
Climate, where the *Elaſticity* of the Air
is quite different, and where the *preſſure
of the Atmoſphere* has for want of Vapour
no Force, all his Notion diſſolv'd in its
Native Vapour call'd *Wind*, and flew upward in blew Strakes of a livid Flame
call'd *Blaſphemy*, which burnt up all the
Wit and Fancy of the Author, and left a
ſtrange *ſtench* behind it, that has this unhappy quality in it, that every Body that
Reads the Book, *ſmells the Author*, tho'
he be never ſo far off ; nay, tho' he took
Shipping to *Dublin*, to ſecure his Friends
from the leaſt danger of a Conjecture.

But to return to the happy Regions of
the *Lunar Continent*, I was no ſooner
Landed there, and had lookt about me,
but I was ſurpriz'd with the ſtrange Alteration of the Climate and Country ; and
particularly a ſtrange Salubrity and Fra-
grancy in the Air, which I felt ſo Nou-
riſhing, ſo Pleaſant and Delightful, that
tho' I could perceive ſome ſmall Reſpira-
tion, it was hardly diſcernable, and the
leaſt

leaft requifite for Life, fupplied fo long that the Bellows of Nature were hardly imployed.

But as I fhall take occafion to confider this in a Critical Examination into the Nature, Ufes and Advantages of *Good Lungs*, of which by it felf, fo I think fit to confine my prefent Obfervations to things more particularly concerning the *Eye-fight.*

I was, you may be fure, not a little furprized, when being upon an Eminence I found my felf capable by common Obfervation, to fee and diftinguifh things at the diftance of 100 Miles and more, and feeking fome Information on this point, I was acquainted by the People, that there was *a certain grave Philofopher* hard by, that could give me a very good Account of things.

It is not worth while to tell you this Man's *Lunar Name*, or whether he had a Name, or no ; 'tis plain, 'twas a *Man in the Moon* ; but all the Conference I had with him was very ftrange : At my firft coming to him, he askt me if I came from the

the *World in the Moon* ? I told him, *no* ?
At which he began to be angry, told me
I Ly'd, he knew whence I came as well
as I did ; for he faw me all the way.   I
told him, I came *to the World in the Moon*,
and began to be as furly as he.   It was a
long time before we could agree about it,
he would have it, that I came down from
the Moon ; and I, that I came *up to the
Moon* : From this, we came to Explica-
tions, Demonftrations, Spheres, Globes,
Regions, Atmofpheres, and a Thoufand
odd Diagrams, to make the thing out to
one another.   I infifted on my part, as
that my Experiment qualified me to know,
and challeng'd him to *go back with me* to
prove it.   He, like a true Philofopher,
raifed a Thoufand Scruples, Conjectures,
and Spherical Problems, to Confront me ;
and as for Demonftrations, he call'd 'em
Fancies of my own.   Thus we differ'd a
great many ways ; both of us were certain, and both uncertain ; both right,
and yet both directly contrary ; how to
reconcile this Jangle was very hard, till
at laft this Demonftration happen'd, the
Moon as he call'd it, turning her blind-
fide upon us three Days after the Change,
by which, with the help of his extraordinary

dinary Glaffes, I that knew the Country, perceived that fide the *Sun* lookt upon was *all Moon*, and the other was *all World* ; and either I fancy'd I faw or elfe really faw all the lofty Towers of the Immenfe Cities of *China :* Upon this, and a little more Debate, we came to this Conclufi-on, and there the Old Man and I agreed, That they were *both Moons* and *both Worlds,* this *a Moon* to that, and that *a Moon* to this, like the Sun between two Looking-Glaffes, and fhone upon one another by Reflection, according to the oblique or direct Pofition of each other.

This afforded us a great deal of Plea-fure ; for all the World covet to be found in the right, and are pleas'd when their Notions are acknowledg'd by their Anta-gonifts : It alfo afforded us many very ufeful Speculations, fuch as thefe ;

1. How eafy it is for Men to *fall out,* and yet all fides to be in the *right ?*

2. How Natural it is for *Opinion* to defpife *Demonftration ?*

F   3. How

3. How proper mutual *Enquiry* is to mutual *Satisfaction* ?

From the Obfervation of thefe Glaffes, we alfo drew fome *Puns*, *Crotchets* and *Conclufions*.

1*st*, That the whole World has a *Blind-fide*, a *Dark-fide*, and a *Bright-fide*, and confequently fo has every Body in it.

2*dly*, That the *Dark-fide* of Affairs *to Day*, may be the *Bright-fide to Morrow* ; from whence abundance of ufeful Morals were alfo raifed ; fuch as,

1. No Man's Fate is fo dark, but when the *Sun* fhines upon it, it will return its Rays, and fhine for it felf.

2. All things turn like the *Moon*, *up* to Day, *down* to Morrow, *Full* and *Change*, *Flux* and *Reflux*.

3. Humane Underftanding is like the *Moon* at the Firft Quarter, *half dark*.

3*dly*, The

3*dly*, The *Changing-fides* ought not to be thought fo ftrange, or fo much Condemn'd by Mankind, having its Original from the *Lunar Influence*, and govern'd by the Powerful Operation of Heavenly Motion.

4*thly*, If there be any fuch thing as Deftiny in the World, I know nothing Man is fo predeftinated to, as to be eternally turning round ; and but that I purpofe to entertain the Reader with at leaft a whole Chapter or Section of the Philofophy of *Humane Motion*, Spherically and *Hypocritically Examin'd* and *Calculated*, I fhould inlarge upon that Thought in this place.

Having thus jumpt in our Opinions, and perfectly fatisfied our felves with Demonftration, That thefe Worlds were Sifters, both in Form, Function, and all their Capacities ; in fhort, a pair of *Moons*, and a pair of *Worlds*, equally Magnetical, Sympathetical, and Influential, we fet up our reft as to that Affair, and went forward.

I

I defir'd no better Acquaintance in my
new Travels, than this new Sociate ; never was there fuch a Couple of People
met ; he was the *Man in the Moon* to me,
and I *the Man in the Moon* to him ; he
wrote down all I faid, and made a Book
of it, and call'd it, *News from the World
in the* Moon ; and all the Town is like to
fee *my Minutes* under the fame Title ;
nay, and I have been told, he publifhed
fome fuch bold Truths there, from the
Allegorical Relations he had of me from
our World : That he was call'd before
the Publick Authority, who could not
bear the juft Reflections of his *damn'd Sa-
tyrical way of Writing* ; and there they pu-
nifht the Poor Man, put him in Prifon,
ruin'd his Family ; and not only Fin'd
him *Ultra tenementum*, but expos'd him
in the *high Places of their Capital City*, for
the Mob to laugh at him for a Fool : This
is a Punifhment not unlike *our Pillory*, and
was appointed for *mean Criminals*, Fellows
that Cheat and Couzen People, Forge
Writings, Forfwear themfelves, and the
like ; and the People, that it was expected would have treated this Man very ill,
on the contrary *Pitied him*, wifht thofe
that

that set him there placed in his room, and exprest their Affections, by *loud Shouts* and Acclamations, when he was taken down.

But as this happen'd before my first Visit to that World, when I came there all was over with him, his particular Enemies were disgrac'd and turn'd out, and the Man was not at all the worse receiv'd by his Country-folks than he was before ; and so much for the *Man in the* Moon.

After we had settled the Debate between us, about the Nature and Quality, I desir'd him to show me some Plan or Draft of *this new World* of his ; upon which, he brought me out a pair of very beautiful Globes, and there I had an immediate Geographical Description of the Place.

I found it less by   Degrees than Our *Terrestial Globe*, but more Land and less Water ; and as I was particularly concern'd to see something in or near the same Climate with Our selves, I observ'd a large extended Country to the North, about the Latitude of 50 to 56 Northern Distance ; and enquiring of that Country,

he

he told me it was one of the beſt Countries in all their World : That it was his
Native Climate, and he was juſt a going
to it, and would take me with him.

He told me in General, the Country
was Good, Wholſome, Fruitful, rarely
Scituate for Trade, extraordinarily Ac-
commodated with Harbours, Rivers and
Bays for Shipping; full of Inhabitants ;
for it had been Peopled from all Parts,
and had in it ſome of the Blood of all the
Nations in the *Moon.*

He told me, as the Inhabitants were
the moſt Numerous, ſo they were the
ſtrangeſt People that liv'd ; both their
Natures, Tempers, Qualities, Actions,
and way of Living, was made up of innumerable Contradictions : That they were
the *Wiſeſt* Fools, and the *Fooliſheſt* Wiſe
Men in the World ; the *Weakeſt* Strongeſt,
Richeſt Pooreſt, moſt *Generous* Covetous,
Bold Cowardly, *Falſe* Faithful, *Sober*
Diſſolute, *Surly* Civil, *Slothful* Diligent,
Peaceable Quarrelling, *Loyal* Seditious Nation that ever was known.

Beſides

Befides my Obfervations which I made my felf, and which could only furnifh me with what was prefent, and which I fhall take time to inform my Reader with as much Care and Concifenefs as poffible ; I was beholding to this Old *Lunarian*, for every thing that was Hiftorical or Particular.

And Firft, He inform'd me, That in this new Country they had very feldom any Clouds at all, and confequently no extraordinary Storms, but a conftant Serenity, moderate Breezes cooled the Air, and conftant Evening Exhalations kept the Earth moift and fruitful ; and as the Winds they had were various and ftrong enough to affift their Navigation, fo they were without the Terrors, Dangers, Shipwrecks and Deftructions, which he knew we were troubled with in this our *Lunar* World, as he call'd it.

The firft juft Obfervation I made of this was, That I fuppos'd from hence the wonderful Clearnefs of the Air, and the Advantage of fo vaft Optick Capacities they enjoy'd, was obtained : *Alas* ! fays the

Old

Old Fellow, *You fee nothing to what fome
of our* Great Eyes *fee in fome Parts of this
World, nor do you fee any thing compar'd to
what you may fee by the help of fome new Invented Glaffes, of which I may in time let
you fee the Experiment ; and perhaps you may
find this to be the reafon why we do not fo
abound in Books as in your* Lunar World ;
and that except it be fome extraordinary
Tranflations *out of your Country, you will
find but little in our Libraries, worth giving you a great deal of Trouble.*

We immediately quitted the Philofophical Difcourfe of Winds, and I began
to be mighty Inquifitive after thefe Glaffes and Tranflations, and

1*ft*, I underftood here was a ftrange
fort of Glafs that did not fo much bring
to the Eye, as by I know not what wonderful Operation carried out the Eye to
the Object, and quite varies from all our
Doctine of Opticks, by forming feveral
ftrange *Phænomena* in Sight, which we are
utterly unacquainted with ; nor could
Vifion, Rarification, or any of our School-
mens fine Terms, ftand me in any ftead
in this cafe ; but here was fuch Additions
of

of *piercing Organs*, Particles of *Transpa-renee, Emiffion, Tranfmiffion, Mediums,* Contraction of *Rays*, and a Thoufand Applications of things prepar'd for the wondrous Operation, that you may be fure are requifite for the bringing to pafs fomething yet unheard of on this fide the *Moon*.

Firft we were inform'd, by the help of thefe Glaffes, ftrange things, which pafs in our World for Non-Entities, is to be feen, and very Perceptible ; for Example :

State Polity, in all its Meanders, Shifts, Turns, Tricks, and Contraries, are fo exactly Delineated and Defcrib'd, That they are in hopes in time to draw a pair of Globes out, to bring all thofe things to a certainty.

Not but that it made fome Puzzle, even among thefe Clear-fighted Nations, to determine what *Figure* the Plans and Drafts of this undifcover'd *World of Myfte-ries* ought to be defcrib'd in : Some were of Opinion, it ought to be an *Irregular Centagon*, a Figure with an Hundred *Cones*

or

or Angles : Since the *Unaccountables* of this State-Science, are hid in a Million of *undiscover'd Corners* ; as the Craft, Subtilty and Hypocrify of Knaves and Courtiers have concealed them, never to be found out, but by this wonderful *D - - - l-**fcope*, which feem'd to threaten a perfect Difcovery of all thofe *Nudities*, which have lain hid in the Embrio, and falfe Conceptions of *Abortive Policy*, ever fince the Foundation of the World.

Some were of Opinion, this Plan ought to be Circular, and in a Globular Form, fince it was on all fides alike, full of *dark Spots*, untrod Mazes, *waking Mifchiefs*, and fleeping Myfteries ; and being delineated like the Globes difplay'd, would difcover all the Lines of Wickednefs to the Eye at one view : Befides, they fancied fome fort of Analogy in the Rotundity of the Figure, with the continued Circular Motion of all Court-Policies, in the ftated Round of Univerfal Knavery.

Others would have had it *Hyrogliphical* as by a *Hand in Hand*, the Form reprefenting the Affinity between *State Policy* here, and *State Policy* in the Infernal Regions, with fome unkind Similies between the Oeconomy of Satan's Kingdom, and thofe

thofe of moft of the Temporal Powers on Earth ; but this was thought too unkind. At laft it was determin'd, That neither of thefe Schemes were capable of the vaft Defcription ; and that, therefore, the Drafts muft be made fingle, tho' not dividing the Governments, yet dividing the Arts of Governing into proper diftinct Schemes, *viz.*

1. A particular Plan of *Publick Faith* ; and here we had the Experiment immediately made : The Reprefentation is quallified for the Meridian of any *Country*, as well in *our World* as *theirs* ; and turning it to'ards *our own World*, there I faw plainly an *Exchequer fhut up*, and 20000 Mourning Families felling their *Coaches, Horfes, Whores, Equipages*, &c. for Bread, the Government ftanding by laughing, and looking on : Hard by I faw the *Chamber* of a great City fhut up, and Forty Thoufand *Orphans* turn'd a-drift in the World ; fome had no *Cloaths*, fome no *Shoes*, fome no *Money* ; and ftill the City Magiftrates calling upon other Orphans, to *pay their Money in*. Thefe things put me in mind of the Prophet *Ezekiel*, and methoughts I heard the fame Voice that fpoke to him, calling me, and telling me, *Come hither,*

and

aud I'll show thee greater Abominations than these : So looking still on that vast Map, by the help of these Magnifying-Glasses, I saw *huge Fleets hir'd for Transport-Service, but never paid* ; vast Taxes *Anticipated*, that were never Collected ; others Collected and *Appropriated*, but Misapplied : Millions of *Talleys* struck to be Discounted, and the Poor paying 40 *per Cent*, to receive their Money. I saw huge Quantities of Money *drawn in*, and little or none *issued out* ; vast Prizes taken *from the Enemy*, and then taken away again at home by *Friends* ; Ships *sav'd* on the Sea, and sunk in the *Prize Offices* ; Merchants *escaping* from Enemies at Sea, and be *Pirated* by *Sham Embargoes, Counterfeit Claims, Confiscations*, &c a-shoar : There we saw *Turkey-Fleets* taken into Convoys, and Guarded to the very Mouth of the Enemy, and then *abandon'd for their better Security* : Here we saw Monf. *Pouchartrain* shutting up the Town-house of *Paris*, and plundring the Bank of *Lyons.*

2. Here we saw the State of the War among Nations ; Here was the *French* giving Sham-thanks for Victories they
never

never got, and fome body elfe adreffing and congratulating *the fublime Glory of running away :* Here was *Te Deum* for Sham-Victories by Land ; and there was Thankfgiving for *Ditto by Sea :* Here we might fee two Armies fight, both run a-way, and *both come and thank GOD for nothing :* Here we faw a Plan of a late War like that in *Ireland* ; there was all the Officers *curfing* a Dutch *General*, be-caufe the damn'd Rogue would fight, and *fpoil a good War*, that with decent Ma-nagement and *good Husbandry*, might have been *eek't out* this Twenty Years ; there was whole Armies hunting two *Cows* to one *Irifhman*, and driving of black Cattle declar'd the *Noble End of the War :* Here we faw a Country full of Stone Walls and ftrong Towns, where every Campaign, the Trade of War was carried on by the Soldiers, with the fame Intriguing as it was carried on in the Council Chambers ; there was Millions of Contributions rai-fed, and vaft Sums Collected, but no *Taxes leffen'd* ; whole *Plate Fleets* furpriz'd, but no *Treafure found* ; vaft Sums *loft* by Enemies, and yet never *found* by Friends, Ships loaded with Volatile Silver, that came away *full*, and gat home *empty* ; whole

Voyages

Voyages made to beat *No body*, and plunder *Every body* ; two Millions robb'd from the honeft Merchants, and not a Groat fav'd for the honeft Subjects : There we faw Captains Lifting Men with the Governments Money, and letting them go again for their own ; Ships fitted out at the Rates of Two Millions a Year, to fight but once in Three Years, and then *run away* for want of Powder and Shot.

There we faw *Partition Treaties* damned, and the whole given away, *Confederacies* without *Allies*, *Allies* without *Quota's*, *Princes* without *Armies*, *Armies* without *Men*, and *Men* without *Money*, *Crowns* without *Kings*, *Kings* without *Subjects*, more *Kings* than *Countries*, and more *Countries* than were worth fighting for.

Here we could fee the King of *France* upbraiding his Neighbours with difhonourably affifting his Rebels, *though the Mifchief was, they did it not neither* ; and in the fame Breath, affifting the *Hungarian* Rebels againft the Emperor ; M. Ld N. refufing fo difhonourable an Action, as to aid the Rebellious *Camifars*, but Leaguing with the Admirant *de Caftile*, to Invade

vade the Dominions of his Mafter to whom he fwore Allegiance : Here we faw Pro. teftants fight againſt Proteſtants, *to help Papiſts*, Papiſts againſt Papiſts *to help Proteſtants*, Proteſtants call in Turks, to keep Faith againſt Chriſtians *that break it :* Here we could fee *Swedes* fighting for Revenge, and call it Religion ; *Cardinals* depofing their Catholick Prince, to introduce the Tyranny *of a Lutheran*, and call it Liberty ; *Armies* Electing Kings, and call it Free Choice ; *French* conquering *Savoy*, to fecure the Liberty of *Italy*.

3. The Map of State Policy contains abundance of Civil Tranſactions, no where to be difcover'd but in this *wonderful Country*, and by this prodigious Invention : As firſt, it ſhows an Eminent Prelate running in every body's Debt to relieve the Poor, and bring to *God* Robbery for *Burnt-Offering :* It opens a Door to the Fate of Nations; and there we might fee the *Duke of S--y* bought three times, and his Subjects fold every time ; *Portugal* bought twice, and neither time worth *the Earneſt* ; *Spain* bought once, but loth to go with the *Bidder* ; *Venice* willing to be Bought, if there had been any Buyers ;

Bavaria

Bavaria Bought, and run away with the
Money ; the Emperor *Bought* and *Sold*,
but Bilkt the Chapman ; the *French* buying Kingdoms he can't *keep*, the *Dutch*
keep Kingdoms they never *Bought* ; and
the *English* paying their Money without
Purchase.

In Matters of Civil Concerns, here was
to be feen *Religion* with no out-fide, and
much *Out-fide* with no Religion, much
Strife about *Peace*, and no Peace in *the
Defign :* Here was Plunder without *Violence*, Violence without *Perfecution*, Confcience without *Good Works*, and Good
Works without *Charity* ; Parties cutting
one anothers Throats *for God's fake*, pulling down Churches *de propoganda fide*, and
making Divifions by way of *Affociation*.

Here we have *Peace and Union* brought
to pafs *The Shorteft Way*, Extirpation and
Deftruction prov'd to be the Road to
Plenty and *Pleafure :* Here all the Wife
Nations, a Learned Author would have
Quoted, *if he could have found them*, are
to be feen, who carry on Exclufive Laws
to the general Safety and Satisfaction of
their Subjects.

Occa-

Occasional Bills may have here a particular Hiftorical, Categorical Defcription : But of them by themfelves.

Here you might have the Rife, Original, Lawfulnefs, Ufefulnefs, and Neceffity of *Paffive Obedience*, as fairly reprefented as a Syftem of Divinity, and as clearly demonftrated *as by a Geographical Defcription* ; and which exceeds our mean Underftanding here, 'tis by the wonderful Affiftance of thefe Glaffes, plainly difcerned to be Coherent *with Refiftance, taking Arms, calling in Foreign Powers, and the like.* --- Here you have a plain Difcovery of *C.* of *E.* Politicks, and a Map of Loyalty : Here 'tis as plainly domonftrated as the Nofe in a Man's Face, *provided he has one,* that a Man may *Abdicate,* drive away, and *Dethrone* his Prince, and yet be abfolutely and intirely free from, and innocent of the leaft *Fracture,* Breach, Incroachment, or Intrenchment, upon the Doctrine of *Non-Refiftance :* Can *fhoot* at his Prince without any Defign to *kill him, fight* againft him without raifing *Rebellion,* and take up Arms, without leaving War againft his Prince.

G   Here

Here they can persecute Dissenters, without desiring they should Conform, conform to the Church they would overthrow ; *Pray* for the Prince they *dare not Name,* and *Name* the Prince they *do not pray for.*

By the help of these Glasses strange Insights are made, into the vast mysterious dark World of *State Policy* ; but that which is yet more strange, and requires vast Volumes to descend to the Particulars of, and huge Diagrams, Spheres, Charts, and a Thousand nice things to display is, That in this vast Intelligent Discovery it is not only made plain, that those things are so, but all the vast Contradictions are made Rational, reconciled to Practice, and brought down to Demonstration.

German Clock-Work, the perpetual Motions, the Prim Mobilies of Our short-sighted World, are Trifles to these Nicer Disquisitions.

Here it would be plain and rational, why a Parliament-Man will spend 5000 *l.* to be Chosen, that cannot get a Groat Honestly by *setting there :* It would be
easily

eafily made out to be rational, why he
that *rails moſt* at a Court is ſooneſt receiv'd *into it :* Here it would be very
plain, how great Eſtates are got in *little
Places*, and Double in *none at all.* 'Tis eaſy
to be prov'd honeſt and faithful to Victual
the *French* Fleet out of *Engliſh* Stores, and
let our own Navy want them ; a long
Sight, or a large Lunar Perſpective, will
make all theſe things not only plain in
Fact, but Rational and Juſtifiable to all
the World.

'Tis a ſtrange thing to any body without doubt, that has not been in that
clear-ſighted Region, to comprehend, That
thoſe we call *High-flyers* in *England* are
the only Friends *to the Diſſenters*, and
have been the moſt Diligent and Faithful
in their Intereſt, of any People in the
Nation ; and yet ſo it is, *Gentlemen*, and
they ought to have the Thanks of the
whole Body for it.

In this advanc'd Station, we ſee it
plainly by Reflexion, That the Diſſenters, like a parcel of Knaves, have retain-
ed all the *High-Church-men* in their Pay ;
they are certainly all in their *Penſion-Roll :*

G 2   Indeed,

Indeed, I could not fee the Money paid
them there, it was too remote ; but I
could plainly fee the thing ; all the
deep Lines of the Project are laid as
true, they are fo *Tackt* and *Confolidated*
together, that if any one will give themfelves leave to confider, they will be moft
effectually convinced, That the *High-
Church* and the *Diffenters* here, are all in
a Caball, a meer Knot, a piece of Clock-
work ; the Diffenters are the Dial-Plate,
and the High-Church the Movement, the
Wheel within the Wheels, the Spring and
the Screw to bring all things to Motion,
and make the *Hand* on the *Dial-plate*
point which way the *Diffenters* pleafe.

For what elfe have been *all the Shams*
they have put upon the *Governments,*
Kings, States, and People they have been
concern'd with ? What Schemes have
they laid on purpofe *to be broken ?* What
vaft Contrivances, on purpofe to be ridicul'd and expos'd ? *The Men are not Fools,*
they had never V---d to *Confolidate* a
B--- but that they were willing to fave
the Diffenters, and put it into a pofture, in which they *were fure it would
mifcarry.* I defy all the Wife Men of
the

the *Moon* to fhow another good reafon for it.

Methinks I begin to pity my Brethren, the moderate Men of the Church, that they cannot fee into this *New Plot*, and to wifh they would but get up into our *Confolidator*, and take a Journey to the *Moon*, and there, by the help of thefe Glaffes, they would fee the *Allegorical*, *Symbollical*, *Hetrodoxicallity* of all this Matter ; it would make immediate Converts of them ; they would fee plainly, that to *Tack* and *Confolidate*, to make *Exclufive Laws*, to *perfecute* for Confcience, *difturb*, and *diftrefs* Parties ; thefe are all *PhanatickPlots*, meer Combinations againft the Church, to bring her into Contempt, and to fix and eftablifh the Diffenters to the end of the Chapter : But of this I fhall find *occafion* to fpeak *Occafionally*, when an *Occafion* prefents it felf, to examine a certain *Occafional Bill*, tranfacting in thefe Lunar Regions, fome time before I had the Happinefs to arrive there.

In examining the Multitude and Variety of thefe *moft admirable Glaffes* for the affifting the *Opticks*, or indeed the Forma-

tion

tion of a new perceptive Faculty ; it was you may be sure moſt ſurprizing, to find there, that Art had exceeded Nature ; and the Power of Viſion was aſſiſted to that prodigious Degree, as even to diſtinguiſh *Non-Entity it ſelf* ; and in theſe ſtrange Engines of Light it could not but be very pleaſing, to diſtinguiſh plainly betwixt *Being* and *Matter*, and to come to a De-termination, in the ſo long Canvaſt Diſ-pute of Subſtance, *vel Materialis, vel Spi-ritualis* ; and I can ſolidly affirm, That in all our Contention between *Entity* and *Non-Entity*, there is ſo *little worth med-dling with*, that had we had theſe Glaſſes ſome Ages ago, we ſhould have left trou-bling our Heads with it.

I take upon me, therefore, to aſſure my Reader, That whoever pleaſes to take a Journey, or Voyage, or Flight up to theſe *Lunar Regions*, as ſoon as ever he comes aſhear there, will preſently be con-vinc'd, of the Reaſonableneſs of *Immate-rial Subſtance*, and the *Immortality*, as well as *Immateriality* of the Soul : He will no ſooner look into theſe Explicating Glaſſes, but he will be able to know the ſeparate meaning of *Body, Soul, Spirit,*
Life,

Life, *Motion*, *Death*, and a Thousand things that *Wise-men* puzzle themselves about here, becaufe they are not *Fools enough to underftand*.

Here too I find Glaffes for the *Second Sight*, as our Old Women call it. This *Second Sight* has been often pretended to in *Our Regions*, and fome Famous Old Wives have told us, they can fee *Death*, the *Soul*, *Futurity*, and the Neighbourhood of them, in the Countenance : By this *wonderful Art*, thefe good People unfold ftrange Myfteries, *as* under fome *Irrecoverable* Difeafe, to foretell *Death* ; under *Hypocondriack* Melancholy, to prefage *Trouble of Mind* ; in pining Youth, to predict *Contagious Love* ; and an Hundred other Infallibilities, *which never fail to be true as foon as ever they come to pafs*, and are all grounded upon the fame Infallibility, by which a Shepherd may always know when any one of his Sheep *is Rotten*, viz. *when he fhakes himfelf to pieces*.

But all this Guefs and Uncertainty is a Trifle, to the vaft Difcoveries of thefe *Explicatory Optick-Glaffes* ; for here are feen the Nature and Confequences of Se-

cret

cret Myfteries : Here are read ftrange
Myfteries relating to *Predeftination*, *Eter-*
nal Decrees, and the like : Here 'tis plainly prov'd, That *Predeftination* is, in fpight
of all Enthufiaftick Preterces, fo intirely
committed into Man's Power, that whoever pleafes to *hang himfelf to Day*, won't
Live till to Morrow ; no, though *Forty*
Predeftination Prophets were to tell him,
His time was not yet come. Thefe abftrufe
Points are commonly and folemnly Dif-
cufs'd here ; and thefe People are fuch
Hereticks, that they fay *God's Decrees* are
all fubfervient to the means of his *Provi-*
dence ; That what we call Providence is
a fubjecting all things to the great *Chain*
of Caufes and Confequences, by which that
one Grand Decree, That all Effects fhall
Obey, without referve to their proper
moving Caufes, fupercedes all *fubfequent*
Doctrines, or pretended Decrees, or Predeftination in the World : That by this
Rule, he that *will kill himfelf*, G O D,
Nature, Providence, or Decree, will not
be concern'd *to hinder him*, but *he fhall*
Die ; any Decrees, Predeftination, or
Fore-Knowledge of Infinite Power, *to the*
contrary in any wife, notwithftanding that it
is in a Man's Power to throw himfelf into
the

the Water, *and be Drown'd* ; and to kill another Man, *and he shall Die*, and to say, God appointed it, is to make him the Author of Murther, and to injure the Murtherer in putting him to Death for what he could not help doing.

All these things are *received Truths* here, and no doubt would be so every where else, if the Eyes of Reason were open'd to the Testimony of Nature, or if they had the helps of these most *Incomparable Glasses.*

Some pretended, by the help of these *Second-sight Glasses,* to see the common Periods of Life ; and Others said, they could see a great way beyond *the leap in the Dark :* I confess, all I could see of the first was, that holding up the Glass against the Sea, I plainly saw, as it were on the edge of the Horizon, these Words,

*The Verge of Life and Death is here.
'Tis best to know where' tis, but not how far.*

As to seeing *beyond Death,* all the Glasses I lookt into for that purpose, *made but little of it* ; and these were the only *Tubes* that I found Defective ; for here I
could

could difcern nothing but Clouds, Mifts, and thick dark hazy Weather ; but revolving in my Mind, that I had read a *certain Book* in our own Country, called, *Nature* ; it prefently occurr'd, That the Conclufion of it, to all fuch as gave themfelves the trouble of making out thofe foolifh things call'd Inferences, was always *Look up* ; upon which, turning one of their Glaffes *Up,* and erecting the Point of it towards the *Zenith,* I faw thefe Words in the Air, *REVELATION,* in large Capital Letters.

I had like to have rais'd the Mob upon me for looking *upright* with this Glafs ; for this, they faid, was prying into the Myfteries of the Great *Eye* of the World ; That we ought to enquire no farther than he has inform'd us, and *to believe* what he had left us *more Obfcure :* Upon this, I laid down the Glaffes, and concluded, that we had *Mofes* and the *Prophets,* and fhould be never the likelier to be taught by *One come from the* Moon.

In fhort, I found, indeed, they had a great deal more Knowledge of things than we in this World ; and that *Nature, Science,*

ence, and *Reafon*, had obtained great Improvements in the *Lunar World* ; but as to *Religion*, it was the fame equally refign'd to and concluded in *Faith* and *Redemption* ; fo I fhall give the World no great Information of thefe things.

I come. next to fome other ftrange Acquirements obtained by the helps of thefe Glaffes ; and particularly for the difcerning the *Imperceptibles* of Nature ; fuch as, the *Soul*, *Thought*, *Honefty*, *Religion*, *Virginity*, and an Hundred other nice things, too fmall for humane Difcerning.

The Difcoveries made by thefe Glaffes, as to the *Soul*, are of a very diverting Variety ; fome *Hieroglyphical*, and *Emblematical*, and fome Demonftrative.

The *Hieroglyphical* Difcoveries of the Soul make it appear in the *Image of its Maker* ; and the Analogy is remarkable, even in the very *Simily* ; for as they reprefent the Original of Nature as *One Great Eye*, illuminating as well as difcerning all things ; fo the *Soul*, in its *Allegorical*, or *Hieroglyphical* Refemblance, appears

pears as a *Great Eye,* embracing the Man,
enveloping, operating, and informing every Part ; *from whence* thofe fort of People who we falfly call *Politicians,* affect-
ing fo much to put out *this Great Eye,* by
acting againft their common Underftandings, are very aptly reprefented by *a great
Eye, with Six or Seven pair of Spectacles on* ;
not but that the Eye of their Souls may
be clear enough of it felf, as to the common Underftanding ; but that they happen to have occafion to look fometimes
fo many ways at once, and to judge, conclude, and underftand *fo many contrary
ways* upon one and the fame thing; that
they are fain to put double Glaffes upon
their Underftanding, as we look at the
Solar Ecclipfes, to reprefent 'em in *different
Lights,* leaft *their Judgments* fhould not
be wheadled into a Compliance with the
Hellifh Refolutions of their Wills ; and this
is what I call the Emblematick Reprefentation of the Soul.

As for the Demonftrations of the *Soul's
Exiftence,* 'tis a plain cafe, by thefe *Ex-
plicative Glaffes,* that *it is,* fome have pretended to give us the Parts ; and we have
heard of Chyrurgeons, that could read
an

an Anatomical Lecture on the Parts of the Soul ; and thefe pretend it to be a Creature in form, whether *Camelion* or *Salamandar*, Authors have not determin'd ; nor is it compleatly difcover'd *when* it comes into the Body, or *how* it goes out, or *where* its Locality or Habitation is, while 'tis a Refident.

But they very aptly fhow it, like a Prince, in his Seat, in the middle of *his Palace the Brain*, iffuing out his inceffant Orders to innumerable Troops of *Nerves*, *Sinews*, *Mufcles*, *Tendons*, *Veins*, *Arteries*, *Fibres*, *Capilariy*, and *ufeful Officers*, call'd *Organici*, who faithfully execute all the Parts of *Senfation*, *Locomotion*, *Concoction*, &c. and in the Hundred-Thoufandth part of *a Moment*, return with particular Meffages for *Information*, and demand New *Inftructions*. If any part of *his Kingdom*, *the Body*, fuffers a Depredation, or an Invafion of the Enemy, the Expreffes fly to the Seat of the Soul, *the Brain*, and immediately are order'd back *to fmart*, that the Body may of courfe fend more Meffengers *to complain* ; immediately other Expreffes are difpatcht to the Tongue, with Orders *to cry out*, that the Neighbours

may

may come in and help, or Friends fend
for the Chyrurgeon : Upon *the Application*, and a Cure, *all is quiet*, and the
fame Expreffes are difpatcht to the Tongue
to be hufh, and fay no more of it till farther Orders : All this is as plain to be
feen in thefe Engines, *as the Moon* of *Our
World* from the World in the *Moon*.

As the Being, Nature, and Scituation
of *humane Soul* is thus *Spherically* and *Mathematically* difcover'd, I could not find
any Second Thoughts about it in all their
Books, whether of their own Compofition
or by Tranflation ; for it was a General
received Notion, That there could not
be a greater Abfurdity in humane Knowledge, than to imploy the Thoughts in
Queftioning, what is as plainly known
by its Confequences, as if feen with *the
Eye* ; and that to doubt the Being or Extent of the Soul's Operation, is to *imploy
her againft her felf*; and therefore, when
I began to argue with my Old Philofopher, againft the Materiality and Immortality of this Myftery we call *Soul*, he
laught at me, and told me, he found we
had none of their Glaffes in our World ;
and

and bid me fend all our *Scepticks, Soul-Sleepers*, our *Cowards, Bakers, Kings* and *Bakewells*, up to him into the *Moon*, if they wanted Demonſtrations; where, by the help of their Engines, they would make it plain to them, that the *Great Eye* being one vaſt Intellect, *Infinite* and *Eternal*, all *Inferior Life* is a Degree of *himſelf*, and as exactly repreſents him as one little *Flame* the whole Maſs of *Fire* ; That it is therefore uncapable of Diſſolution, being like its Original in Duration, as well as in its Powers and Faculties, but that it goes and returns by *Emiſſion, Regreſſion*, as the *Great Eye* governs and determines ; and this was plainly made out, by the Figure I had ſeen it in, *viz.* an *Eye*, the exact Image of its Maker : 'Tis true, *it was darkned* by Ignorance, Folly and Crime, and therefore oblig'd *to wear Spectacles* ; but tho' theſe were Defects or Interruptions in its Operation, they were none in its Nature ; which as it had its immediate Efflux from *the Great Eye*, and its return to him muſt partake of himſelf, and could not but be of a Quality *uncomatable*, by Caſualty or Death.

From

From this Difcourfe we the more willingly adjourned our prefent Thoughts, *I
being clearly convinced of the Matter* ; and
as for our Learned Doctors, with their
Second and Third *Thoughts*, I told him I
would recommend them *to the Man in the*
Moon for their farther Illumination, which
if they refufe to accept, it was but juft
they fhould remain *in a Wood*, where *they
are*, and are *like to be*, puzzling themfelves
about Demonftrations, fquaring of Circles,
and converting *oblique* into *right Angles*,
to bring out a Mathematical *Clock-Work
Soul*, that will go till the *Weight is down*,
and then ftand ftill till *they know not who*
muft wind it up again.

However, I cannot pafs over a very
ftrange and extraordinary piece of Art
which this Old Gentleman inform'd me
of, and that was an Engine *to fcrew a Man
into himfelf :* Perhaps our Country-men
may be at fome Difficulty to comprehend
thefe things by my dull Defcription ; and
to fuch I cannot but recommend, a Journey *in my Engine to the* Moon.

This

This *Machine* that I am fpeaking of, contains a multitude of *ftrange Springs* and *Screws*, and a Man that puts himſelf into it, is very infenſibly carried into *vaſt Speculations*, *Reflexions*, and *regular Debates with himſelf :* They have a very hard Name for it in thoſe Parts ; but if I were to give it an *Engliſh* Name, it ſhould be call'd, *The Cogitator*, or *the Chair of Reflection*.

And Firſt, The Perſon that is ſeated here feels ſome pain in paſſing ſome *Negative Springs*, that are wound up, effectually to ſhut out all *Injecting, Diſturbing* Thoughts ; and the better to prepare him for the Operation that is to follow, and this is without doubt a very rational way ; for when a Man can *abſolutely ſhut out all manner of thinking*, but what he is upon, he ſhall think the more Intenſly upon the one object before him.

This Operation paſt, here are *certain Screws* that draw *direct Lines* from every *Angle of the Engine to the Brain of the Man*, and at the ſame time, other direct Lines to his Eyes ; at the other end of

H   which

which Lines, there are Glaffes which
convey or reflect the Objects the Perfon is
defirous to *think upon*.

Then the main Wheels are turn'd, which
wind up according to their feveral Offices ; *this* the Memory, *that* the Underftanding, a *third* the Will, a *fourth* the
thinking Faculty ; and thefe being put
all into regular Motions, pointed by direct Lines to their proper Objects, and
perfectly uninterrupted by the Interven-
tion of Whimfy, Chimera, and a Thoufand fluttering *Dæmons* that Gender in
the Fancy, but are effectually Lockt out
as before, affift one another to receive
right Notions, and form juft Ideas of the
things they are directed to, and from
thence the Man is impower'd to make
right Conclufions, *to think and act like
himfelf*, fuitable to the fublime Qualities
his Soul was originally bleft with.

There never was a Man went into one
of thefe *thinking Engines*, but he came
wifer out than he was before ; and I am
perfuaded, it would be a more effectual
Cure to our *Deifm, Atheifm, Scepticifm*,
and all other *Scifms*, than ever the *Italian's*
Engine,

Engine, for curing the Gout by cutting off the Toe.

This is a moſt wonderful Engine, and performs admirably, and my Author gave me extraordinary Accounts of the good Effeȼts of it ; and I cannot but tell my Reader, That our Sublunar World ſuffers Millions of Inconveniencies, for want of this thinking Engine : I have had a great many Projeȼts in my Head, how to bring our People to regular thinking, but 'tis in vain without this Engin ; and how to get the Model of it I know not ; how to ſcrew up the Will, the Underſtanding, and the reſt of the Powers ; how to bring the Eye, the Thought, the Fancy, and the Memory, into Mathematical Order, and obedient to Mechanick Operation ; help *Boyl, Norris, Newton, Manton, Hammond, Tillotſon,* and all the Learned Race, help *Phyloſophy, Divinity, Phyſicks, Oeconomicks,* all's in vain, a Mechanick Chair of Refleȼtion is the only Remedy that ever I found in my Life for this Work.

As to the Effeȼts of Mathematical thinking, what Volumes might be writ of it will more eaſily appear, if we conſider the

wondrous

wondrous Ufefulnefs of this Engine in all
humane Affairs ; as of *War*, *Peace*, *Juftice*,
Injuries, *Paffion*, *Love*, *Marriage*, *Trade*,
Policy, and *Religion*.

When a Man has been fcrew'd into himfelf, and brought by this Art to a Regularity of Thought, he never commits any
Abfurdity after it ; his Actions are fqua-
red by the fame Lines, for Action is but
the Confequence of Thinking ; and he
that acts before he thinks, fets humane
Nature with the bottom upward.

M. would never have made his Speech,
nor the famous *B- - - -ly* wrote a Book, if
ever they had been in this thinking Engine : One would have never told us of
Nations he never faw, nor the other told
us, he had feen a great many, and was
never the Wifer.

H. had never ruin'd his Family to Mar-
ry Whore, Thief and Beggar-Woman, in
one Salliant Lady, after having been told
fo honeftly, and fo often of it by the very Woman her felf.

Our

Our late unhappy Monarch had never trufted the *Englifh* Clergy, when they preacht up that Non-Refiftance, which he muft needs fee they could never Practice; had his Majefty been fcrew'd up into this *Cogitator*, he had prefently reflected, that it was againft Nature to expect they fhould ftand ftill, and let him tread upon them : That they fhould, whatever they had preacht or pretended to, hold open their Throats to have them be cut, and tye their own Hands from refifting the Lord's Anointed.

Had fome of our Clergy been fcrew'd in this Engine, they had never turned Martyrs for their Allegiance to the Late King, only for the Lechery of having Dr. *S*------- in their Company.

Had our Merchants been manag'd in this Engine, they had never trufted their *Turkey* Fleet with a famous Squadron, that took a great deal of care to Convoy them fafe into the Enemies Hands.

Had fome People been in this Engine, when they had made a certain League in

the

the World, in order to make amends for
a better made before, they would certainly have confider'd farther, before they had
embarkt with a Nation, that are neither
fit to go abroad nor ftay at Home.

As for the Thinking practis'd in Noble
Speeches, *Occafional Bills*, Addreffings a-
bout Prerogative, Convocation Difputes,
Turnings in and Turnings out at Ours,
and all the Courts of *Chriftendom*, I have
nothing to fay to it.

Had the Duke of *Bavaria* been in our
Engine, he would never have begun a
Quarrel, which he knew all the Powers
of *Europe* were concern'd to fupprefs, and
lay all other Bufinefs down till it was done.

Had the Elector of *Saxony* paft the O-
peration of this Engine, he would never
have beggar'd a Rich Electorate, to ruin
a beggar'd Crown, nor fold himfelf for a
Kingdom hardly worth any Man's taking:
He would never have made himfelf lefs
than he was, in hopes of being really no
greater; and ftept down from a Proteftant
Duke, and Imperial Elector, to be a No-
minal Mock-King with a fhadow of Power,
and

and a Name without Honour, Dignity or Strength.

Had Monf. *Tallard* been in our Engine, he would not only not have attackt the Confederates when they paſt the Morafs and Rivulet in his Front, but not have attackt them at all, nor have ſuffer'd them to have attackt him, it being his Bufinefs not to have fought at all, but have linger'd out the War, till the Duke of *Savoy* having been reduced, the Confederate Army muſt have been forced to have divided themfelves of courfe, in order to defend their own.

Some that have been very forward to have us proceed *The Shorteſt Way* with the *Scots*, may be faid to ftand in great need of this Chair of Reflection, to find out a juſt Caufe for fuch a War, and to make a Neighbour-Nation making themfelves fecure, a fufficient Reafon for another Neighbour-Nation to fall upon them : Our Engine would prefently fhow it them in a clear fight, by way of Paralel, that 'tis juſt with the fame Right as a Man may break open a Houfe, becaufe the People bar and bolt the Windows.

If

If fome-body has chang'd Hands there from bad to worfe, and open'd inftead of clofing Differences in thofe Cafes, the *Cogitator* migyt have brought them, by more regular Thinking, to have known that was not at all the Method of bringing the S---s to Reafon.

Our *Cogitator* would be a very neceffary thing to fhow fome People, That Poverty and Weaknefs is not a fufficient Ground to opprefs a Nation, and their having but little Trade, cannot be a fufficient Ground to equip Fleets to take away what they have.

I cannot deny, that I have often thought they have had fomething of this Engine in our Neighbouring *Antient Kingdom*, fince no Man, however we pretend to be angry, but will own they are in the right of it, as to themfelves, to Vote and procure Bills for their own Security, and not to do as others demand without *Conditions* fit to be accepted : But of that by it felf.

There are abundance of People in Our World, of all forts and Conditions, that
.ftand

stand in need of our thinking Engines, and *to be screw'd into themselves a little,* that they might think as directly as they speak absurdly : But of these also in a Class by it self.

This Engine has a great deal of Philosophy in it, and particularly, 'tis a wonderful Remedy against *Poreing* ; and as it was said of Monf. *Jurieu* at *Amsterdam,* that he us'd to *lose himself in himself* ; by the Assistance of this piece of Regularity, a Man is most effectually secur'd against *bewildring Thoughts,* and by direct thinking, he prevents all manner of dangerous wandring, since nothing can come to more speedy Conclusions, than that which in right Lines, points to the proper Subject of Debate.

All sorts of *Confusion of Thoughts* are perfectly avoided and prevented in this case, and a Man is never troubled with *Spleen, Hyppo,* or *Mute Madness,* when once he has been thus under the Operation of *the Screw* : It prevents abundance of Capital Disasters in Men, in private Affairs ; it prevents *hasty Marriages, rash Vows, Duels, Quarrels,* Suits at *Law,* and most sorts of *Repentance.*

Repentance. In the State, it saves a Government from many Inconveniences ; it checks immoderate *Ambition,* stops *Wars, Navies* and *Expeditions* ; especially it prevents Members making *long Speeches* when they have *nothing to say* ; it keeps back Rebellions, Insurrections, Clashings of Houses, *Occasional Bills, Tacking,* &c.

It has a wonderful Property in our Affairs at Sea, and has prevented many a *Bloody Fight,* in which a great many honest Men might have lost their Lives that are now useful Fellows, and help to Man and manage Her Majesty's Navy.

What if some People are apt to charge Cowardice upon some People in those Cases? 'Tis plain *that* cannot be *it*, for he that dare incur the Resentment of the *English* Mob, shows more Courage than would be able to carry him through Forty Sea-fights.

'Tis therefore for want of being in this Engine, that we censure People, because they don't be knocking one another on the Head, like the People at the *Bear-Garden* ; where, if they do not see the

Blood

Blood run about, they always cry out, *A Cheat* ; and the poor Fellows are fain to cut one another, that they may not be pull'd a pieces ; where the Case is plain, they are *bold for fear*, and pull up Courage enough to Fight, becaufe they are afraid of the People.

This Engine prevents all forts of *Lunacies*, *Love-Frenzies*, and *Melancholy-Madnefs*, for preferving the Thought in right Lines to direct Objects, it is impoffible any *Deliriums*, *Whimfies*, or *fluttering Air* of Ideas, can interrupt the Man, he can never be Mad ; for which reafon I cannot but recommend it to my Lord *S---*, my Lord *N---*, and my Lord *H-----*, as abfolutely neceffary to defend them from the State-Madnefs, which for fome Ages has poffeft their Families, and which runs too much in the Blood.

It is alfo an excellent Introduction to Thought, and therefore very well adapted to thofe People whofe peculiar Talent and Praife is, That *they never think at all.* Of thefe, if his Grace of *B---d* would pleafe to accept Advice from the *Man in the Moon*, it fhould be to put himfelf into
this

this Engine, as a Soveraign Cure to the known Difeafe call'd the *Thoughtlefs Evil.*

But above all, it is an excellent Remedy, and very ufeful to a fort of People, who are always *Travelling* in Thought, but never *Deliver'd* into Action ; who are fo exceeding bufy at Thinking, they have no leifure for Action ; of whom the late Poet fung well to the purpofe ;

- - - - *Some modern Coxcombs, who*
Retire to Think, 'caufe they have nought to do ;
For Thoughts were giv'n for Actions Government,
Where Action ceafes, Thought Impertinent :
The Sphere of Action is Life's Happinefs,
And he that Thinks beyond, Thinks like an Afs.

Rocheft. Poems, *p. 9.*

Thefe Gentlemen would make excellent ufe of this Engine, for it would teach 'em to difpatch one thing before they begin another ; and therefore is of fingular ufe to honeft *S- - - -*, whofe peculiar it was, to be always beginning Projects, but never finifh any.

The Variety of this Engine, its Ufes, and Improvements, are Innumerable, and
the

the Reader muſt not expeƈt I can give
any thing like a perfeƈt Deſcription of it.

There are yet another ſort of Machine,
which I never obtained a ſight of, till the
laſt Voyage I made to this Lunar Orb,
and theſe are called *Elevators :* The Mechanick Operations of theſe are wonderful, and helpt by Fire ; by which the
Sences are raiſed to *all the ſtrange Extreams*
we can imagine, and whereby the Intelligent Soul is made to converſe with its
own Species, whether embody'd or not.

Thoſe that are rais'd to a due pitch in
this wondrous Frame, have a clear Proſ-
peƈt into the World of Spirits, and converſe with *Viſions, Guardian-Angels, Spirits departed,* and what not : And as this
is a wonderful Knowledge, and not to be
obtained, but by the help of this Fire ;
ſo thoſe that have try'd the Experiment,
give ſtrange Accounts of *Sympathy, Prex-
iſtence* of Souls, *Dreams,* and the like.

I confeſs, I always believ'd a converſe
of Spirits, and have heard of ſome who
have experienced ſo much of it, as they
could obtain upon *no Body elſe* to believe.

I never ſaw any reaſon to doubt the
Exiſtent State of the Spirit before embody'd, any more than I did of its Immortality

tality after it fhall be uncas'd, and the
Scriptures faying, the Spirit returns to
God that gave it, implies *a coming from,*
or how could it be call'd *a return.*

Nor can I fee a reafon why Embodying
a Spirit fhould altogether Interrupt its
Converfe with the World of Spirits, from
whence it was taken ; and to what elfe
fhall we afcribe *Guardian Angels,* in which
the Scripture is alfo plain ; and from
whence come *Secret Notices,* Impulfe of
Thought, preffing *Urgencies of Inclination,*
to or from this or that altogether Invo-
luntary ; but from fome *waking kind Af-*
fiftant wandring Spirit, which gives fecret
hints to its Fellow-Creature, of fome approaching Evil or Good, which it was
not able to forefee.

For Spirits without the helps of Voice converfe.

I know we have fupplied much of this
with *Enthufiafm* and *conceited Revelation* ;
but the People of this World convince us,
that it may be all Natural, by obtaining
it in a Mechanick way, *viz.* by forming
fomething fuitable to the fublime Nature, which working by Art, fhall only
rectify the more *vigorous Particles* of the
Soul,

Soul, and work it up to *a suitable Eleva-tion.* This Engine is wholly applied to the Head, and Works by Injection ; the chief · Influence being on what we call *Fancy*, or Imagination, which by the heat of strong Ideas, is fermented to a strange heighth, and is thus brought to see back-ward and forward every way, beyond it self : By this a Man fancies himself *in the Moon*, and realizes things there as distinct-ly, as if he was actually talking to *my Old Phylosopher.*

This indeed is an admirable Engine, 'tis compos'd of *an Hundred Thousand* ra-tional Consequences, *Five times the num-ber* of Conjectures, Supposes, and Proba-bilities, besides an innumerable Company of fluttering Suggestions, and Injections, which hover round the Imagination, and are all taken in as fast as they can be Con-cocted and Digested there : These are form'd into Ideas, and some of those so well put together, so exactly shap'd, so well drest and set out by the Additional Fire of Fancy, that it is no uncommon thing for the Person to be intirely decei-ved by himself, not knowing *the brat of his own Begetting*, nor be able to distin-guish between Reality and Representa-tion :

tion: From hence we have fome People
talking to Images of their own forming,
and feeing more Devils and Spectres than
ever appear'd: From hence we have weaker Heads not able to bear the Operation,
feeing imperfect Vifions, as of Horfes and
Men without Heads or Arms, *Light* without *Fire*, hearing *Voices* without *Sound*,
and Noifes without *Shapes*, as their own
Fears or Fancies broke the *Phænomena* before the intire Formation.

But the more Genuine and perfect Ufe
of thefe vaft Elevations of the Fancy,
which are perform'd, as I faid, by the
Mechanick Operation of Innate Fire, is
to guide Mankind to as much Fore-fight
of things, as either by Nature, or by the
Aid of any thing Extranatural, may be
obtain'd ; and by this exceeding Knowledge, a Man fhall forebode to himfelf
approaching Evil or Good, fo as to avoid
this, or be in the way of that ; and what
if I fhould fay, That the Notices of thefe
things are not only frequent, but conftant,
and require nothing of us, but to make
ufe of this *Elevator*, to keep our Eyes,
our Ears, and our Fancies open to the
hints ; and obferve them ;

You

You may suppose me, if you please, come by this time into those Northern Kingdoms I mention'd before, where my Old Philosopher was a Native, and not to trouble you with any of the needful Observations, Learned Inscriptions, &c. *on the way*, according to the laudable practices of the Famous Mr. *Br---mly*, 'tis sufficient to tell you I found there an *Opulent, Populous, Potent* and *Terrible People*.

I found them at War with one of the greatest Monarchs of the *Lunar* World, and at the same time miserably rent and torn, mangl'd and disorder'd among themselves.

As soon as I obſerv'd the Political posture of their Affairs, (for here a Man sees things mighty soon by the helps of such a Masterly Eye-sight as I have mention'd) and remembring what is said for our Instruction, *That a Kingdom divided against its self cannot stand* ; I ask'd the Old Gentleman if he had *any Estate* in that Country ? He told me, no great matter ; but ask'd me why I put that Question to him ? *Because*, said I, *if this*

I   *People*

People go on fighting and snarling at all the
World, and one among another in this man-
mer, they will certainly be Ruin'd and Un-
done, either subdu'd by some more powerful
Neighbour; whilst one Party will stand still
and see the t'others Throat cut, tho' their
own Turn immediately follows, or else they
will destroy and devour one another. Therefore I told him I would have him Turn
his Estate into Money, and go some
where else; or go back to the other
World with me.

No, no, reply'd the Old Man, *I am*
in no such Fear at this Time, the Scale
of Affairs is very lately chang'd here, says
he, *in but a very few Years.*

I know nothing of that, said I, *but I*
am sure there never was but one spot of
Ground in that World which I came from,
that was divided like them, and that's that
very Country I liv'd in. Here are three
Kingdoms of you in one spot, said I, One *has*
already been Conquer'd and Subdu'd, the
t'other *suppress'd its Native Inhabitants,*
and planted it with her own, and now
carries it with so high a Hand over them
of her own Breed, that *she limits their*
Trade,

Trade, stops their Ports, when the Inhabitants have made their Manufactures, these wont give them leave to send them abroad, impose Laws upon them, refuse to alter and amend those they would make for themselves, make them pay Customs, Excifes, and Taxes, and yet pay the Garrisons and Guards that defend them, themselves; Press their Inhabitants to their Fleets, and carry away their Old Veteran Troops that should defend them, and leave them to raise more to be serv'd in the same manner, will let none of their Mony be carry'd over thither, nor let them Coin any of their own; and a great many such hardships they suffer under the Hand of this Nation as meer Slaves and Conquer'd People, tho' the greatest part of the Traders are the People of the very Nation that treats 'em thus.

On the other hand, this creates Eternal Murmurs, Heart-burnings and Regret, both in the Natives and the Transplanted Inhabitants; the first have shewn their Uneasiness by frequent Insurrections and Rebellions, for Nature prompts the meanest Animal to struggle for Liberty; and these struggles have often been attended with great Cruelty, Ra-

I 2   vages,

vages, Death, Maffacres, and Ruin both
of Families and the Country it felf: As
to the Tranfplanted Inhabitants, they
run into Clandeftine Trade, into corref-
ponding with their Mafters Enemies,
Victualling their Navies, Colonies and
the like, receiving and importing their
Goods in fpight of all the Orders and Directions to the contrary.

Thefe are the effects of Divifions, and
Feuds on that fide ; on the other hand
there is a Kingdom *Entire* Unconquer'd
and *Independent*, and for the prefent, under the fame Monarch with the reft.----
But here their Feuds are greater than
with the other, and *more dangerous by far*
becaufe National : This Kingdom joins
to the North part of the firft Kingdom,
and Terrible Divifions ly among the
two Nations.

The People of thefe two Kingdoms
are call'd if you pleafe for diftinction
fake, for I cannot well make you underftand their hard Names, *Solunarians*
and *Nolunarians*, thefe to the *South* and
thofe to the *North*, the *Solunarians* were
divided in their Articles of Religion ;
the

the Governing Party, or the Eſtabliſh'd
Church, I ſhall call the *Solunarian*
Church; but the whole Kingdom was
full of a ſort of Religious People call'd
Crolians, who like our Diſſenters in *Eng-*
land profeſs divers ſub-divided Opinions
by themſelves, and cou'd not, or wou'd
not, let it go which way it will, joyn
with the Eſtabliſh'd Church.

On the other hand, the Eſtabliſh'd
Church in the Northern Kingdom was
all *Crolians,* but full of *Solunarians* in
Opinions, who were Diſſenters there, as
the *Crolians* were Diſſenters in the South,
and this unhappy mixture occaſion'd
endleſs Feuds, Diviſions, Sub-diviſions
and Animoſities without Number, of
which hereafter.

The Northern Men are Bold, Terrible
Numerous and *Brave,* to the laſt Degree,
but Poor, and by the Encroachments of
their Neighbours, growing poorer every
Day.

The Southern are equally Brave, more
Numerous and Terrible, but Wealthy
and *care not for Wars,* had rather ſtay at

I 3   Home

Home and Quarrel with one another,
than go Abroad to Fight, making good
an Old Maxim, *Too Poor t'Agree, and yet
too Rich to Fight.*

Between these the Feud is great, and
every Day growing greater ; and those
People who pretend to have been in the
Cogitator or *thinking Engine* tell us, all the
lines of Consequences in that Affair point
at a fatal period between the Kingdoms.

The Complaints also are great, and
back'd with fiery Arguments on both
sides ; the Northern Men say, the *Solunarians* have dealt unjustly and unkindly
by them in several Articles ; but the
Southern Men reply with a most powerful Argument, *viz.* they are *Poor*, and
therefore ought to be Oppress'd, Suppress'd, or *any thing.*

But the main Debate is like to lye upon the Article of Choosing *a King*, both
the Nations being under one Government at present, but the Settlement
ending in the Reigning Line, the Northern Men refuse to joyn in Government
again , unless they have a rectification
of some Conditions in which, they say,
they have the worst of it.   In

In this cafe, even the Southern Men themfelves, fay, they believe the *Nolunarians* have been in the *Chair of Reflection*, the *thinking Engine*, and that having fcrew'd their Underftandings into a Direct Pofition to thatMatter before them, they have made a right Judgment of their own Affairs, and *with all their Poverty* ftand on the beft Foot *as to Right*.

But as the matter of this Northern Quarrel comes under a Second Head, and is more properly the Subject of a Second Voyage to the *Moon*; the Reader may have it more at large confider'd in another Clafs, and fome farther Enlightnings in that Affair than perhaps can be reafonably expected of me here.

But of all the Feuds and Brangles that ever poor Nation was embroil'd in, of all the Quarrels, the Factions and Parties that ever the People of any Nation thought worth while to fall out for, none were ever in *reality* fo light, in *effect* fo heavy, in *appearance* fo great, in *fubftance* fo fmall, in *name* fo terrible, in *nature* fo trifling, as thofe for which this Southern

I 4   Country

Country was altogether by the Ears among themſelves.

And this was one Reaſon why I ſo earneſtly enquir'd of my *Lunarian Phi-loſopher*, whether he had an Eſtate in that Country or no. But having told him the Cauſe of that enquiry, he re-ply'd, there was one thing in the Na-ture of his Country-men which ſecur'd them from the ruin which uſually at-tended *divided Nations*, *viz.* that if any Foreign Nation thinking to take the ad-vantage of their Inteſtine Diviſions *fell upon them* in the higheſt of all their Feuds, they'd lay aſide their Parties and Quarrels and preſently *fall in together* to beat out the common Enemy ; and then no ſooner had they obtain'd *Peace abroad*, by their Conduct and Bravery, but they would fall to cutting one anothers Throats again at home *as naturally* as if it had been their proper Calling, and that for Trifles too, *meer Trifles*.

Very well, ſaid I to *my learned Self*, pretty like my own Country ſtill, that whatever Peace they have *abroad*, are ſure to have none *at home*.

To

To come at the hiſtorical Account of theſe *Lunarian* Diſſentions, it will be abſolutely neceſſary to enter a little into the Story of *the Place*, at leaſt as far as relates to the preſent Conſtitution, both of the People, the Government, and the Subject of their preſent Quarrels.

And firſt we are to underſtand, that there has for ſome Ages been carry'd on in theſe Countries, a private feud or quarrel among the People, about a thing call'd by them *Upogyla*, with us very vulgarly call'd *Religion*.

This Difference, as in its Original it was not great, nor indeed upon Points accounted among themſelves Eſſential, ſo it had never been a Difference of any height, if there had not always been ſome one thing, or other, hapning in the State which made the Court-Polititians think it neceſſary to keep the People buſy and embroil'd, to prevent their more narrow Inſpection into Depredations and Encroachments on their Liberties, which was always making on them by the Court.

'Tis

'Tis not deny'd but there might be a Native want of Charity in the Inhabitant, adapting them to Feud, and particularly qualifying them to be always Piquing one another ; and fome of their own Nation, who by the help of the famous Perfpectives before-mentioned, pretend to have feen farther into the Infides of Nature and Conftitution than other People, tell us the crofs Lines of Nature which appear in the make of thofe particular People, fignify a direct *Negative* as to the Article of *Charity* and good Neighbour-hood.

'Twas particularly unhappy to this wrangling People, that Reafons of State fhould always fall in, to make that uncharitablenefs and continual quarrelling Humour neceffary to carry on the Publick Affairs of the Nation, and may pafs for a certain Proof, that the State was under fome Difeafes and Convulfions, which, like a Body that digefts nothing fo well as what is hurtful to its Conftitution, makes ufe of thofe things for its Support, which are in their very Nature, fatal to its being, and

and muft at laft tend to its Deftruction.

But as this however enclin'd them
to be continually *Snarling* at one another, fo as in all Quarrels it generally
appears one Side muft go down.

The prevailing Party therefore always kept the Power in their Hands,
and as the *under* were always Subject
to the lafh they foon took care to hook
their Quarrel into the Affairs of State,
and fo join *Religious* Differences, and
Civil Differences together.

Thefe things had long embroil'd the
Nation, and frequently involv'd them
in bitter Enmities, Feuds, and Quarrels,
and once in a tedious, ruinous, and bloody
War in their own Bowels, in which, contrary to all expectation, this *leffer Party*
prevail'd.

And fince the allegorick Relation
may bear great Similitude with our
European Affairs on this fide *the Moon* :
I fhall for the eafe of Expreffion, and
the better Underftanding of the Reader,

er, frequently call them by the same
Names our unhappy Parties are call'd
by in *England*, as *Solunnarian Church-
men*, and *Crolian Diffenters*, at the same
time defiring my Reader to obferve,
that he is *always to remember* who it is
we are talking of, and that he is *by no
means* to underftand me of any Perfon,
Party, People, Nation, or Place on
this fide the Moon , any Expreffion,
Circumftance, Similitude, or Appearance *to the contrary in any wife notwithftanding.*

    This premis'd, I am to tell the Read-
er that the laft Civil War in this *Lunar*
Country ended in the Victors confounding their own Conquefts by their inteft-
ine Broils, they being as is already noted a moft Eternally Quarrelling Nation ;
upon this new Breach, they that firft
began the War, turn'd about, and plead-
ing that they took up Arms to regulate
the Government , not to overthrow it,
fell in with the Family of their Kings,
who had been banifh'd , *and one of
them deftroy'd* , and reftor'd the Crown
to the Family, and the Nation to the
Crown, juft *for all the World* as the *Pref-
byterians*

byterians in *England* did, in the Cafe of King *Charles* the Second.

The Party that was thus reftor'd, accepted the return the others made to their Duty, and their Affiftance in reftoring the Family of their Monarch, but abated not a Tittle of the old Ran-cour againfl them *as a Party* which they entertain'd at their firft taking Arms, not allowing the return they had made to be *any attonement at all* for the Crimes they had been guilty of before. 'Tis true they pafs'd an Act or Grant of *Ge-neral Pardon*, and Oblivion, as in all fuch Cafes is ufual, and as without which the other would never ha' come in, or have join'd Powers to form the Refto-ration they were bringing to pafs, but the old Feud of Religion continu'd with this addition, that the *Diffenters* were *Re-bels*, *Murtherers*, *King-killers*, Enemies to *Monarchy* and Civil Government, lovers of Confufion, popular, anarchial Go-vernments, and movers of Sedition ; that this was in their very *Nature* and *Principles*, and the like.

In

In this Condition, and under thefe
Mortifications this Party of People liv'd
juft an *Egyptian* Servitude, *viz.* of 40
Years, in which time they were frequently vex'd with Perfecution, *Ha-
rafs'd*, Plunder'd, *Fin'd*, Imprifoned, and
very hardly Treated, infomuch that they
pretend to be able to give an account
of vaft Sums of their Country-Mony,
levy'd upon them on thefe Occafions,
amounting as I take it to 2 Millions of
Lunatians, a Coin they keep their Accounts by there, and much about the
value of our Pound Sterling ; befides
this they were hook't into a great many Sham Plots, and Sworn out of their
Lives and *Eftates* in fuch a manner, that
in the very next Reign the Government
was fo fenfible of their hard treatment,
that they revers'd feveral Sentences by
the fame Authority that had Executed
them ; a moft undeniable Proof they
were afham'd of what had been done ;
at laft, the Prince who was reftor'd as
abovefaid, dyed, and his Brother mount-
ed the Throne ; and now began *a third
Scene* of Affairs, for this Prince was
neither *Church-man*, nor *Diffenter*, but
of a different Religion from them all,
known

known in that Country by the Name of
Abrogratzianifm, and this Religion of his
had this one abfolutely neceffary Confequence in it, that a Man could not be
fincerely and heartily of this, but he muft
be an Implacable hater of both the o-
ther. As this is laid down as a previ-
ous Suppofition, we are with the fame
Reafon to imagine this Prince to be entirely bent upon the Suppreffion and
Deftruction of both the other, if not
abfolutely as to Life and Eftate, yet *entirely* as to Religion.

To bring this the more readily to pafs
like a true Polititian, had his Methods
and Particulars been equally Politick
with his Generals, he began at the right
End, *viz.* to make the Breach between
the *Solunnarian Church*, and the *Crolian
Diffenters* as wide as poffible, and to do
this it was refolv'd to fhift Sides, and
as the Crown had always took part
with the Church, crufh'd, humbl'd,
perfecuted, and by all means poffible
mortify'd the Diffenters, as is noted in
the Reign of his Predeceffor. This
Prince refolv'd to carefs, cherifh, and
encourage the *Crolians* by all poffible
Arts

Arts and outward Endearments, not fo
much that they purpos'd them any real
Favour, *for the deftruction of both was
equally determin'd,* nor fo much that they
expected to draw them over to *Abro-
gratrianifm*, but Two Reafons may
be fuppos'd to give Rife to this Project.

1. The *Lunarian Church* Party had all
along Preach'd up for a part of their Religion, that *Abfolute undifputed Obedience,*
was due from every Subject to their
Prince without any *Referve,* Reluctance
or *Repining*; that as to Refiftance, it was
Fatal to *Body, Soul, Religion, Juftice* and
Government; and tho' the Doctrine was
Repugnant to *Nature,* and to the very
Supreme Command it felf, yet he that
refifted, receiv'd to himfelf Damnation,
juft *for all the World* like our Doctrine of
Paffive Obedience. Now tho' thefe *Solunarian* Church-Men did not abfolutely
believe all they faid themfelves to be
true, yet they found it neceffary to pufh
thefe things to the üttermoft Extremities, becaufe they might the better fix
upon the *Crolian Diffenters,* the Charge
of profeffing lefs Loyal Principles than
they. For as to the *Crolians,* they profefs'd

fefs'd openly they would pay Obedience
to the Prince, as far as the Laws directed, *but no farther.*

Thefe things were run up to ftrange
heights, and the People were always
falling out about what they would do,
or wou'd not do, if things were *fo or fo,*
as they were not, and *were never likely to
be* ; and the hot Men on both fides were
every now and then going together by
the Ears about *Chimeras,* Shadows, *May-
be's* and *Suppofes.*

The hot Men of the *Solunarian Church*
were for knocking the *Crolians* in the
Head, becaufe as they faid they were
Rebels, their *Fathers* were Rebels, and
they would certainly turn Rebels again
upon occafion.

The *Crolians* infifted upon it, that they
had nothing to do with what was done
before they were Born, that if they were
Criminal, becaufe their Fathers were fo,
then a great many who were now of the
Solunarian Church were as Guilty as they,
feveral of the beft Members of that

K   Church

Church having been Born of *Crolian*
Parents.

In the matter of Loyalty they infifted
upon it, they were as Loyal as the *Solunarians*, for that they were as Loyal as
Nature, Reafon and the Laws both of
God and Man requir'd, and what the
other talk'd of *more*, was but a meer
pretence, and fo it would be found if
ever their Prince fhould have occafion
to put them to the Tryal, that he that
pretended to go beyond the Power of
Nature and Reafon, *muft indeed go beyond
them*, and they never defir'd to be brought
into the extream, but they were ready
at any time to fhew fuch Proofs, and
give fuch Demonftrations of their Loyalty, as would fatisfy any reafonable
Prince, and *for more they had nothing to
fay*.

In this pofture of Affairs, this new
Prince found his Subjects when he came
to the Crown, the *Solunarian Church* Carefs'd him, and notwithftanding his being Devoted to the *Abrogratzian Faith*,
they Crown'd him with extraordinary
Acclamations.

They

They were the rather enclin'd to
puſh this forward by how much they
thought it would ſingularly mortify the
Crolians, and all the ſorts of *Diſſenters*,
for they had all along declar'd their abhorrence of the *Abrogratzians* to ſuch a
Degree that they publickly endeavour'd
to have got a general Concurrence of
the whole Nation in the Publick *Cortez*,
or *Dyet* of the Kingdom, to have joyn'd
with them in Excluding this very Prince
by Name, and all other Princes that
ſhould ever embrace the *Abrogratzian*
Faith.

And it wanted but a very little of bringing it to paſs, for almoſt all the Great
Men of the Nation, tho' *Solunarians*, yet
that were Men of *Temper*, Moderation,
and *Fore-ſight*, were for this excluſive
Law. But the *High Prieſts* and *Patri-*
archs of the *Solunarian Church* prevented
it, and upon pretence of this *Paſſive O-*
bedience Principle, made their Intereſt
and gave their Voices for Crowning, or
Entailing the Crown and Government
on the Head of one of the moſt Implacable Enemies both to their Religion
and

and Civil Right that ever the Nation
faw ; *but they liv'd to Repent it too late.*

This Conqueſt over the *Crolians* and
the *Moderate Solunarians,*if it did not ſuppreſs them entirely, it yet gave the other
Party ſuch an aſcendant over them,
that they made no Doubt when that
Prince came to the Crown, they had
done ſo much to oblige him, that he
could deny them nothing, and therefore
in expeĉtation they ſwallow'd up the
whole Body of the *Crolians* at once, and
began to talk of nothing leſs than Ba-
niſhing them to theNorthern part of the
Country, or to certain Iſlands, and
Countries a vaſt way off, where formerly great numbers of them had fled for
ſhelter in like Caſes.

And this was the more probable by
an unhappy Stroke theſe *Crolians* attempted to ſtrike, *but miſcarry'd* in at the
very beginning of this Prince's Reign:
for as they had always profeſt an averſion to this Prince on account of his Religion, as ſoon as their other King was
dead, they ſet up one of his Natural
Sons againſt this King, which the *Solu-*
narian

narians had fo joyfully Crown'd. This youngPrince invaded his Dominions,and great Numbers of the moft zealous *Crolians* joyn'd him.---- But to cut the Story fhort, he was entirely routed by the Forces of the new Prince, for all the *Solunarian Church* joyn'd with him againſt the *Crolians* without any refpeɔ̌t to the Intereſt of Religion, fo they over-threw their Brethren: The young in-vaded Prince was taken and put to Death openly, and *Great Cruelties* were exercis'd in cold Blood upon the poor unhappy People that were taken in the Defeat!

Thus a fecond time thefe Loyal *Solu-narian Church-men* Eftablifh'd their E-nemy, and built up what they were glad afterwards to pull down again, and to beg the affiftance of thofe very *Crolians* whom they had fo rudely handled, to help them demolifh the Power they had erected themfelves, and which now began to fet its foot upon the Throat of thofe that nourifh'd and fupported it.

Upon this exceeding Loyalty and blind Affiftance given to their Prince,

the

the *Solunarians* made no queſtion but they had ſo Eternally bound him to them, that it would be in their Power to pull down the very Name of *Crolianiſm*, and utterly deſtroy it from the Nation.

But the time came on to Undeceive them, for this Prince, whoſe Principle as an *Abrogratzian*, was to deſtroy them both, as it happened, was furniſh'd with Counſellors and Eccleſiaſticks of his own Profeſſion, ten thouſand Times more bent for their general Ruin, than himſelf.

For abſtracted from the Venom and Rancour of his Profeſſion as an *Abrogratzian*, and from the furious Zeal of his *Bramin*, Prieſts, and Religious People, that continually hung about him, and that prompted him to act againſt his Temper and Inclination, by which he ruin'd all, he was elſe a *forward* and *generous* Prince, and likely to have made his People Great and Flouriſhing.

But his *furious Church-Men* ruin'd all his good Deſigns, and turn'd all his

Pro-

Projects to compass the Introduction of his own Religion into his Dominions.

Nay, and had he not fatally been push'd on by such as really design'd his Ruin, to drive this deep Design on too hastily and turn the Scale of his Mannagement from a close and conceal'd, to an open and profess'd Design, he might have gone a great Way with it.----
----- Had he been content to have let that have been twenty Year a doing, which he impatiently as well as preposterously attempted all at once.------- *Wise Men have thought* he might in time have suppreft the *Solunarian Religion*, and have set up his own.

To give a short Scheme of his Proceedings, and with them of the reason of his Miscarriage.

1. Having defeated the Rebellious *Crolians*, as is before noted, and reflecting on the Danger he was in upon the sudden Progress of that Rebellion, for indeed he was within a trifle of Ruin in that Affair; and had not the *Crolians* been deceiv'd by the darkness of the

K 4   Night

Night and led to a large Ditch of Water, which they could not pafs over, they had certainly furpriz'd and overthrown his Army, and cut them in pieces, before they had known who had hurt them. Upon the Senfe of this Danger, he takes up a pretence of neceffity for the being always ready to refift *the Factious Crolians,* as he call'd them, and by that Infinuation hooks himfelf into a *ftanding Army in time of Peace* ;----- nay, and fo eafy were the *Solunarian Church* to yield up any point, which they did but imagin would help to crufh their Brethren the *Crolians,* that they not only confented to this unufual Invafion of their antient Liberties, but fent up feveral *Teftimonials* of their free Confent, nay, and of their Joy of having arriv'd to fo great a Happinefs, as to have a Prince that *fetting afide the formality of Laws* would vouchfafe to Govern them by the glorious Method of a *Standing Army.*------

These *Teftimonials* were things not much unlike *our Addreffes* in *England,* and which when I heard, I could not but remember our Cafe, in the time of the late King *James,* when the City of *Carlifle* in their Addrefs, *Thankt his Majefty* for the Eftablifhing a Standing Army
my

my in *England* in time of Peace, calling it
the *Strength, and Glory* of the Kingdom.

So ſtrong is the Ambition and Envy
of Parties, theſe *Solunarian Gentlemen* not
grudging to put out one of their own
Eyes, ſo they might at the ſame time put
out both the Eyes of their Enemies; the
Crolians rather conſented to this badge
of their own Slavery, and brought
themſelves who were a free People before, under the Power and Slavery of
the Sword.

The eaſe with which this Prince got
over ſo conſiderable a Point as this, made
him begin to be too credulous, and to
perſwade himſelf that the *Solunarian
Church-Men* were really in earneſt, as
to their Pageant-Doctrin of *Non Reſiſtance*, and that as he had ſeen them
bear with ſtrange extravagancies on
the *Crolian* Part, they were real and
·n earneſt when they Preach'd that Men
ought to obey for Conſcience's ſake,
whatever hardſhip were impos'd upon
them, and however unjuſt, or contrary to
the Laws of God, Nature, Reaſon, or
their Country; what Principle in the
World could more readily prompt a
Prince

Prince to attempt what he so earneftly coveted, as this zealous Prince did the reftoring the *Abrogratzian* Faith, for fince he had but two forts of People to do with; one he had crufh'd by force, and had brought the other to profefs it their *Religion*, their *Duty*, and their *Refolution* to bear every thing he thought fit to Impofe upon them, and that they fhould be *Damn'd* if they *refifted*, the Work feem'd half done to his Hand.

And indeed when I reflected on the Coherence of things, I could not fo much blame this Prince for his venturing upon the probability; for whoever was but to go up to this *Lunar World* and read the Stories of that Time, with what Fury the hot Men of the *Solunarian Church* acted againft the *Diffenting Crolians,* and with what warmth they affifted their Prince againft them, and how Cruelly they infulted them after they were defeated in their attempt of Dethroning him, how zealoufly they Preach'd up the Doctrine of abfolute undifputed Refignation to his Will, how frequently they obey'd feveral of his encroachments upon their Liberties, and

and what folemn Proteftations they made
to fubmit to him in any thing, and to
ftand by and affift him in *whatever* he
Commanded them to the *laft Drop*,
much with the fame Zeal and Forward-
nefs, as our *Life-and-Fortune Men* did
here in *England*. I fay, when all this was
confider'd, I could not fo much condemn his Credulity, nor blame him for
believing them, for no Man could have
doubted their Sincerity, but he that at the
fame time muft have Taxt them with
moft unexampled Hipocrifie.

For the *Solunarians* now began to
difcern their Prince was not really on
their fide, that neither in State Matters any more than Religion, he had
any affection for them, and the firft abfolute Shock he gave them, was in Publifhing a general Liberty to the *Crolians*.
'Tis true this was not out of refpect to
the *Crolian* Religion any more than the
Solunarian, but purely becaufe by that
means he made way for an Introduction
of the *Abrogratzian* Religion which now
began to appear publickly in the Country.

But

But however, as this was directly contrary to the expectation of the *Solunarians*, it gave them such a disgust against
their Prince, that from that very time
being disappointed in the Soveraign Authority they expected, they entred into
the deepest and blackest Conspiracy a-
gainst their Prince and his Government
that ever was heard of.

Many of the *Crolians* were deluded
by the new Favour and Liberty they
receiv'd from the Prince to believe him
real, and were glad of the Mortification
of their Brethren; but the more Judici-
ous feeing plainly the Prince's Defign,
declar'd against their own Liberty, because
given them by an illegal Authority,
without the assent of the whole Body
legally assembled.

When the *Solunarians* saw this they
easily reconcil'd themselves to the *Croi-
lians*, at least from the Outside of the
Face, for the carrying on their Defign,
and so here was a Nation full of Plots,
here was the Prince and his *Abrogratzians* plotting to introduce their Religion,
here was a parcel of blind short-sighted
Crolians

Crolians plotting to ruin the *Solunarian Establishment*, and weakly joining with the *Abrogratzians* to satisfy their private Resentments ; and here was the *wiser Crolians* joining heartily with the *Solunarians* of all forts, laying afide private Resentments, and forgetting old Grudges about Religion, in order to ruin the invading Projects of the Prince and his Party.

There was indeed fome verbal Conditions paft between them, and the *Solunarians* willing to bring them into their Party promifed them upon the Faith of their Nation, and the Honour of the *Solunarian Religion*, that there fhould be no more Hatred, Difturbance *or Perfecution* for the fake of Religion between them, but that they would come to a Temper with them, and always be Brethren for the future. They declared that *Perfecution was contrary to their Religion in general, and to their Doctrin in particular* ; and backt their Allegations with fome Truths they have not fince thought fit *to like*, nor much *to regard*.

However by this Artifice, and on
thefe

thefe Conditions, they brought the *Crolians* to join with them in their Refolutions to countermine their defigning
Prince ; thefe indeed were for doing it
by the old way down-right, and to oppofe Oppreffion with Force, a Doctrin
they acknowledg'd, and profeft to join
with all the *Lunar* part of Mankind in
the practice, and began to tell their Brethren how they had impos'd upon themfelves and the World, in pretending to
abfolute Submiffion againft Nature and
univerfal Lunarian Practice.

But a cunning Fellow perfonating a
Solunarian, and who was in the Plot,
gravely anfwer'd them thus, ' Look ye,
' Gentlemen, we own with you that
' *Nature, Reafon, Law, Juftice*, and *Cu-*
' *ftom of Nations* is on your fide, and that
' all Power *Derives* from, *Centers* in,
' and on all Receffes or Demifes of
' Power *returns* to its Great Original the
' *Party Governed :* Nay we own our
' *Great Eye* from whom all the habitable
' Parts of this Globe are inlightned, has
' always directed us to practife what
' Nature thns dictates, always approv'd
' and generally fucceeded the attempt of
' Dethroning Tyrants. But our Cafe
' differs

‘ differs, *we have always pretended to this*
‘ *abſolute undiſputed Obedience*, which we
‘ did indeed to gain the Power of your
‘ Party ; and if we ſhould turn round at
‘ once to your Opinion, tho’ never ſo
‘ right, we ſhould ſo fly in the Face of
‘ our own Doctrin, *Sermons*, innumera-
‘ ble *Pamphlets* and *Pretenſions*, as would
‘ give all our Enemies too great a Power
‘ over us in Argument, and we ſhould
‘ never be able to look Mankind in the
‘ Face: But we have laid our Meaſures
‘ ſo that by prompting the King to *run*
‘ *upon us* in all ſorts of bare-fac’d Ex-
‘ treams and Violences, we ſhall bring
‘ him to exaſperate the whole Nation;
‘ then we may underhand foment the
‘ breach on this ſide, raiſe the Mob upon
‘ him, and by acting on both ſides ſeem
‘ to ſuffer a Force in falling in with the
‘ People, and preſerve our Reputation.

‘ Thus we ſhall bring the thing to
‘ paſs, *betray our Prince*, take Arms a-
‘ *gainſt his Power*, call in *Foreign Force* to
‘ do the Work, and even then keep our
‘ Hands ſeemingly out of the Broil, by
‘ being pretended Sticklers for our for-
‘ mer Prince; ſo ſave our Reputation,
‘ and

' and bring all to pass with Ease and
' Calmness ; while the eager Party of
' the *Abrogratzians* will do their own
' Work by expecting we will do it for
' them.

The *Crolians* aftonish'd both at the
Policy, the Depth, the Knavery and
the Hypocrify of the Defign, left them
to carry it on, owning it was a Mafter-
piece of Craft, and fo ftood ftill to obferve the Iffue, which every way anfwer'd the exactnefs of its Contrivance.

When I faw into the bottom of all this
Deceit, I began to take up new Refolutions of returning back into *our Old World
again*, and going home to *England*, where
tho' I had conceiv'd great Indignation at
the Treatment our *Paffive Obedience Men*
gave their Prince here, and was in hopes
in thefe my remote Travels to have
found out fome Nations of Honour and
Principles. I was fill'd with Amaze-
ment to fee our *Moderate Knaves* fo
much *out-done*, and I was inform'd that
all thefe things were meer Amufements,
Vizors, and Shams, to bring an Innocent Prince into the Snare.

Would

Would any Mortal imagin who has read this short Part of the Story, that all this was *a Solunarian Church Plot*, a meer Conspiracy between these Gentlemen and the *Crolian Dissenters*, only to wheedle in the unhappy Prince to his own Destruction, and bring the popular Advantage of the Mob, to a greater Ascendant on the Crown.

Of all the *Richlieus*, *Mazarines*, *Gondamours*, *Oliver Cromwels*, and the whole Train of Polititians that our World has produc'd, the greatest of their Arts are Follies to the unfathomable depth of these *Lunarian Policies*; and for *Wheedle*, *Lying*, *Swearing*, *Preaching*, *Printing*, &c. what is said in our World by *Priests* and *Polititians*, we thank God *may be believ'd ;* but if ever I believe a *Solunarian Priest* Preaching Non-Resistance of Monarchs, or a *Solunarian Polititian* turning *Abrogratzian*, I ought to be mark'd down for a Fool; nor will ever any Prince in that Country take their Word again, if ever they have their Senses about 'em, but as this is a most extraordinary Scene, so I cannot omit a more particu-

L   lar

lar and fufficient Relation of fome Parts
of it, than I us'd to give.

The *Solunarian Clergy* had carry'd on
their Non-Refiftance Doctrin to fuch Ex-
termities, and had given this new Prince
fuch unufual demonftrations of it, that
he fell abfolutely *into the Snare*, and entirely believ'd them; he had try'd them
with fuch Impofitions as they would
never have born from any Prince in the
World, nor from him neither, had they
not had a deep Defign, and confequently ftood in need of the deepeft Difguife
imaginable; they had yielded to a *Standing Army*, and applauded it as a thing
they had defir'd; they had fubmitted to
levying Taxes upon them by *New Methods*,
and illegal Practices; they had yielded to
the abrogation or fufpenfion at leaft of
their Laws, when the King's abfolute
Will requir'd it;. not that they were
blind, and did not fee what their Prince
was doing, but that the black Defign
was fo deeply laid, they found it was
the only way to ruin him, to pufh him
upon the higheft Extreams, and then
they fhould have their turn ferv'd.----
Thus if he defir'd one illegal Thing of
them,

them, they would immediately grant
two ; one would have thought they had
read our Bible, *and the Command, when a
Man takes away the Cloak, to give him the
Coat alfo.*

Nor was this enough, but they feem'd
willing to admit of the publick Exer-
cife of the *Abrogratzian* Religion in all
Parts ; and when the Prince fet it up
in his own Chappel, they fuffered it to
be fet up in their Cities, and Towns,
and the *Abrogratzian Clergy* began to be
feen up and down in their very Habits ;
a thing which had never been permitted before in that Country, and which
the Common People began to be very
uneafy at But ftill the *Solunarian Clergy*,
and all fuch of the Gentry, efpecially as
were in the Plot , by their Sermons,
printed Books, and publick Difcourfes,
carry'd on this high topping Notion of
abfolute Submiffion, fo that the People
were kept under, and began to fubmit
to all the impofitions of the Prince.

Thefe things were fo acted to the
Life , that not only the Prince , but
none of his *Abrogratzian* Counfellors

L 2   could

could fee the Snare, the Hook was fo
finely covered by the Church-Artificers,
and the Bait fo delicious, that they all
fwallow'd it with eagernefs and delight.

But the Confpirators willing to make
a fure game of it, and not thinking the
King, or all his Counfellors would
drive on fo faft as they would have
them, tho' they had already made a fair
Progrefs for the Time, refolv'd to play
home, and accordingly they perfuade
their Prince, that they will not only
fubmit to his Arbitrary Will, in Matters
of State, and Government, but in Matters of Religion ; and in order to carry
this Jeft on, *one of the heads of their Politicks,* and a Perfon of great Eftem for
his Abilities in Matters of State, being
without queftion one of the ableft Heads
of all the *Solunarian* Nobility, *pretended to
be converted,* and turn'd *Abrogratzian.* This
immediately took as they defir'd, for the
Prince carefs'd him, and entertain'd him
with all poffible endearments, preferr'd
him to feveral Pofts of Honour and Advantage; always kept him near him,
confulted him in all Emergencies, took
him with him to the *Abrogian* Sacrifices,
and

and he made no Scruple publickly to
appear there, and by thefe degrees and
a *fuper-achitophalian* Hypocrifie, fo in-
finuated himfelf into the credulous
Prince's favour, that he became his only
Confident, and abfolute Mafter of all
his Defigns.

Now the Plot had its defir'd effect,
for he pufh'd the King upon all manner
of Precipitations; and if even the *Abrogratzians* themfelves who were about
the King, interpos'd for more *temperate
Proceedings,* he would call them Cowards, Strangers, ignorant of the Temper of the *Lunarians,* who when they
were a going, might be driven, but if
they were fuffered to cool and confider,
would face about and fall off.

Indeed the Men of Prudence and E-
ftates among his own Party, I mean the
Abrogratzians in the Country, frequently warn'd him to take more *moderate
Meafures,* and to proceed with more
Caution; told him he would certainly
ruin them all, and himfelf, and that
there muft be fome Body about his Majefty that pufh'd him upon thefe Ex-

tremes

tremes, on purpofe to fet all the Nation
in a Flame, and to overthrow all the
good Defigns, which with Temper and
good Conduct, might be brought to
Perfection.

Had thefe wary Councils been obferv'd, and a Prudence and Policy agreeable to the mighty confequence of Things
been practis'd, the *Solunarian Church* had
run a great rifque of being over thrown,
and to have funk gradually in the *Abro-*
*gianErrors,*the People began to be drawn
off gradually, and the familiarity of the
thing made it appear lefs frightful to un-
thinking People, who had entertain'd
ftrange Notions of the monftrous things
that were to be feen in it, fo that common Vogue had fill'd the Peoples Minds
with ignorant Averfions, that 'tis no abfurdity to fay,I believe there was 200000
People who would have fpent the laft
drop of their Blood againft *Abrogratzian-*
ifm, that did not know whether it was a
Man or a Horfe.

This thing confider'd well, would
of it felf have been fufficient to have
made the Prince and his Friends *wary,*
and

and to have taught them to suit
their Measures to the Nature and Cir-
cumstances of Things before them; but
Success in their beginnings blinded their
Eyes, and they fell into this *Church
Snare* with the most unpitied willingnefs
that could be imagin'd.

The first thing therefore this new
Counsellor put his Master upon, in order to the beginning his more certain
Ruin, was to introduce several of his
Abrograzians into Places of all kinds,
both in the *Army*, *Navy*, *Treasure*, and *Civil
Affairs*, tho' contrary to some of the general Constitutions of Government ; he
had done it into the *Army* before, tho'
it had disgusted several of his Military
Men, but now he push'd him upon
making it Universal, and still the *Passive
Solunarians* bore it with patience.

From this tamenefs and submission,
his next Step was to argue that he might
depend upon it the *Solunarian Church*
had so sincerely embrac'd the Doctrine
of *Non-Resistance*, that they were now
ripen'd not only to sit still, and see their
Brethren the *Crolians* suppress'd, but to

L 4 stand

ftand ftill and be oppreft themfelves, and he might affure himfelf the Matter was now ripe, he might do juft what he wou'd himfelf with them, they were prepar'd to bare any thing.

This was the fatal Stroke, for having poffeft the Prince with the belief of this, he let loofe the Reins to all his long conceal'd Defires. Down went their *Laws*, their *Liberties*, their *Corporations*, their *Churches*, their *Colleges*, all went to wreck, and the eager *Abrograzians* thought the Day their own. The *Solunarians* made no oppofition, but what was contain'd within the narrow circumference of Petitions, Addreffes, *Prayers, and Tears*; and thefe the Prince was prepar'd to reject, and upon all occafions to let them know he was *refolv'd to be obey'd*.

Thus he drove on by the treacherous Advice of his new Counfels, till he ripen'd all the Nation for the *general Defection* which afterward follow'd.

For as the Encroachments of the Prince pufh'd efpecially at their Church Liber-

Liberties, and threatned the overthrow
of all their Ecclefiaftical Privileges, the
Clergy no fooner began to feel that they
were like to be the firft Sacrifice, but
they immediately threw off the Vizor,
and beat the *Concionazimir* ; this is a
certain Eeclefiaftick *Engine* which is u-
fual in cafes of general Alarm, as the
Churches Signal of *Univerfal Tumult*.

This is truly a ftrange Engine, and
when a Clergy-Man gets into the In-
fide of it, and beats it, *it Roars*, and
makes fuch a terrible *Noife* from the feveral Cavities, that 'tis heard a long
way ; and there are always a competent
number of them plac'd in all Parts fo
conveniently, that the Alarm is heard
all over the Kingdom in one Day.

I had fome Thoughts to have given
the Reader a *Diagram* of this piece of
Art, but as I am but a bad Drafts Man,
I have not yet been able fo exactly to
defcribe it, as that a Scheme can be
drawn, but to the beft of my Skill, take
it as follows. 'Tis a *hollow Veffel*, large
enough to hold the biggeft Clergy-Man
in the Nation ; it is generally *an Octogon*

[154]

in Figure, *open before*, from the *Waſt* upward, but whole *at the Back*, with *a Flat* extended over it for *Reverberation*, or doubling the Sound; *doubling* and *redoubling*, being frequently thought neceſſary to be made uſe of on theſe occaſions; 'tis very Mathematically contriv'd, erected on *a Pedeſtal of Wood* like a Windmil, and has a pair of winding Stairs up to it, like thoſe at the great Tun at *Hiedlebergh*.

I could make ſome *Hierogliphical* Diſcourſes upon it, from theſe References, thus. 1. That as it is erected on a Pedeſtal like a Wind-Mill, ſo it is no new thing for the Clergy, who are the only Perſons permitted to make uſe of it, to make it *turn round with the Wind*, and ſerve to all the Points of the Compaſs. 2. As the *Flat* over it aſſiſts to encreaſe the Sound, by forming a kind of hollow, or cavity proper to that purpoſe, ſo there is a certain natural hollowneſs, or emptineſs, made uſe of ſometimes in it, by the Gentlemen of the Gown, which ſerves exceedingly to the propogation of all ſorts of *Clamour*, *Noiſe*, *Railing*, and *Diſturbance*. 3. As the Stairs to it go wind-

winding up like thofe by which one mounts to the vaft Tun of Wine at *Hiedlebergh*, which has no equal in *our World*, fo the ufe made of thefe afcending Steps, is not altogether different, being frequently employ'd to raife People up to all forts of *Enthufiafms*, fpiritual *Intoxications*, mad and *extravagant Action*, high exalted *Flights*, *Precipitations*, and all kinds of *Ecclefiaftick Drunkennefs* and *Exceffes*.

The found of this Emblem of emptinefs, the *Concionazimir*, was no fooner heard over the Nation, but all the People difcover'd their readinefs to *join in* with the Summons, and as the thing had been concerted before, they fend over their Meffengers to demand Affiftance from a powerful Prince beyond the Sea, one of their own Religion, and who was allied *by Marriage* to the Crown.

They made their Story out fo plain, and their King had by the contrivance of their *Achitophel* rendred himfelf fo fufpected to all his Neighbours, that this Prince, without any hefitation, refolv'd to join with them, and accordingly makes vaft Preparations to invade their King. Dur-

During this interval their Behaviour was quite altred at home, the Doctrin of *abſolute Submiſſion* and *Non-Reſiſtance* was heard no more among them, the *Concionazimir* beat daily to tell all the People they ſhould ſtand up to Defend the Rights of the Church, and that it was time to look about them for the *Abrograzians* were upon them. The eager Clergy made this *Eccleſiaſtick Engine* ſound as loud and make all the Noiſe they could, and no Men in the Nation were ſo forward as they to acknowledge that it was a State-Trick, and they were drawn in to make ſuch a ſtir about the pretended Doctrins of *abſolute Submiſſion*, that they did not ſee the Snare which lay under it, that now their Eyes were opened, and they had learnt to ſee the Power and Superiority of Natural Right, and would be deceiv'd no longer. *Others* were ſo honeſt to tell the Truth, that they knew the emptineſs and weakneſs of the pretence all along, and knew what they did when they Preacht it up, *viz. to ſuppreſs and pull down the Crolians:* But they thought their Prince who *they always* ſerv'd in crying up that Doctrin, and whoſe Excluſion

clufion was prevented by i , would ha'
had more Gratitude, or at leaft more
Senfe, than to try the Experiment *upon
them*, fince whatever to ferve his Defigns and their own, *which they always
thought well united*, they were willing to
pretend, he could not but fee they *always knew better* than to fuffer the practice of it in their own Cafe. That
fince he had turn'd the Tables upon
them, 'tis true he had them at an advantage and might pretend *they were
Knaves*, and perhaps had an opportunity
to call them fo with fome reafon; but
they were refolv'd, fince he had drove
them to the neceffity of being one or
t'other, tho' he might call them Knaves,
they would take care he fhould have no
reafon to *call them Fools* too.

Thus the Vapour of abfolute Subjection was loft on a fuddain, and as if it
had been preparatory to what was coming after, the Experiment was quickly
made; for the King perfuing his Encroachments upon the Church, and being poffeft with a Belief that purfuant
to their open Profeffions they would
fubmit to any thing, he made a beginning

ning with them, in sending his positive
Command to one of his Superintendent
Priests, or *Patriarchs*, to forbid a certain
Ecclesiastick to officiate any more till
his Royal Pleasure was known.

Now it happen'd *very unluckily* that
this Patriarch, tho' none of the most
Learned of his Fraternity, yet had always been a mighty zealous Promoter
of this blind Doctrin of *Non-Resistance*,
and had not a little triumph'd over and
insulted the *Crolian Dissenters* upon the
Notion of *Rebellion*, antimonarchical
Principles and Obedience, with a reserve
for the Laws, and the like, as a scanda-
lous practice, and comprehensive of Fa-
ction, Sedition, dangerous to the
Church and State, and the like.

This Reverend Father was singl'd out
as the first Mark of the King's Design;
the *deluded Prince* believ'd he could not
but comply, having so publickly pro-
fest his being *all Submission* and *absolute
Subjection*; but as this was *all Conceit*,
he was pusht on to make the Assault
where he was most certain to meet a
repulse; and this Gentleman had long
since

since thrown off the Mask, so his first
Order was disobey'd.

The *Patriarch* pretended to make
humble Remonstrances, and to offer his
Reasons why he could not in Consci-
ence, *as he call'd it*, comply. The King,
who was now made but a meer Engine,
or Machine, screw'd up or down by this
false Counsellor to act his approaching
Destruction with his own Hand , *was
prompted* to resent this Repulse with the
utmost Indignation, to reject all manner
of Submissions, Excuses or Arguments, or
any thing but an immediate, absolute
compliance, according to the Doctrin so
often inculcated ; and this he run on so
high, as to put *the Patriarch in Prison* for
Contumacy.

The *Patriarch* as absolutely refus'd to
submit, and offer'd himself to the Deci-
sion of the Law.

Now it was always a sacred Rule in
these *Lunar Countries*, that both *King*
and *People* are bound to stand by the ar-
bitrimnet of *the Law* in all Cases of
Right or Claim , whether publick or
pri-

private; and this has been the reason
that all the Princes have endeavour'd to
cover their Actions with pretences of
Law, *whatever really has been in their De-*
sign; for this reason the King could not
refuse to bring the Patriarch to a Tryal,
where the Humour of the People first
discover'd it self, for here *Passive Obedi-*
ence was Try'd and Cast, the Law prov'd
to be superior to the King, the Patriarch
was acquitted, his Disobedience to the
King *justify'd*, and the King's Command
prov'd unjust.

The Applause *of the Patriarch*, the
Acclamations of the People, and the general Rejoycings of the whole Nation at
this Transaction, gave a black prospect
to the *Abrograzians*; and a great many
of them came very honestly and humbly
to the King and told him, if he continued to go on by these Measures he
would ruin them all; they told him
what general Alarm had been over the
whole Nation by the Clamours of the
Clergy; and the beating of the *Conciona-*
zimir in all Parts, inform'd him how the
Doctrin of *absolute Obedience* was ridicul'd in all Places, and how the Clergy
began

began to preach it back again *like a Witches Prayer*, and that it would infallibly raise the Devil of Rebellion in all the Nation, they besought him to content himself with the liberty of their Religion, and the freedom they enjoy'd of being let into Places and Offices of Trust and Honour, and to wait all reasonable Occasions to encrease their Advantages, and gradually to gain Ground; they entreated him to consider the impossibility of reducing so mighty, so obstinate, and so resolute a Nation all at once. They pleaded how rational a thing it was to expect that by Degrees and good Management, which by precipitate Measures would be endanger'd and overthrown.

Had these wholsome Counsels taken place in the King's Mind he had been King to his last hour, and the *Solunarians* and *Crolians* too had been all undone, for he had certainly incroach'd upon them gradually, and brought that to pass in time which by precipitant Measures he was not likely to effect.

It was therefore a master-piece of Po-
M   licy

licy in the *Solunarian* Church-men to place a feign'd Convert near their Prince, who shou'd always biafs him with contrary Advices, puff him up with vaft profpect of Succefs, prompt him to all Extreams, and always Fool him with the certainty of bringing Things to pafs his own way.

Thefe Arts made him fet light by the repulfe he met with in the Matter of the *Patriarch*, and now he proceeds to make two Attacks more upon the Church ; one was by putting fome of his *Abrograzian Priefts* into *a College* among fome of the *Solunarian Clergy* ; and the other was to oblige all the *Solunarian Clergy* to read a certain Act of his Council, in which his Majefty admitted all the *Abrograzians*, *Crolians*, and all forts of Diffenters, to a freedom of their Religious Exercifes, *Sacrifices*, *Exorcifms*, *Dippings*, *Preachings*, &c. and to prohibit the *Solunarians* to Moleft or Difturb them.

Now as this laft was a bitter reproach to the *Solunarian Church* for all the ill Treatment the *Diffenting Crolians* had receiv'd from them, and as it was expreft preſt in the Act that all ſuch Treatment was Unjuſt and Unchriſtian, ſo for them to read it in their Temples, was to acknowledge that they had been guilty of moſt unjuſt and irreligious Dealings to the *Crolians*, and that their Prince had taken care to do them Juſtice.

The matter of introducing the *Abrograzians* into the Colleges or Seminaries of the *Solunarian Prieſt*, was actually againſt the Sacred Conſtitutions and Foundation-Laws of *thoſe Seminaries*.

Wherefore in both theſe Articles they not only diſobey'd their Prince, but they oppos'd him with thoſe *trifling Things call'd Laws*, which they had before declar'd had no Defenſive Force againſt their Prince; theſe they had recourſe to now, inſiſted upon the Juſtice and Right devolv'd upon them by the Laws, and abſolutely refus'd their compliance with his Commands.

The Prince, puſht upon the Tenters before, receiv'd their Denial with exceeding Reſentment, and was heard with deep regret, to break out in Ex-

cla-

clamations at their unexpected faithlefs
Proceedings, and fometimes to exprefs
himfelf thus: *Horrid Hypocrify! Sur-
prizing Treachery! Is this the abfolute Subjection which in fuch numerous Teftimonials
or Addreffes you profeft, and for which you
fo often and fo conftantly branded the poor*
Crolians, *and told me that your Church
was wholly made up of Principles of Loyalty
and Obedience! But I'll be fully fatisfied
for this Treatment.*

In the minute of one of thofe Excur-
fions of his Paffion, came into his Pre-
fence the feemingly revolted *Lazarian
Noble Man,* and falling in with his prefent Paffions, prompts him to a fpeedy
Revenge ; and propos'd his erecting *a
Court of Searches,* fomething like the *Spa-
nifh* Inquifition, giving them plenipo-
tentiary Authority to hear and determine all Ecclefiaftical Caufes abfolutely, and without Appeal.

He empower'd thefe Judges to place
by his abfolute Will, all the *Abrograzian*
Students in the *Solunarian College,* and
tho' they might make a formal Hearing
for the fake of the Form, yet that by
Force it fhould be done.   He

He gave them Power to difplace all thofe *Solunarian Clergy*-Men that had refus'd to read his Act of Demiffion to the *Abrograzian, and Crolian Diffenters,* and 'twas thought he defign'd to keep their Revenues in *Petto,* till he might in time fill them up to fome of his own Religion.

The Commiffion accordingly began to act, and difcovering a full Refolution to fulfil his Command, they by Force proceeded with the Students of the *Solunarian College*; and it was very remarkable, that even fome of the *Solunarian Patriarchs* were of this number, who turn'd out their Brethren the *Solunarian Students,* to place *Abrograzians in their room.*

This indeed they are faid to have repented of fince, but however, thefe it feems were not of the Plot, and therefore did not forefee what was at hand.

The reft of the *Patriarchs* who were all in the Grand Defign, and faw things ripening for its Execution, upon the apprehenfion of this *Court of Searches* be-

ginning

ginning with them, make an humble
Addrefs to their Prince, containing the
Reafons why they could not comply
with his Royal Command. ------

The incens'd King upbraided them
with his having been told by them of
their abfolute and *unreferv'd Obedience*, and refufing their Submiffions or
their Reafons, *fent them all to Jail*, and refolv'd to have brought them before his
new *High Court of Searches*, in order, as
was believ'd, to have them all difplac'd.

And now all began to be in a Flame,
the Sollicitations of the *Solunarian Party*, having obtain'd powerful Relief A-
broad, they began to make fuitable preparations at Home. The Gentry and
Nobility who the Clergy had brought
to join with them, furnifh'd themfelves
with Horfes and Arms, and prepar'd with
their Tenants and Dependants to join
the Succours as foon as they fhould Arrive.

In fhort, the Forreign Troops they
had procur'd, Arriv'd, Landed, and
publifh'd a long Declaration of all the
Grievances which they came to redrefs.
No

No fooner was this Forreign Army
arriv'd with the Prince at the head of
them, but the face of Affairs *altred on a
fuddain.* The King indeed, like a brave
Prince, drew all his Forces together,
and marching out of his Capital City,
advanc'd above 500 *Stages,* things *they
meafure Land with in thofe Countries,* and
much about *our Furlong,* to meet his E-
nemy.

He had a gallant Army well appointed
and furnifh'd, and all things much fupe-
rior to his Adverfary, but alas the Poifon
of Difobedience was gotten in there, and
upon the firft *March* he offer'd to make towards the Enemy one of *his great Captains*
with a ftrong Party of his Men went over
and revolted.

This Example was applauded all over
the Nation, and by this time one of the Patriarchs, even the fame mention'd before
that had fo often preacht Non-Refiftance
of Princes, lays by his Sacred Veftments,
Mitre, and Staff, and exchanging his
Robes for a Soldier's Coat, mounts on
Horfeback, and in fhort, appears in Arms
againft his Lord.----- Nor was this all,
but the *Treacherous Prelate* takes along

M 4   with

with him feveral *Solunarian Lords,* and
Perfons of the higheft Figure, and of
the Houfhold, and Family of the King,
and with him went the King's own
Daughter, his principle Favourites and
Friends.

At the News of this, the poor deferted Prince loft all Courage, and a-
bandoning himfelf to Defpair, he caufes
his Army to retreat without fighting
a Stroke, quits them and the Kingdom
at once, and takes Sanctuary with fuch
as could efcape with him, in the Court
of a Neighbouring Prince.

I have heard this Prince exceedingly
blam'd, for giving himfelf up to Defpair fo foon. ----- That he thereby a-
bandon'd the beft and faithfulleft of his
Friends, and Servants, and left them
to the Mercy of the *Solanarians*; that
when all thofe that would have forfak-
en him were gone, he had Forces e-
qual to his Enemies; that his Men were
in Heart, frefh and forward; that he
fhould have ftood to the laft; retreated
to a ftrong Town, where his Ships rod,
and which was over againft the Terri-
tories of his great Allie, to whom he
might

might have deliver'd up the Ships which were there, and have thereby made him Superior at Sea to his Enemies, and he was already much Superior at Land; that there he might have been reliev'd with Forces too ſtrong for them to match, and at leaſt might have put it to the Iſſue of a fair Battle.------ Others, that he might have retreated to his own Court, and capital City, and taking poſſeſſion of the Citadel, which was his own, might ſo have aw'd the Citizens who were infinitely Rich, and Numerous, with the apprehenſions of having their Houſes burnt, they would not have dar'd to have declar'd for his Enemies, for fear of being reduc'd to heaps and ruins; and that at laſt he might have ſet the City on Fire in 500 Places, and left the *Solunarian Church-Men* a Token to remember their *Non-Reſiſting Doctrine by,* and yet have made an eaſy Retreat down the Harbour, to other Forts he had below, and might with eaſe have deſtroy'd all the Shipping as he went.

'Tis confeſs'd had he done either, or both theſe things, he had left them a dear bought Victory, but he was de-
priv'd

priv'd of his Counfellor, for as foon
as things came to this height, *the Achitophel* we have fo often mention'd, *left
him alfo,* and went away ; all his *Abrograzian Priefts too forfook him,* and he was
fo bereft of Counfel that he fell into
the Hands of his Enemies as he was
making his efcape, but he got away a-
gain, not without the connivance of
the Enemy, who were willing enough
he fhould go ; fo he got a Veffel to carry him over to the Neighbouring Kingdom, and all his Armies, Ships, Forts,
Caftles. Magazines, and Treafure, fell
into his Enemies Hands.

The Neighbouring Prince entertain'd
him very kindly, Cherifh'd him, Suc-
cour'd him, and furnifh'd him with Armies and Fleets for the recovery of his
Dominions, which has occafion'd a tedious War with that Prince, which continues to this Day.

Thus far *Paffive Doctrins,* and Abfolute Submiffion ferv'd a Turn, *bubl'd
the Prince,* wheedled him in to take their
Word who profefs'd it, 'till he laid his
Finger upon the Men themfelves, and
that

that unravell'd all the Cheat; they were the firſt that call'd in Forreign Power, and took up Arms againſt their Prince.

Nor did they end here, but all this Scene being over, and the Forreign Prince having thus deliver'd them, and their own King being thus chac'd away, the People call themſelves together, and *as Reaſon good*, having been deliver'd by him from the Miſeries, Brangles, Oppreſſions, and Diviſions of the former Reign, they thought they could do no leſs than to Crown their Deliverer; and having Summon'd a general Aſſembly of all their *Capital Men*, they gave the Crown to this Prince who had ſo generouſly ſav'd them.

And here again, I heard the firſt King exceedingly blam'd for quitting his Dominions, for had he ſtaid here, tho' he had actually been in their Hands, unleſs they wou'd have Murther'd him, they could never have proceeded to the Extremeties they did reach to, nor cou'd they ever have Crown'd the other Prince, he being yet alive, and in his own Dominions.

But

But by quitting the Country, they fix'd a legal Period to their Obedience, he having deferted their Protection, and Defence, and openly laid down the Adminiftration.

But as thefe fort of Politicks cannot be decided by us, unlefs we know the Conftitutions of thofe *Lunar Regions*, fo we cannot pretend to make a Decifion of what might, or might not have happen'd.

It remains to examine how thofe *Solunarians* behav'd themfelves, who had fo earneftly cryed up the Principles of Obedience, and abfolute Submiffion.

Nothing was fo Ridiculous, now they faw what they had done, they began to repent, and upon recollection of Thoughts fome were fo afham'd of themfelves, that having broken their Doctrin, and being now call'd upon to tranfpofe their Allegiance, truly they ftopt in the mid-way, and *fo became Martyrs on both fides*.

I can liken thefe to nothing fo well as to thofe Gentlemen of our *Englifh Church*,

Church, who tho' they broke into the Principles of PaſſiveObedience by joining, and calling over the P. of O. yet ſuffer'd deprivations of Benefices, and loſs of their Livings, *for not taking the Oath*; as if they had not as *effectually perjur'd themſelves* by taking up Arms againſt their King, and joyning a Forreign Power, as they could poſſibly do afterward, by Swearing to live quietly under the next King.

But theſe nice Gentlemen are infinitely outdone in theſe Countries, for theſe *Solunarians* by a true Church turn, not only refuſe to tranſpoſe their Allegiance, but pretend to wipe their Mouths as to former taking Arms, and return to their old Doctrins of abſolute Submiſſion, boaſt of Martyrdom, and boldly reconcile the contraries of *taking up Arms,* and *Non-Reſiſtance,* charging all their Brethren with Schiſm, Rebellion, Perjury, and the *damnable Sin of Reſiſtance.*

Nor is this all, for as a great many of theſe *Solunarian Church*-Men had no affection to this new Prince, but were

not

not equally furnifh'd, or qualify'd for
Martyrdom with their Brethren; they
went to certain Wife Men, who being
cunning at *fplitting Hairs,* and making
diftinctions, might perhaps furnifh them
with *fome mediums between Loyalty and
Difloyalty*; they apply'd themfelves with
great dilligence to thefe Men, and they
by deep Study, and long Search, *either
found or made* the quainteft Device for
them that ever was heard of.

By this unheard of Difcovery, to their
great Joy and Satisfaction, they have
arriv'd at a Power, which all the Wife
Men in our World could never pretend
to, and which 'tis thought, could the
defcription of it be regularly made, and
brought down hither, would ferve for
the Satisfaction and Repofe of a great
many tender Confciences, who are very uneafy at *Swearing to fave their Benefices.*

Thefe great Mafters of Diftinction,
have learn't to diftinguifh between
active Swearing, and *paffive* Swearing,
between *de facto* Loyalty, and *de jure*
Loyalty, and by this decent acquire-
ment

ment they obtain'd the Art of reconciling *Swearing Allegiance without Loyalty*, and *Loyalty without Swearing*, so that native and original Loyalty may be preserv'd pure and uninterrupted, in spight of all *subsequent Oaths*, *to prevailing Usurpations*.

Many are the Mysteries, and vast the Advantages of this new invented Method, *Mental Reservations*, *Inuendoes*, and Double Meanings *are Toys to this*, for they may be provided for in the litteral terms of an Oath, but no Provision can be made against this; for these Men after they have taken the Oath, make no Scruple to declare, *they only Swear to be quiet, as long as they can make no Disturbance*; that they are left at liberty still to espouse the Interest and Cause of their former Prince, they nicely distinguish between *Obedience* and *Submission*, and tell you a *Slave taken into Captivity*, tho' he Swears *to live peaceably*, does not thereby renounce his *Allegiance* to his natural Prince, nor abridge himself of a Right to attempt his own Liberty *if ever opportunity present*.

Had

Had thefe neat Diftinctions been found
out before, none of our *Solunarian Clergy,*
no nct the *Patriarchs* themfelves furely
would have ftood out, and fuffer'd fuch
Depredations on their Fortunes and
Characters as they did ; they wou'd never have been fuch Fools to have been
turn'd out of their Livings for not
Swearing, when they might have learnt
here that they *might have fwore to one
Prince, and yet have retain'd their Allegiance to another* ; might have taken an
Oath to the new, without impeachment
of their old Oaths to the abfent Prince.
------- *It is great pity thefe Gentlemen
had not gone up to the* Moon *for Inftruction
in this difficult* Cafe.

There they might have met with excellent Logicians, Men of moft fublime Reafons, Dr. *Overall,* Dr. *Sherlock,*
and all our nice Examiners of thefe
things wou'd appear to be no Body to
them ; for as the People in thefe Regions
have an extraordinary *Eye-fight,* and the
clearnefs of the Air contributs much to
the help of their *Opticks,* fo they have
without doubt a proportion'd clearnefs of
difcerning, by which they fee as far *in-*
to

to Mill-ftones, and all forts of Solids, as the nature of things will permit, but a-bove all, their Faculties are bleft with two exceeding Advantages.

1. *With an extraordinary diftinguifhing Power*, by which they can diftinguifh *even Indivifibles*, part Unity it felf, *di-vide Principles*, and *diftinguifh Truth* into fuch and fo many *minute Particles*, till they dwindle it away into a very Nofe of Wax, and mould it into any Form they have occafion for, by which means they can diftinguifh themfelves into or out of any Opinion, either in Religion, Politicks or Civil Right, that their pre-fent Emergencies may call for.

2. Their reafoning Faculties have this further advantage, that upon occafion *they can fee clearly for themfelves*, and *pre-vent others from the fame difcovery*, fo that when they have occafion to fee any thing which prefents for their own Ad-vantage, they can fearch into the Parti-culars, make it clear to themfelves, and yet let it remain dark and myfterious to all the World befides. Whether this is perform'd by their exceeding Penetra-

N   tion,

tion, or by cafting an artificial Veil over
the Underftandings of the Vulgar, *Authors have not yet determin'd*; but that the
Fact is true, admits of no Difpute.

And the wonderful Benefit of thefe
Things in point of Difpute is extraordinary, for they can fee clearly they have
the better of an Argument, when all the
reft of the World think they have not
a Word to fay for themfelves: 'Tis plain
to them that this or that proves a thing,
when Nature, by common Reafoning,
knows no fuch Confequences.

I confefs I have feen fome weak Attempts at this extraordinary Talent,
particularly in the Difputes in *England*
between the *Church and the Diffenter*, and
between the *High and Low Church*,
wherein People have tollerably well
convinc'd themfelves when no Body elfe
could fee any thing of the Matter, as
particularly the famous Mr. *W---ly* about
the *Antimonarchical Principles taught in
the Diffenters Accademies*; ditto in *L----fly*,
about the Diffenters *burning the City*,
and fetting Fire to their own Houfes to
deftroy their Neighbours; and *another
famous*

famous Author, who prov'd that *Christo-pher Love* loft his Head for attempting to pull down Monarchy by reftoring King *Charles* the Second.

Thefe indeed are fome faint Refem-blances of what I am upon; but alas! thefe are tender fort of People, that han't obtain'd *a compleat Victory over their Confciences*, but fuffer *that Trifle* to reproach them all the while they are do-ing it, to rebel againft their refolv'd Wills, and check them in the middle of the Defign, from which Interruptions arife Palpitations of the Heart, Sicknefs and fqueamifhnefs of Stomach; and thefe have proceeded to *Caftings and Vo-mit*, whereby they have been forc'd fometimes to throw up fome fuch un-happy Truths as have confounded all the reft, and flown in their own Faces fo violently, as in fpight of Cuftom has made them blufh and look downward; and tho' in kindnefs to one another they have carefully lickt up *one anothers Filth*, yet this unhappy fqueamifhnefs of Sto-mach has fpoil'd all the Defign, and turn'd the Appetites of their Party, to the no fmall prejudice of a Caufe that

N 2   ftood

ftood in need of more Art and *more Face*
to carry it on as it fhou'd be with a
thoro'-pac'd *Cafe-harden'd Policy*, fuch as
I have been relating, is compleatly obtain'd in thefe Regions, where the Arts
and Excellencies of fublime Reafonings
are carried up to all the extraordinaries
of *banifhing Scruples*, reconciling Contradictions, *uniting Oppofites*, and all the
neceffary Circumftances requir'd in a
compleat Cafuift.

'Tis not eafily conceivable to what
extraordinary Flights they have carry'd
this ftrength of Reafoning, for befides
the diftinguifhing nicely between Truth
and Error, they obtain a moft refin'd
Method of diftinguifhing *Truth it felf into
Seafons and Circumftances*, and fo can bring
any thing to be Truth, when it ferves
the turn that happens juft then to be
needful, and make the fame thing to be
falfe at another time.

And this method of *circumftantiating
Matters of Fact* into Truth or Falfhood,
fuited to occafion, is found admirably
ufeful to the folving the moft difficult
Phænomena of State, for by this Art the
Solu-

Solunarian Church made Perfecution be
againft their Principles at one time, and
reducible to Practice at another. They
made *taking up Arms*, and calling in
Foreign Power to depofe their Prince,
*confiftent with Non-Refiftance, and Paffive
Obedience*; nay they went farther, they
diftinguifht between a *Crolian*'s taking
Arms, and a *Solunarians*, and fairly
prov'd this to be *Rebellion*, and that to
be *Non-Refiftance*.

Nay, and which exceeded all the Power of human Art in the higheft degrees
of Attainment that ever it arriv'd to
on *our fide the Moon*; they turn'd the
Tables fo dexteroufly, as to argument
upon one fort of *Crolians*, call'd *Preftarians*: that tho' they repented of the
War they had rais'd in former Times,
and protefted againft the violence offer'd
their Prince; and after another Party
had *in fpight of them* Beheaded him, *took
Arms* againft the *other Party*, and never
left contriving their Ruin, till they had
brought in his Son, and fet him upon the
Throne again.

Yet by this moft dextrous way of

Twift-

Twisting, Extending, Contracting, and *Distinguishing* of Phrases and Reasoning, they presently made it as plain as the Sun at Noon Day; that these *Presbarians* were *King-killers,* Common-wealths Men, *Rebels,* Traytors and *Enemies to Monarchy*; that they *restor'd* the Monarchy only in order *to Destroy it,* and that they Preach'd up *Sedition, Rebellion* and the like: This was prov'd so plain by these *sublime Distinctions,* that they convinc'd themselves and their Posterity of it, by a rare and newly acquir'd Art, found out *by extraordinary Study,* which proves the wonderful power of *Custom,* insomuch, that let any Man by this method *tell a Lye over a certain number of times,* he shall arrive to a Satisfaction *of its certainty,*tho' he knew it to be *a Fiction before,* and shall freely *tell it for a Truth all his life after.*

Thus the *Presbarians* were call'd the Murtherers of *the Father,* tho' they restor'd *the Son,* and all the Testimonials of their Sufferings, Protests and Infurrections to prevent his Death, *signify'd nothing,* for this method of *Distinguishing* has that powerful Charm in it, that all
those

thofe Trifles we call Proofs and Demonftration were of no ufe in that Cafe.
Cuftom brought the Story up to a Truth,
and in an inftant all the *Crolians* were
hookt in under the general Name of
Preftarians, at the fame time to hook all
Parties in the Crime.

Now as it happen'd at laft that thefe
Solunarian Gentlemen found it neceffary
to *do the fame thing themfelves*, viz. To
lay afide their Loyalty, *Depofe*, *Fight* a-
gainft, *fhoot Bullets* at, and throw Bombs
at their King till they frighted him away,
and *fent him abroad to beg his Bread.* The
Crolians began to take Heart and tell
them, now they ought *to be Friends with
them*, and tell them no more of *Rebellion* and *Difloyalty* ; nay, they carry'd it
fo far as to challenge them to bring *their
Loyalty to the Teft* , and compare
Crolian Loyalty and *Solunarian Loyalty* together , and fee who had *rais'd more
Wars*, taken up Arms *ofteneft*, or appear'd in *moft Rebellions* againft their
Kings ; nay, who had *kill'd moft Kings*,
the *Crolians* or the *Solunarians*, for there
having been then newly fought a great
Battle between the *Solunarian Church-*

N 4 *Men*

Men under their new Prince, and the Armies of Foreign Succours under *their old King*, in which their *old King* was beaten and forc'd to flie a second time, the *Crolians* told them that every Bullet they shot at the Battle was as much *a murthering their King*, as cutting off the Head *with a Hatchet* was a killing his Father.

These Arguments in our World would have been unanswerable, but when they came to be brought to *the Test of Lunar Reasoning*, alas they signify'd nothing; they *distinguisht* and *distinguisht* till they brought the *Prestarian War* to be meer Rebellion, *King-killing*, Bloody and *Unnatural*; and the *Solunarian* fighting against their King, and *turning him adrift* to seek his Fortune, *no prejudice at all to their Loyalty*, no, nor to the famous Doctrine of *Passive Obedience*, and Absolute Subjection.

When I saw this, I really bewail'd the unhappiness of some of our Gentlemen in *England*, who standing exceedingly in need of such a wonderful Dexterity of Argument to defend their share *in our*

our late Revolution, and to reconcile it
to their *anticedent* and *subsequent* Conduct, should not be furnish'd from this
more *accurate World* with the suitable
Powers, in order the better to defend
them against the *Banter* and *just Raillery*
of their ill-natur'd Enemies *the Whigs*.

By this they might have attained suitable reserves of Argument to distinguish
themselves *out of their Loyalty*, and *into
their Loyalty*, as occasion presented to
dismiss *this* Prince, and entertain *that*,
as they found it to their purpose ; but
above all, they might have learnt a way
how to justify *Swearing* to one King and
Praying for another, *Eating* one Prince's
Bread and *doing* another Prince's *Work*,
Serving one King they don't *Love* and
Loving another they don't *Serve*; they
might easily reconcile the Schisms of the
Church, and prove they are still Loyal
Subjects *to King James*, while they are
only forc'd Bonds-Men to the *Act of Settlement*, for the sake of that comforta-
ble Importance, call'd *Food and Rai-
ment* ; and thus their Reputation might
have been sav'd, which is most *unhappily
tarnish'd* and blur'd, with the malicious
At-

Attacks of *the Whigs* on one Hand, and
the *Non-Jurants* on the other.

These Tax them as above with Rebellion by their own Principles, and
contradicting the Doctrin of *Passive Submission* and Non-Resistance, by taking
up Arms against their Prince, calling in
a *Foreign Power*, and deposing him:
They charge them with killing the
Lord's Anointed, by Shooting at him *at
the Boyn*, where if he was not kill'd it
was his own fault, at least 'tis plain *'twas
none of theirs*.

On the other Hand, the *Non Jurant
Clergy* charge them with *Schism*, declare
the whole Church of *England Schisma-
ticks*, and breakers off from the general
Union of the Church, in renouncing
their Allegiance, and Swearing to *another Power*, their former Prince being *yet
alive*.

'Tis confest all *the Answers* they have
been able to make to these things, are
very weak and *mean*, unworthy Men of
their Rank and Capacities, and 'tis pity
they should not be assisted by some kind
Com-

Communication of these *Lunar Arguments* and *Distinctions*, without which, and till they can obtain which, a *Conforming Jacobite* must be the absurdest Contradiction in Nature; a thing that admits of no manner of Defence, no, not by the *People themselves*, and which they would willingly abandon, but that they can find no side to join with them.

The *Dissenting Jacobites* have some Plea for themselves, for let their Opinion be never so repugnant to their own Interest, or general Vogue, they are *faithful to some thing*, and they wont joyn with these People, because they have *Perjur'd their Faith*, and yet pretend to adhere to it at the same time. The *Conforming Whigs* won't receive them, because they pretend to rail at the Government they have Sworn to, and espouse the Interest they have Sworn against; so that these *poor Creatures* have but one way left them, which is *to go along with me*, next time I Travel *to the Moon*, and that will most certainly do their Business, for when they come down again, they will be quite *another sort of Men*, the Distinctions, the
Pow-

Power of Argument, they way of Reafoning, they will be then furnifh'd with
will quite change *the Scene of the World
with them*, they'll certainly be able to
prove they are the only People, both *in
Juftice*, in *Politicks* and in *Prudence*; that
the extremes of every fide are *in the
Wrong*, they'll prove their Loyalty preferv'd, untainted, thro' all the *Swear-
ings*, *Fightings*, *Shootings* and the like,
and no Body will be able *to come to the
Teft with them*; fo that upon the whole,
they are all diftracted if they don't *go up
to the Moon* for Illumination, and that
they may eafily do in the next *Confolidator*.

But as this is a very long Digreffion,
and for which I am to beg my Reader's
Pardon, being an Error I flipt into from
my abundant refpect to thefe Gentlemen, and for their particular Inftruction, I fhall endeavour to make my
Reader amends, by keeping more clofe
to my Subject.

To return therefore to the Hiftorical
part of the *Solunarian Church-Men*, in
the World in the Moon.

Ha-

Having as is related *Depos'd their King*, and plac'd the Crown upon the Head of the Prince that came to their affiftance, a new Scene began all over the Kingdom.

1. *A terrible and bloody War* began thro' all the parts of the *Lunar World*, where their banifh'd Prince and his new Allie had any Intereft; and the new King having a univerfal Character over all the Northern Kingdoms of the Moon, he brought in a great many Potent *Kings*, *Princes*, *Emperors* and *States*, to take part with him, and fo it became the moft general War that had happen'd in thofe Ages.

I did not trouble my felf to enquire into the particular Succeffes *of this War*, but at what had a more particular regard to the Country from whence I came, and *for whofe Inftruction* I have defign'd *thefe Sheets*, the Strife *of Parties*, the Internal Feuds at home, and their *Analogy to ours*; and whatever is inftructively to be deduced from them, was the Subject of immediate Inquiry.

No

No fooner was this Prince plac'd on
the Throne, but according to his Promifes to them that invited him over, he
conven'd the Eftates of the Realm, and
giving them free Liberty to *make, alter,
add* or *repeal,* all fuch Laws as they
thought fit, it muft be *their own fault*
if they did not Eftablifh themfelves upon fuch Foundation of *Liberty,* and
Right, as they defir'd; for he gave them
their *full Swing,* never interpos'd *one
Negative* upon them for feveral Years,
and let them do almoft every thing they
pleas'd.

This *full Liberty* had like to have
fpoil'd all, for as is before noted, this
Nation had *one unhappy Quality* they
could never be broke of, always to *be
falling out* one among another.

The *Crolians,* according to Capitulati-
on, demanded the full Liberty and Toleration of Religion, which the *Solunarians*
had condition'd with them for, when they
drew them off from joyning with the
old King, and when they promis'd to
come *to a Temper,* and to *be Brethren in
Peace and Love ever after.*

Nor

Nor were the *Solunarian* Church-Men backward, either to remember, or perform the Conditions but by the confent of the King, who had been by agreement made *Guarantee of their former Stipulations,* an Act was drawn up in full Form, and as compleat, as both fatisfy'd the defires of the *Crolians,* and teftify'd the Honefty and Probity of the *Solunarians,* as they were abftractedly and *moderately* confider'd.

During the whole Reign of this King, this *Union of Parties* continu'd without any confiderable Interruption, there was indeed *brooding Mifchiefs* which hovered over every accident, in order to *generate Strife,* but the Candor of the Prince, and the Prudence of his Minifters, kept it under for a long time.

At laft an occafion offer'd it felf, which gave an unhappy Stroke to the Nation's Peace. The King thro' *innumerable Hazards,* terrible *Battles* and *a twelve Years War,* had reduc'd his powerful Adversary to fuch a neceffity of Peace, that he became content to abandon *the fugitive King,* and to own the Title of this

War-

Warlike Prince; and upon thefe, among various other Conditions, *very Honourable for him*, and his Allies, and by which vaft Conquefts were furrendred, and *difgorg'd to the Lofers*, a Peace was made to the Univerfal Satisfaction of all thofe Parts of *the Moon* that had been involv'd in a tirefome and expenfive War.

This Peace was no fooner made, but the Inhabitants of this unhappy Country, according *to the conftant Practice* of the Place, fell out in the moft horrid manner among themfelves, and with the very Prince that had done all thefe *great things for them*; and I cannot forget how the Old Gentleman I had thefe Relations from, being once deeply engag'd in Difcourfe with *fome Senators of* that Country, and hearing *them 'reproach the Memory of that Prince* from whom they · *receiv'd fo much*, and on the foot of whofe *Gallantry* and *Merit* the Conftitution *then fubfifted*, it put him into fome heat, and he told them to their Faces that they were guilty both of *Murther and Ingratitude.*

I

I thought the Charge was very high, but as they return'd upon him, and challeng'd him to make it out, he anſwer'd he was *ready to do it*, and went on thus.

His Majeſty, *ſaid he*, left a quiet, retir'd, compleatly happy Condition, *full of Honour*, belov'd of his Country, *Vallu'd* and *Eſteem'd*, as well *as Fear'd* by his Enemies, to come over hither at your own Requeſt, to deliver you from the Encroachments and Tyranny *as you call'd it*, of your Prince.

Ever ſince he came hither, he has been your meer *Journy-Man*, your *Servant*, your *Souldier of Fortune*, he has *Fought* for you, *Fatigu'd* and *Harras'd* his Perſon, and *rob'd himſelf* of all his Peace *for you*; he has been in a conſtant Hurry, and run thro' *a Million of Hazards for you*; he has converſ'd with Fire and Blood, *Storms at Sea*, Camps and Trenches aſhore, and given himſelf no reſt for *twelve Years*, and all for *your Uſe*, Safety and Repoſe: In requital of which, he has been always treated with *Jealouſies* and *Suſpitions*, with *Reproaches*, and *Abuſes of all Sorts*, and on all Occa-

O   ſions,

fions, till the ungrateful Treatment of
the *Solunarians* eat into *his very Soul*,
tir'd it with ferving *an unthankful Nation*, and abfolutely *broke his Heart* ; for
which reafon I think him *as much Murther'd* as his Predeceffor was, *whofe Head
was cut off* by his Subjects.

I could not when this was over, but
ask the *Old Gentlemen*, what was the
reafon of his Exclamation, and how it
was the People treated their Prince upon this occafion ?

He told me it was a grievous Subject,
and a long one, and too long to rehearfe,
but he would give me a fhort Abridg-
ment of it; and not to look back into his
Wars, in which he was abominably ill
ferv'd, *his Subjects conftantly ill treated
him* in giving him Supplies *too late*, that
he cou'd not get into the Field, nor forward his Preparations *in time* to be ready for his Enemies, who frequently were
ready to infult him in his Quarters.

By giving him *fham Taxes* and *Funds,
that raifed little or no Mony*, by which he
having borrow'd Mony of his People
by

by Anticipation, the Funds not anfwer-
ing, he contracted fuch *vaft Debts* as the
Nation *could never Pay*, which brought
the War *into difrepute*, funk the Credit
of his Exchequer, and fill'd the Nation
with Murmurs and Complaint.

By betraying his Counfel and well laid
Defigns to his Enemies, *felling their Native Country to Foreigners*, retarding their
Navies and Expeditions, till the Enemies were provided to receive them,
betraying their Merchants and Trade,
fpending vaft Sums to fit out Fleets,
juft time enough to go Abroad, and do
nothing, and then *get Home again.*

But as thefe were too numerous Evils,
and too long to repeat, the particular
things he related to in his Difcourfe,
were thefe that follow.

There had been *a hafty Peace* concluded with a furious and powerful Enemy,
the King *forefaw it would be of no continn-
uace,* and that the demife of a neighbour-
ingKing,who by all appearance could not
live long, would certainly embroil them
again, ----- He faw that Prince keep up

nume-

numerous Legions of Forces, in order
to be in a posture to break the Peace
with advantage. This the King fairly
represented to them, and told them the
necessity of keeping up *such a Force*, and
for such a Time, at least as might be
necessary to awe the Enemy from putting any affront upon them in case of
the Death of that Prince, which they
daily expected.

!VS

The Party who had all along malign'd
the Prosperity of this Prince, *took fire
at the Offer*, and here began another
State Plot, which tho' it hookt in two
or three sets of Men for different Ends,
yet altogether join'd in affronting and
ill treating their Prince, upon this Article of the Army.

The Nation had been in danger enough
from the designs of former Princes invading their Priviledges, and putting themselves in a Posture to Tyrannize by the
help *of standing Forces*, and the Party
that first took Fire at this Proposal tho'
the very same Men who in the time of an
Abrogratzian Prince, were for caressing
him, and *giving him Thanks for his Standing*

ing *Army*, as has been noted before, were the very People that began the outcry against this Demand, and *so specious were the Pretences* they made, that they drew in the very *Crolians themselves* upon the pretence of Liberty, and Exemption from Arbitrary Methods of Government *to oppose their King*.

It griev'd this good Prince to be suspected of Tyrannick Designs, and that by a Nation who he had done so much, and ventur'd so far to save *from Tyranny, and Standing Armies*; 'twas *in vain* he represented to them the pressing occasion; *in vain* he gave them a Description of *approaching Dangers*, and the threatning posture of the Enemies Armies; *in vain* he told them of the probabilities of renewing the War, and how keeping but *a needful Force* might be a means of preventing it; *in vain* he propos'd the subjecting what Force should be necessary to the Absolute Power, both as to Time and Number of their own *Cortez* or *National Assembly*.

It was all one, the Design being form'd in the Breasts of those who were *neither*

Friends

Friends to the Nation, nor the *King,* thofe
Reafons which would have been of
Force in another Cafe, made them the
more eager; *bitter Reflections were made
on the King,* and fcurrilous Lampoons
publifh'd upon the Subject of Tyrants,
and Governing by Armies.

Nothing could be more ungrateful to
a generous Prince, nor could any thing
more deeply affect this King, *than
whom* none ever had a more *genuine, fin-
gle-hearted Defign for the Peoples good,* but
above all, like *Cæfar* in the Cafe of *Bru-
tus,* it heartily mov'd him to find himfelf pufh'd at by thofe very People whom
he had all along feen, pretending to adhere to *his Intereft,* and the *Publick Benefit,* which he had always taken care
fhould *never be parted,* and to find thefe
People join againft this Propofal, *as a
Defign againft their Liberties,* and as a
Foundation of Tyranny *heartily and fen-
fibly afflicted him.*

It was a ftrange Miftery, and not eafily
unriddled, that thofe Men who had always a known averfion to the Intereft
of the depos'd King fhould fall in with
this

this Party, and thofe that were Friends
to the general Good, never forgave it
them.

All that could be faid to excufe them,
was the Plot I am fpeaking of, that by
carrying this Point for that Party, they
hookt in thofe forward People to join
in a popular Cry of Liberty and Property, *things they were never fond of be-*
fore, and to make fome Settlement of the
Peoples Claims *which they always had op-*
pos'd, and which they would *fince have*
been very glad to have repeal'd.

So great an Afcendant had the *Per-*
fonal Spleen of this Party over their o-
ther Principles, that they were content
to *let the Liberties of the People be declar'd*
in their higheft Claims, rather than not
obtain this one Article, which they
knew would *fo exceedingly mortify their*
Prince, and ftrengthen the Nations E-
nemies. They freely join'd in *Acts of*
Succeffion, Abjuration, Declaration of the
Power and *Claims of the People,* and the
Superiority of their Right to the Princes
Prerogative, and abundance of fuch
things, *which they could never be otherwife*
brought to.　　　O 4　　　'Tis

Tis true thefe were great things, but 'twas thought all this might have been obtain'd *in Conjunction with their Prince*, rather than by putting Affronts and Mortifications upon the Man that had next to the Influence of Heaven, been the only Agent of reftoring them to a Power and Capacity of enjoying, as well as procuring, fuch things as National Priviledges.

'Twas vigorofly alledg'd that *Standing Armies in times of Peace, were inconfiftent with the Publick Safety*, the Laws and Conftitutions of all the Nations *in the Moon*.

But thefe Allegations were ftrenuoufly anfwer'd, that it was true without the confent of the great National Council, it was fo, but *that being obtain'd*, it was not illegal, and publick Neceffities might make that confent, not only legal, but convenient.

'Twas all to no purpofe, the whole was carry'd with a Torrent of Clamour and Reflection againft the good Prince, *who confented*, becaufe he would in nothing oppofe

oppofe the Current of the People ; but withal, told them plainly what would be the confequences of their Heat, *which they have effectually found true fince* to their Coft, and to the lofs of fome Millions of Treafure.

For no fooner was this Army broke, *which was the beft ever that Nation faw,* and was juftly the Terror of the Enemy, but the great Monarch we mention'd before , broke all Meafures with this Prince and the Confederate Nations, a Proof what juft apprehenfions they had of his Conduct, at the head of fuch an Army. For *they broke with contempt,* a Treaty which the Prince *upon a profpect of this unkindnefs of his People* had entred into with the Enemy, and which he engag'd in, if poffible, to prevent *a new War*, which he forefaw he fhould be very unfit to begin, or carry on, and which they would never have dar'd to break had not *this Feud* happen'd.

It was but a little before I came into this Country, when *fuch repeated Accounts came,* of the Incroachments, Infults and Preparations of their *great powerful*

erful Neighbour, that all the World faw
the neceffity of a War, and the very
People *who were to feel it moft* apply'd to
the Prince to begin it.

He was forward enough tô begin it,
and in compliance with his People, refolv'd on it ; but *the Grief* of the ufage
he had receiv'd, the unkind Treatment
he had met with from thofe very People
that brought him thither, had *funk fo*
deep upon his Spirits, that he could never recover it ; but being very weak in
Body and Mind, and join'd to a flight hurt
he receiv'd by a fall from his Horfe, *he
dyed,* to the unfpeakable grief of all his
Subjects that wifh'd well to their Native Country.

This was the melancholly Account
of this great Prince's end, and I have been
told that at once every Year, there is a
kind *of Faft,* or folemn Commemora-
tion kept up for the Murther of that former Prince, who, as I noted, *was Beheaded by his Subjects* ; So it feems fome
of the People, who are of Opinion this
Prince was Murther'd by the ill Treatment of his Friends, a way which I muft
own,

own, *is the cruelleft of Deaths,* keep the
fame Day, to commemorate his Death,
and this is a Day, in which it feems *both
Parties are very free with one another,* as to
Rallery and ill Language.

But the Friends of this laft Prince
have a double advantage, for they alfo
commemorate the Birth Day of this
Prince, and are generally very merry
on that Day; and the cuftom is at their
Feaft on that Day, juft like our drinking
Healths, they pledge one another *to the
immortal Memory of their Deliverer;* as
the Hiftorical part of this Matter was
abfolutely neceffary to introduce the fol-
Remarks, and to inftruct the Ignorant in
thofe things, I hope it *fhall not be thought
a barren Digreffion,* efpecially when I
fhall tell you that it is a moft exact Reprefentation of what is yet to come in
a Scene of Affairs, of which I muft
make a fhort Abftract, by way of Introduction.

The deceas'd Prince we have heard of,
was fucceeded by his Sifter in-Law, the
fecond Daughter of the banifh'd Prince,
a Lady of *an extraordinary Character,* of
the

the Old Race of their Kings, *a Native* by
Birth, *a Solunarian* by Profeſſion ; exceeding *Pious, Juſt* and *Good,* of an *Honeſty* peculiar to her ſelf, and for which
ſhe was juſtly belov'd of all ſorts and
degrees of her Subjects.

This Princeſs having the Experience
of her *Father* and *Grand-father* before her,
join'd to her own Prudence and Honeſty of Deſign ; it was no wonder if ſhe
prudently ſhun'd all manner of *raſh
Counſels,* and endeavour'd to carry it
with a ſteady Hand between her con-
tending Parties.

At her firſt coming to the Crown,
ſhe made *a ſolemn Declaration* of her re-
ſolutions for *Peace* and juſt Government ;
ſhe gave the *Crolians* her Royal Word,
that ſhe would inviolably preſerve the
Toleration of their Religion and Worſhip,
and always afford them *her Protection,*
and by this ſhe hop'd they would *be
eaſy.*

But *to the Solunarians,* as thoſe among
whom ſhe had been Educated , and
whoſe Religion ſhe had always profeſs'd,

fefs'd, been train'd up in, and Pioufly perfued ; fhe exprefs'd her felf *with an uncommon Tendernefs*, told them they fhould be the Men of her Favour, and thofe that were *moft zealous* for that Church fhould have moft of her Countenance; and fhe back'd this foon after with an unparallel'd Act of Royal Bounty to them, freely parting with a confiderable Branch *of her Royal Revenue*, for the *poor Priefts* of that Religion, of which there were many in the remote Parts of her Kingdom.

What vaft Confequences, and prodigioufly differing from the Defign, may Words have when miftaken and mifayplyed by the Hearers. Never were fignificant Expreffions fpoken from a fincere, honeft and generous Principle, with a fingle Defign to ingage all the Subjects in *the Moon*, to Peace and Union, fo perverted, mifapply'd and turn'd by a Party, to a meaning directly contrary to the Royal Thoughts of the Queen: For from this very Expreffion, *moft Zealous*, grew all the Divifions and Subdivifions in the *Solunarian Church*, to the Ruin of their own Caufe, and the vaft advan-

advantage of the *Crolian* Intereft. The eager Men of the Church, efpecially thofe we have been talking of, *haftily* çatch'd at this Expreffion of the Queen, *Moft Zealous*, and Millions of fatal Conftructions, and unhappy Confequences they made of it, fome of which are as follows.

1. *They took it to imply* that the Queen whatever fhe had faid to *the Crolians*, really defign'd *their Deftruction*, and that thofe that were of that Opinion, muft be meant by the *Moft Zealous* Members of the *Solunarian* Church, and they could underftand *Zeal* no otherwife than their *own way*

2. From this Speech, and their miftaking the Words *Moft Zealous*, arofe an unhappy Diftinction among the *Solunarians* themfelves, fome *Zealous*, fome *More Zealous*, which afterwards divided them into two moft oppofite Parties, being fomented by an accident of a Book publifh'd *on an Occafion*, of which prefently.

The

The Confequences of this miftake, appear'd prefently in the *Moft Zealous*, in their offering all poffible Infults to the *Crolian Diffenters*, Preaching them down, *Printing* them down, and *Talking* them down, as a People not fit to be fuffer'd *in the Nation*, and now they thought they had the Game fure.

Down with the *Crolians* began to be all the Cry, and truly the *Crolians themfelves* began to be uneafy, and had nothing to rely upon *but the Queens Promife*, which however her Majefty always made good to them.

The other Party proceeded fo far, that they begun to Infult *the very Queen her felf*, upon the Matter of her Word, and one of her College-Priefts told her plainly in Print, fhe could not be a true Friend to *the Solunarian Church*, if fhe did not declare War againft, and root out all the *Crolians* in her Dominions.

But thefe Proceedings met *with a Check*, by a very odd accident: A certain *Author* of thofe Countries, a *very mean, obfcure and defpicable Fellow*, of no great

great share of Wit, but that had a very *unlucky way of telling his Story*, seeing which way things were a going, writes a Book, and *Perfonating this high Solunarian Zeal*, mufters up all their Arguments, *as if* they were his own, and ftrenuoufly pretends to prove that *all the Crolians* ought to be Deftroy'd, *Hang'd, Banifh'd*, and the D----l and all. As this Book was a perfect Surprize to all the Country, fo the Proceedings about it on all fides were as extraordinary.

The *Crolians* themfelves were furpriz'd at it, and fo clofely had the Author couch'd his Defign, that they never faw *the Irony of the Stile*, but began to look about them, to fee which way they fhould fly to fave themfelves.

The *Men of Zeal* we talk'd of, were fo blinded with the Notion which *fuited fo exactly with their real Defign*, that they hugg'd the Book, *applauded the unknown Author*, and plac'd the Book next their *Oraclar Writings*, or Laws of Religion.

The Author was all this while conceal'd, and the Paper had all the effect he wifh'd for.   For

For as it caus'd *thefe firft* Gentlemen
to carefs, applaud and approve it, and
thereby difcover'd their real Intention,
fo it met with Abhorrence and Deteſta-
tion in all the Men of *Principles, Prudence* and *Moderation* in the Kingdom,
who tho' they were *Solunarians* in Religion, yet were not for Blood, Defola-
tion and Perfecution of their Brethren,
but *with the Queen* were willing they
fhould enjoy their Liberties and Eftates,
they behaving themſelves *quietly and
peaceably* to the Government.

At laſt it came out that it was writ
by *a Crolian*; but *good* God! what a Clamour was rais'd at the poor Man, the
Crolians flew at him like Lightning, *ignorantly and blindly*, not feeing that he had
facrific'd himfelf and his Fortunes in
their behalf; they *rumag'd his Character*
for Reproaches, tho' they could find little that way to hurt him; they plenti-
fully loaded him with ill Language and
Railing, and took a great deal of pains
to let the World fee their *own Ignorance
and Ingratitude.*

The *Minifters of State*, tho' at that time

P   *of*

of the fiery Party, yet feeing the general Deteftation of fuch a Propofal, and how ill *it would go down with the Nation*, tho' they approv'd the thing, yet began to fcent the Defign, and were alfo oblig'd to declare againft it, for fear of being thought of the fame Mind.

Thus the Author was Profcrib'd by Proclamation, and a *Reward* of 50000 *Hecato's*, a fmall imaginary Coin in thofe Parts, put upon his Head.

The *Cortez* of the Nation being at the fame time affembled join'd in Cenfuring the Book, and thus *the Party* blindly damn'd *their own Principles* for meer fhame of the practice, not daring to own the thing in publick which they had underhand profeft, and the fury of all Parties fell *upon the poor Author*.

The Man fled the firſt popular Fury, but at laft being betraid fell into the Hands of the publick Miniftry.

When they *had him* they hardly knew *what to do with him*; they could not proceed againft him as Author of a Propofal

for

for the Deſtruction of *the Crolians*, becauſe it appear'd he was *a Crolian himſelf*; they were loth to charge him with
ſuggeſting that the *Solunarian Church-
men* were guilty of ſuch a Deſign, leaſt
he ſhould bring *their own Writings to
prove it true*; ſo they fell to *wheadling
him* with good Words to throw himſelf
into their Hands and ſubmit, giving him
that *Gew-gaw* the *Publick Faith* for a Civil
and Gentleman-like *Treatment*; the Man,
believing *like a Coxcomb* that they ſpoke
as they meant, *quitted his own Defence*,
and threw himſelf on the Mercy *of the
Queen as he thought*; but they abuſing
their Queen with falſe Repreſentations,
Perjur'd all their Promiſes with him, and
treated him in a moſt barbarous manner,
on pretence that there were *no ſuch Promiſes made*, tho' he prov'd it upon them
by the Oath of the Perſons to whom
they were made.

Thus they laid him under *a heavy Sentence*, Fin'd him more than they thought
him able to pay, and order'd him to be
expos'd to the Mob in the Streets.

Having him at this Advantage they
ſet

fet upon him with their Emiffaries to
difcover to them his Adherents, *as they
call'd them*, and promis'd him great
Things on one Hand, threatning him
with his utter Ruin on the other; and
the *Great Scribe* of the Country, with
another of their great Courtiers, took
fuch a low Step as to go to him *to the
Dungeon* where they had put him, to fee
if they could tempt him *to betray his
Friends.* - The *Comical Dialogue* between
them there the Author of this
has feen *in Manufcript*, exceeding *diverting*, but having not time to 'Tranflate it 'tis omitted for the prefent ; tho'
he promifes to *publifh it in its proper Sea-
fon* for publick Inftruction.

However for the prefent it may fuf-
fice to tell the World, that neither by
Promifes of Reward or fear of Punifhment
they could prevail upon him to difcover
any thing, and fo it remains a Secret to
this day.

The Title of this unhappy Book was
The fhorteft way with the Crolians. The
Effects of it were various, as will be
feen in our enfuing Difcourfe: As to the
Au-

Author nothing was more unaccountable than the Circumftances of his Treatment ; for he met with all *that Fate* which
they muft expect *who attempt to open the
Eyes of a Nation wilfully blind.*

The *hot Men of the Solunarian Church*
damn'd him without *Bell,* *Book,* or *Can-
dle ;* the more *Moderate* pitied him, but
lookt on as unconcern'd : *But the Croli
ans,* for whom he had run this Venture,
us'd him worft of all ; for they not only
abandon'd him, but *reproacht him as an
Enemy* that would ha' them deftroy'd :
So one fide rail'd at him becaufe they
did underftand him, and the other becaufe
they did not.

Thus the Man funk under the general
Neglect, was ruin'd and undone, and
left a Monument of what every Man
muft expect that ferves a good Caufe,
profeft by an *unthankful People.*

And here it was I found out that my
Lunar Philofopher was *only fo* in Difguife, and that *he was no Philofopher, but
the very Man* I have been talking of.

From

From this Book, and the Treatment its
Author receiv'd, for they us'd him with
all poſſible Rigour, a new Scene of Parties came upon the Stage, and this
Queen's Reign began to be fill'd with
more Diviſions and Feuds than any before her.

Theſe Parties began to be ſo numerous
and violent that *it endanger'd the Publick
Good*, and gave great Diſadvantages to
the general Affairs abroad.

The Queen invited them all to *Peace
and Union*, but 'twas in vain; nay, one
had the Impudence to publiſh that to
procure Peace and Union it was neceſſary to ſuppreſs *all the Crolians*, and have
no Party but one, and then all muſt be
of a Mind.

From this heat of Parties all the moderate Men fell in with their Queen,
and were heartily *for Peace and Union*:
The other, who were now diſtinguiſh'd
by the Title of *High Solunarians*, call'd
theſe all *Crolians* and *Low Solunarians*,
and began to Treat them with more
Inveteracy than they us'd to do the *Crolians*,

lians themfelves, calling them *Traytors* to
their Country, *Betrayers* of their Mother,
Serpents harbour'd in the Bofom, who bite,
fting and hifs at the Hand that fuccour'd
them ; and in fhort the Enmity grew
fo violent, that from hence proceeded
one of the *fubtileft, foolifheft, deep, fhal-
low* Contrivances and *Plots* that ever
was hatcht or fet on foot by any Party
of Men in the whole Moon, at leaft who
pretended *to any Brains*, or to half a
degree *of common* Underftanding.

There had always been Diflikes and
Diftafts between even the moft moderate *Solunarians* and the *Crolians*, as I
have noted in the beginning of this
Relation , and thefe were deriv'd
from *Diffenting in Opinions of Religion*,
ancient Feuds, private Intereft, Education, and the like; and the *Solunarians*
had frequently, on pretence of fecuring
the Government , made Laws to ex-
clude the *Crolians* from any part of the
Adminiftration , unlefs they fubmitted
to fome *Religious Tefts* and Ceremonies
which were prefcrib'd them.

Now as *the keeping them out of Offices*
was more the Defign than the *Conver-*

fion

fion of the Crolians to the *Solunarian*
Church, the *Crolians*, at leaft many of
them, *fubmitted to the Teft*, and frequently Conform'd to qualify themfelves for
publick Employments.

The moft moderate of the Solunarians
were in their Opinion againft this practice, and the *High Men* taking advantage of them, *drew them in* to Concur in
making a Law with yet more Severity
againft them, effectually to keep them
out of Employment.

The low Solunarians were eafy to be
drawn into this Project, as it was only
a Confirming former Laws of their own
making, and all Things run fair *for the
Defign*; but as the *High Men* had further
Ends in it than barely reducing the *Crolians* to Conformity, they coucht fo many grofs Claufes into their Law, that
even the *Grandees of the Solunarians*
themfelves could not comply with; nay
even the *Patriarchs* of the *Solunarian*
Church declar'd againft it, as tending
to Perfecution and Confufion.

This Difappointment *enrag'd the Party*,
and

and that very Rage entirely ruin'd their
Project; for now the *Nobility*, the *Patriarchs*, and all the wise Men of the Nation, joining together against these *Men
of Heat and Fury*, the Queen began to
see into their Designs, and *as she was of a
most pious and peaceable Temper*, she con-.
ceiv'd a just Hatred of so wicked and
barbarous a Design, and immediately
dismiss'd from her Council and Favour
the Great Scribe, and several others who
were Leaders in the Design, *to the great
mortification of the whole Party*, and utter
Ruin of the intended Law against *the
Crolians*.

Here I could not but observe, as I
have done before in the Case of the ba-
nish'd King, how *impolitick these high
Solunarian Church-men acted* in all their
Proceedings, for had they contented
themselves *by little and little* to ha' done
their Work, they had done it effectually;
but pushing at Extremities they over-
shot themselves, and *ruin'd all.*

For *the Grandees* and *Patriarchs* made
but a *few trifling Objections* at first, nay and
came off, and yielded some of them too;
and

and if thefe would ha' confented to ha'
parted with fome Claufes which they
have willingly left out fince, they had
had it pafs'd ; but thefe were *as hot Men
always are*, too eager and fure of their
Game, they thought all was their own,
and fo they loft themfelves.

If they rail'd at the *low Solunarian
Churchmen* before, they doubled their
Clamors at them now, all the *Patriarchs*,
and all the Nobility and *Grandees*, nay
even the *Queen* her felf came under their
Cenfure, and every Body who was not of
their Mind were *Preftarians* and *Crolians*.

As this Rage of theirs was implacable,
fo, as I hinted before, it drove them into
another *Subdivifion of Parties*, and now began *the Myfterious Plot* to be laid which I
mention'd before; for the *Cortez* being
fummon'd, and the Law being propofed,
fome of thefe *high Solunarians* appear'd in
Confederacy with the *Crolians*, *in perfect
Confederacy* with them, a thing no Body
would have imagin'd could ever ha' been
brought to pafs.

Now as thefe forts of Plots muft always be carry'd very nicely, fo thefe
high

high Gentlemen who Confederated with the *Crolians*, having, to fpight the other, refolv'd effectually to prevent the paffing the Law againft *the Qualification of the Crolians*, it was not their Bufinefs immediately to declare themfelves *againft* it as a Law, but by ftill loading it with fome Extravagance or other, and pufhing it on to fome intolerable Extreme, *fecure its mifcarriage.*

In the managing this Plot, one of their *Authors* was fpecially employ'd, and *that all that was really true of the* Crolian Diffenters might be ridicul'd, his Work was to draw *monftrous Piĉtures* of them, which no Body could believe ; this took immediately , for now People began to look at their Shooes to fee if they were not *Cloven Footed* as they went a long Streets ; and at laft finding they were really fhap'd like the reft *of the Lunar Inhabitants*, they went back *to the Author*, who was a Learned Member of a certain Seminary, or Brother-hood of *the Solunarian Clergy*, and enquir'd if he were *not Mad*, Diftraĉted and *Raving*, or *Moon-blind*, and in want of the thinking Engine ; but finding all things *right there*, and that he

was

was in his Senfes, efpecially in a Morn-
ing when he was a little *free from*, &c.
that he was a Good, Honeft, Jolly,
Solunarian Prieft, and no room could be
found for an Objection there. Upon all
thefe Scarches it prefently appear'd, and
all Men concluded it was a meer *Fanatick Crolian Plot* ; that this *High Party
of all* were but Pretenders, and meer
Traytors to the *True High Solunarian
Church-Men*, that wearing the fame
Cloth had herded among them *in Difguife*, only to wheedle them into fuch
wild Extravagancies as muft of neceffity confufe their Councils, expofe their
Perfons, and ruin their Caufe. ---- According to the like Practice, put upon
their *Abrograzian* Prince, and of which
I have fpoken before.

And fince I am upon the detection of
this *moft refin'd Practice*, I crave leave
to defcend to fome particular Inftances,
which will the better evince the Truth
of this Matter, and make it appear
that either this was really *a Crolian Plot*,
or elfe all thefe People were *perfectly
Diftracted* ; and as their Wits in *that Lu-*
nar

nar World are much higher ſtrain'd *than ours,* ſo their Lunacy, where it happens, muſt according to the Rules *of Mathematical Nature,* bear aŋ extream Equal in proportion.

This College Fury of a Man was the firſt on whom this uſeful Diſcovery was made, and having *writ ſeveral Learned Tracts* wherein he invited the People *to Murther* and Deſtroy *all the Crolians,* Branded all the *Solunarian Patriarchs, Clergy* and *Gentry* that would not come into *his Propoſal,* with the name of *Cowards, Traytors* and *Betrayers* of *Lunar Religion;* having beat the *Concionazimir* at a great Aſſembly of the Cadirs, *or Judges,* and told them *all the Crolians* were *Devils,* and they were *all Perjur'd* that did not uſe them as ſuch: He carry'd on Matters *ſo dexterouſly,* and with ſuch ſurprizing Succeſs, that he fill'd even *the Solunarians* themſelves with Horror at his Propoſals.----- And as I happen'd to be in one of their publick Halls where all ſuch Writings *as are new* are laid a cer-tain time to be read by *every Comer,* I ſaw a little *knot of Men* round a Table, where one was reading *this Book.* **There**

There were two *Solunarian High Priests*
in their proper Veftments, one *Privy
Councellor* of the State, one other *Noble
Man*, and one who had *in his Hat* a Token, to fignifie that he poffeft one of the
fine Feathers of the *Confolidator*, of
which I have given the Defcription already.

The Book being read by one of the ha-
bited Priefts, he ftarts up with fome
warmth, *by the Moon, fays he*, I have
found this Fellow out, he is certainly a
Crolian, a meer *Preftarian Crolian*,
and is crept into our Church only *in
Difguife*, for 'tis certain all this is *but
meer Banter* and Irony to expofe us, and
to ridicule the *Solunarian* Intereft.

The Privy Councellor took it prefently,
whether he is *a Crolian* or no, fays he, I
cannot tell, but he has certainly *done
the Crolians fo much Service*, that if they
had hir'd him to act for them, they
could not have defir'd he fhould ferve
them better.

Truly, fays *the Man of the Feather*, I
was always for pulling down *the Crolians*,
for

for I thought them dangerous to the State; but this Man has brought the Matter *nearer to my View*, and shown me *what destroying them is*, for he put me upon examining the Consequences, and now I find it would be *lopping off the Limbs of the Government*, and laying it at the Mercy of the Enemy *that they might lop off its Head*; I assure you he has done *the Crolians* great Service, for whereas abundance of our Men *of the Feather* were for routing the *Crolians*, they lately fell down to 134 or thereabouts.

All this confirm'd the first Man's Opinion that *he was a Crolian in Disguise*, or an Emissary employ'd by them to ruin the Project of their Enemies; for *these Crolians are damn'd cunning People in their way*, and they have Mony enough to engage Hirelings to their side.

Another Party concern'd in *this Plot* was an old *cast-out Solunarian Priest*, who, tho' professing himself a *Solunarian*, was turn'd out for adhering to the *Abrograzian King*, a mighty Stickler for the Doctrin of *absolute Subjection*.

This

This Man draws *the most monstrous Pi-cture of a Crolian* that could be invented, he put him in a *Wolf's Skin* with long *Asses Ears*, and hung him all over full of *Associations, Massacres, Persecutions, Re-bellions*, and *Blood.* Here the People began to *stare* again, and a *Crolian* cou'd not go along the Street but they were always looking for the *long Ears*, the *Wolf's Claws*, and the like; 'till at last nothing of these Things appearing, but the *Crolians* looking and acting like *other Folks*, they begun to examine the Mat-ter, and found this was *a meer Crolian Plot* too, and *this Man* was hir'd to run these extravagant lengths to point out the right meaning.

The Discovery being made, People ever since understand him that when he talks of the Dissenters *Associations, Murthers, Persecutions,* and the like, he means that his Readers should look back to the *Murthers, Oppressions* and *Persecutions* they had suffered for several past years, and the *Associations* that were now forming to bring them into the same Condition again.

From

From this famous Author I could not
but proceed to obferve the farther Progrefs of this moft refin'd piece of Cunning, among the *very great Ones, Grandees, Feathers,* and *Confolidators* of the
Country... For thefe *Cunning Crolians*
manag'd their Intriegues fo nicely, that
they brought about a Famous Divifion
even among the *High Solunarian Party
themfelves;* and whereas the Law of Qualification was reviv'd again, and in
great Danger of being compleated; thefe
fubtle *Crolians* brought over One Hundred and Thirty Four *of the Feathers* in
the Famous *Confolidator* to be of their
fide, and to *Contrive the utter Deftruction
of it; and thus fell the Defign* which the
High Solunarian Church Men had laid
for the Ruin of *the Crolians Intereft,*
by their own Friends firft joyning in
all the Extremes they had propofed, and
then pufhing it fo much farther, and to
fuch *mad Periods* that the very higheft
of them *ftood amaz'd* at the Defign,
ftartled, flew back and made a *full ftop;*
they were willing to Ruin the *Crolians,*
but they were not willing to Ruin the
whole Nation. The more thefe Men
began to confider, the more furioufly
thefe Plotters carry'd on their Extrava-
Q   gances

gances; at laſt they made *a General puſh*
at a thing in which they knew if the
other *High Men* joyn'd, they muſt throw
all into Confuſion, bring a *Foreign Enemy*
on their Backs, *unravel all the Thread of
the War,* fight all their Victories *back
again,* and involve the whole Nation in
Blood and *Confuſion.*

They knew well enough that moſt of
the *High Men* would heſitate at this,
they knew if they did not the *Grandees*
and *Patriarchs* would reject it, and ſo
they plaid the *fureſt Game* to blaſt and
overthrow this Law, that could poſſibly
be plaid.

If any Man, *in the whole World in the
Moon,* will pretend this was not *a Plot,*
a *Crolian Deſign,* a meer *Conſpiracy to deſtroy the Law,* let him tell me for what
other end could theſe Men offer ſuch extreams as they needs muſt know would
meet with immediate oppoſition, things
that they knew all the Honeſt Men, all
the *Grandees,* all the *Patriarchs,* and almoſt all the *Feathers* would oppoſe.

From

From hence all the Men of any fore-sight brought it to this pass, as is before Noted, that either these One Hundred and Thirty Four were *Fools* or *Mad-Men*, or that it was a *Phanatick Crolian Plot* and Conspiracy to Ruin the make-ing this Law, which the rest of the *So-lunarian Church Men* were very forward to carry on.

I heard indeed some Men Argue that this could not be, the breach was too wide between *the Crolians* and these Gentlemen ever to come to such an A-greement; but *the Wiser Heads* who ar-gu'd the other way, always brought them, as is noted above, to this pinch of Argument; that either it must be so, be *a Fanatick Crolian Plot*, or else the *Men of Fury* were all *Fools, Madmen,* and fitter for an *Hospital,* than a State-House, or a *Pulpit.*

It must be allow'd, these *Crolians* were Cunning People, thus to wheedle in these *High Flying Solunarians* to break the Neck of their dear Project.

But upon the whole, for ought I cou'd

see

fee, whether it went one way or t'other, all the Nation efteem'd the other People *Fools* ------ *Fools of the moft extraordinary Size in all the Moon, for either way* they pull'd down what they had been many Years a Building.

I cannot fay that this was in kindnefs to the *Crolians,* but in meer Malice to the *Low Solunarian Party,* who had the Government in their Hands, for *Malice always carries Men on to monftrous Extremes.*

Some indeed have thought it hard to call this a Plot, and a Confederacy *with the Crolians.* ------ But I cannot but think it the *kindeft thing that can be faid of them,* and that 'tis impoffible thofe People who pufh'd at fome imaginary Things in *that Law,* could but be in a Plot as aforefaid, or be perfectly *Lunatick,* down right Mad-Men, or Traytors to their Country, *and let them choofe which Character they like.*

I cannot in Charity but fpare them their *Honefty,* and their *Senfes,* and attribute it all to their Policy.

When

When I had underftood all things at large, and found the exceeding depth of the Defign; I muft confefs the Dif-. covery of thefe things *was very diverting*, and the more fo, when I made the proper Reflections upon the *Analogy there feem'd to be* between *thefe Solunarian High Church-Men* in the Moon, and ours here in *England*; *our High Church-Men* are no more to compare to *thefe*, than the Hundred and Thirty Four, are to the *Confolidators*.

Ours can Plot now and then a little among themfelves, but then 'tis all *Grofs* and *plain Sailing*, down right *taking Arms*, calling in Foreign Forces, *Affaffinations* and *the like*; but thefe are nothing to the more Exquifite Heads in *the Moon*. For they have the fubtilleft Ways with them, that ever were heard of. They can *make War* with a Prince, on purpofe to *bring him to the Crown*; fit out *vaft Navies againft him*, that he may have the more leifure *to take their Merchant Men*; make *Defcents* upon him, on purpofe to come Home and do *nothing*; if they have a mind to a Sea Fight, they carefully fend out Admirals

Q 3   that

that care not to come within half a
Mile of the Enemy, that coming off
safe they may have *the boasting Part* of
the Victory, and *the beaten Part both
together.* I r

'Twould be endless to call over the
Roll of their sublime Politicks. They
*damn Moderation in order to Peace and U-
nion,* set the House *on Fire* to save it
from *Desolation,* Plunder to avoid Perse-
cution, and *consolidate Things* in order
to their more *immediate Dissolution.*

Had our *High Church-Men* been Masters of these excellent Arts, they had
long ago brought their Designs to
pass.

The exquisite Plot of these *High Solunarians* answer'd the *Crolians End,* for it
broke all their Enemies Measures, the Law
vanish'd, the Grandees could hardly be
perswaded to read it, and when it was
propos'd to be read again, *they hiss at it,*
and threw it by with Contempt.

Nor was this all; for it not only lost
them their Design as to this Law, but it
abso

absolutely broke the Party, and just as it
was with *Adam* and *Eve,* as soon as *they
Sinn'd* they *Quarrell'd,* and fell out with
one another ; so, as soon as things came
to this height, *the Party fell out one a-
mong another,* and even the *High Men* themselves were divided, some were for *Consolidating,* and some not for *Consolidating,* some were for *Tacking,* and some
not for *Tacking,* as they were, or were
not let into the Secret.

If this *Confusion of Languages,* or Interest, lost them the real Design, it cannot be a wonder ; have we not always
seen it *in our World,* that dividing an
Interest, weakens and exposes it ? Has
not a great many both good and bad Designs been render'd Abortive in *this our
Lower World,* for want of *the Harmony
of Parties,* and the Unanimity of those
concern'd in the Design ?

How had the *knot of Rebellion* been
dissolv'd in *England,* if it had not been
untied by the very Hands *of those that
knit it* ? All the contrary Force
had been entirely broken and subdu'd,
and the *Restoration of Monarchy* had ne-

ver

ver happen'd in *England*, if *Union and Agreement* had been found among the managers of that Age.

The Enemies of the prefent Eftablifh-ment have fhown fufficiently that they perfectly underftand the *fhorteft way* to our infallible Deftruction, when they bend their principle Force at dividing us into Parties, and keeping thofe Par-ties at the utmoft variance.

But this is not all, the Author of this cannot but obferve here that as *England* is unhappily divided among Parties, fo it has this one Felicity even to be found in the very matter of her Misfortunes, that thofe Parties are all again fubdi-vided among themfelves.

How eafily might the Church have crufht and fubdu'd the Diffenters if they had been all as mad as one Party, if they had not been *fome High* and *fome Low* Church-men? And what Mifchief might not that one Party ha' done in this Nation, had not they been divided again into *Jurant Jacobites* and *Non-Ju-rant,* into *Confolidators* and *Non-Confoli-dators?*

dators? From whence 'tis plain to me, that *juſt as it is in the Moon* theſe *Conſolidating Church-men* are meer Confederates with the *Whigs*; and it muſt be ſo, unleſs we ſhould ſuppoſe them meer *mad Men* that don't know what they are a doing, and who are the Drudges of their Enemies, and kno' nothing of the Matter.

And from this *Lunar Obſervation* it preſently occur'd to my Underſtanding, that *my Maſters the Diſſenters* may come in for a ſhare among the *Moon-blind* Men of this Generation, ſince had they done for their own Intereſt what the *Laws fairly admits to* be done, had they been *united among themſelves*, had they form'd themſelves into a *Politick Body* to have acted in a publick, united Capacity *by general Concert*, and as Perſons that had but one Intereſt *and underſtood it*, they had never been ſo often Inſulted by every riſing Party, they had never had ſo many *Machines* and *Intrigues to ruin and ſuppreſs them*, they had never been ſo often *Tackt* and *Conſolidated* to Oppreſſion and Perſecution, and yet never have rebell'd or broke the Peace, incurr'd

curr'd the Difpleafure of their Princes,
or have been upbraided with Plots, Infurrections and *Antimonarchical Princi-*
ples; when they had made Treaties and
Capitulations with the Church *for Tem-*
per and *Toleration*, the Articles would
have been kept, and thefe would have
demanded Juftice with an Authority
that would upon all Occafions *be refpe-*
cted.

Were they united in *Civil Polity* in
Trade and *Intereft*, would they *Buy and*
Sell with *one another*, abftract their *Stocks*,
erect *Banks* and *Companies* in Trade *of*
their own, lend their Cafh to the Government *in a Body*, and as a *Body.*

If I were to tell them what Advantages the *Crolians* in the *Moon* make of
this fort of management, how the Government finds it their Intereft to treat
them civilly, and ufe them like Subjects
of Confideration ; how upon all Occafions fome of the *Grandees* and *Nobility*
appear as Protectors of the *Crolians*, and
treat with their Princes in their Names,
prefent their Petitions, and make Demands from the Prince of fuch Loans
and

and *Sums of Mony* as the publick Occafions require ; and what abundance of
Advantages are reapt from fuch a Union, both to their own Body as a Party,
and to the Government alfo they would
be convinc'd ; wherefore I cannot but
veryearneftly defire of the Diffenters and
Whigs *in my own Country*, that they would
take a Journy in my *Confolidator* up to the
Moon, they would certainly fee there
what vaft Advantages they lofefor want
of a *Spirit of Union*, and a concert of Meafures among themfelves.

The *Crolians in the Moon* are Men of
large Souls, and Generoufly ftand by one
another *on all Occafions* ; it was never
known that they deferted any Body
that fuffer'd for them, *my Old Philofopher excepted*, and that was a furprize
upon them.

The Reafon of the Difference is plain,
our Diffenters here have not the Advantage of *a Cogitator*, or *thinking Engine*, as they have *in the Moon*.----- We
have the *Elevator* here, and are lifted
up pretty much, but *in the Moon* they
always go into the *Thinking Engine* upon

on every *Emergency*, and in this they out-do us of this World on every Occasion.

In general therefore I muft note that the wifeft Men I found *in the Moon*, when they underftood the Notes I had made as above, of the fub-divifions of our Parties, told me that it was the greateft Happinefs that could ha' been obtained to our Country, for that if our Parties had not been thus divided, *the Nation had been undone.* They own'd that had not their *Solunarian Party* been divided among themfelves, the *Crolians* had been undone, and all the *Moon* had been involv'd *in Perfecution*, and been very probably fubjected to the *Gallunarian Monarch.*

Thus the *fatal Errors of Men* have their advantages, the feperate ends they ferve are not forefeen by their Authors, and they *do good* againft the very *Defign of the People*, and the nature of the Evil it felf.

And now that I may encourage *our People* to that Peace and good Underftading ſtanding among themſelves, which can alone produce their Safety and Deliverance; I ſhall give a brief Account how the *Crolians in the Moon* came to open their Eyes to their own Intereſt, how they came to *Unite*, and how the Fruits of *that Union* ſecur'd them from ever being inſulted again by the *Solunarian Party*, who in time gave over the vain and fruitleſs Attempt, and ſo a univerſal *Lunar Calm* has ſpread the whole *Moon* ever ſince.

If *our People* will not liſten to their own Advantages, nor *do their own Buſineſs*, let them take the conſequences to themſelves, they cannot blame the *Man in the Moon*.

To endeavour to bring this to paſs, as theſe Memoirs have run thro' the general Hiſtory of the Feuds and unhappy Breaches between the *Solunarian* Church and *the Crolian* Diſſenters *in the World of the Moon*, it would ſeem an imperfect and abrupt Relation, if I ſhould not tell you how, and by what Method, *tho' long hid from their Eyes*, the *Crolians* came to underſtand their own Intereſt, and *know their own Strength.* 'Tis

'Tis true, it feem'd a Wonder to me when I confider'd the Excellence and Variety of thofe *perfpective Glaffes* I have mentioned, the clearnefs of the Air, and *confequently of the Head*, in this Lunar World. I fay it was very ftrange the *Cro-lians* fhould ha' been *Moon Blind* fo long as they were, that they could not fee it was always in their Power if they had but purfued their own Intereft, and made ufe of thofe, legal Opportunities which lay before them, to put them-felves in a Pofture, as that the Govern-ment it felf fhould think them a Body too big to be infulted, and find it their Intereft to keep Meafures with them.

It was indeed a long time before they open'd their Eyes to thefe advantages, but bore the Infults of the hair-brain'd Party, with a weaknefs and negligence that was as unjuftifiable in them, as un-accountable to all the Nations of the Moon.

But at laft, as all violent Extremes rouze *their contrary Extremeties*, the folly and extravagance of the *High Soluna-rians* drove the *Crolians* into their Senfes,

fes, and *rouz'd them* to their own Intereft, the occafion was among a great
many others as follows.

The eager *Solunarian* could not on all
occafions forbear to fhow their deep Regret at the Diffenting *Crolians* enjoying
the Tolleration of their Religion, *by a
Law* ---.

And when all their legal Attempts to
leffen that Liberty had prov'd Abortive, her *Solunarian Majefty* on all
Occafions repeating her affurances of
the continuance of her Protection, and
particularly the maintaining this Tolleration Invioiable. They proceeded then
to fhow the remains of their Mallice, in
little Infults, mean and *illegal Methods*,
and continual private Difturbances upon particular Perfons, in which, however the *Crolians* having recourfe to the
Law, always found Juftice on their fide,
and had redrefs with Advantage, of
which the following Inftance is more
than ordinarily Remarkable.

There had been a Law made by *the
Men of the Feather*, that all the meaner
Idle

idle fort of People, who had no fettel'd
way of living fhould go to the Wars,
and the *Lazognians*, a fort of Magiftrates
there, in the nature of our Juftices of
the Peace, were to fend them away by
Force.

Now it happen'd in a certain *Soluna-*
rian Ifland, that for want of a better,
one of their High Priefts was put into
the Civil Adminiftration, and made a
Lazognian.----- In the Neighbourhood of
this Man's Jurifdiction, one of their own
Solunarian Priefts had turn'd *Crolian*,
and whether he had a better Tallent at
performance, or rather was more diligent in his Office is not material, but he
fet up a kind of a *Crolian* Temple in an
old Barn, or fome fuch Mechanick Building, and all the People flock'd after
him.

This fo provok'd his Neighbours *of*
the black Girdle, an Order of Priefts, of
which he had been one, that they refolv'd to fupprefs him let it coft what it
would.

They

They run *strange lengths* to bring this to pass.

They forg'd strange Stories of him, defam'd him, run him into Jayl upon frivolous and groundless Occasions, represented him as a *Monster of a Man*, told their Story *so plain*, and made it *so specious*, that even *the Crolians* themselves *to their Shame*, believ'd it, and took up Prejudices against the Poor Man, which had like to ha' been his Ruin.

They proscrib'd him in Print for Crimes they could never prove, *they branded him* with Forgery, Adultery, Drunkenness, Swearing, breaking Jayl, and abundance of Crimes; but when Matters were examin'd and things came to the Test, they could *never prove the least thing upon him*. ----- In this manner however they continually worryed the poor Man, till they ruin'd his Family and *reduc'd him to Beggary*; and tho' he came out of the Prison they cast him into by the meer force of Innocence, yet they never left persuing him with all sorts of violence. ------ At last they made use of their *Brother of the Girdle*, who was in

R   Com-

Commiſſion as above, and this Man being *High Prieſt* and *Lazonian* too, by the
firſt was a Party, and by the *laſt* had a
Power to act the Tragedy *they had plotted*
againſt the poor Man.

In ſhort, they ſeiz'd him without any
Crime alledg'd, took violently from him
his Licence, as a Crolian Prieſt, by which
the Law juſtify'd what he had done,
pretending it was forg'd, and after very
ill Treating him, *condemn'd him to the
Wars*, delivers him up for a Souldier,
and accordingly carry'd him away.

But it happen'd, to their great Mortification, that this Man found more
Mercy from the *Men of the Sword*, than
from thoſe *of the Word*, and ſo found
means to get out of their Hands, and
afterwards to undeceive all the Moon,
both as to his own Character, and as
to what he had Suffer'd.

For ſome of the *Crolians*, who began
to be made ſenſible of the Injury done
the poor Man, advis'd him to have
recourſe to the Law, and to bring his
Adverſaries before *the Criminal Bar*.

But

But as foon as this was done, *good God!* what a *Scene of Villany* was here opened : The poor Man brought up fuch a Cloud of Witneffes to confront every Article of their Charge, and to vindicate his own Character, that when the very Judges heard it, tho' they were all *Solunarians* themfelves, they held up their Hands, and declar'd in open Court it was the *deepeft Track of Villany* that ever came before them, and that the Actors ought to be made Examples to *all the Moon.*

The Perfons concern'd, us'd all poffible Arts to avoid, or at leaft to delay the Shame, and adjourn the Punifhment, thinking ftill to weary the poor Man out,------ But now his Brethren the *Crolians* began to fee themfelves wounded thro' his Sides, and above all, finding his Innocence clear'd up beyond all manner of difpute, *they efpous'd his Caufe,* and affifted him to profecute his Enemies, which he did, till he brought them all to Juftice, expos'd them to the laft Degree, obtain'd full reparation of all his Loffes, and a publick Decree of

R 2　　　　the

the Judges of his Juſtification *and fu-*
ture Repoſe.

Indeed when I ſaw the Proceedings
againſt this poor Man run to a heighth
ſo extravagant and monſtrous, when I
found *Malice, Forgery, Subornation, Perjury,*
and a thouſand unjuſtifiable Things
which their own Senſe, if they had any,
might ha' been their Protection againſt,
and which any Child *in the Moon* might
ha' told them muſt one time or other
come upon the Stage and expoſe them ; I
began to think theſe People were all in
the Crolian Plot too.

For really ſuch Proceedings as theſe
were the greateſt pieces of Service to
the Crolians as could poſſibly be done;
for as it generally proves in other
Places as well as in the Moon, that
Miſchief unjuſtly contriv'd falls upon the
Head of the Authors, and redounds to
their treble Diſhonour, ſo it was here ;
the barbarity and inhumane Treatment
of this Man, made the ſober and honeſt
Part even of the *Solunarians* themſelves bluſh for their Brethren, and own
that the Puniſhment awarded on them
was juſt.

Thus

Thus *the Crolians* got ground by the
Folly and Madnefs of their Enemies,
and the very Engines and Plots laid to
injure them, ferv'd to bring their Enemies on the Stage, and expofe both
them and their Caufe.

But this was not all, by thefe incef-
faat Attacks on them as a Party, they
began *to come to their Senfes* out of a 50
Year flumber, they found the Law on
their fide, and the Government Moderate
and Juft; they found they might *oppofe
Violence with Law*, and that when
they did fly to the Refuge of Juftice, they
always had the better of their Enemy;
flufht with this Succefs, it put them
upon confidering *what Fools they had been*
all along to bear the Infolence of a few
hot-headed Men, who contrary to the
true Intent and Meaning of the Queen,
or of the Government, *had refolv'd their
Deftruction.*

It put them upon revolving the State
of their own Cafe, *and comparing it
with their Enemies*; upon Examining on
what foot they ftood, and tho' Eftablifh'd upon a firm Law, yet a violent

R 3 Party

Party *pushing at the overthrow of that Establishment*, and diffolving the legal Right they had to their Liberty and Religion ; it put them upon duly weighing the nearnefs of their approaching Ruin and Deftruction, and finding things run fo hard againft them, reflecting upon the Extremity of their Affairs, and how if they had not drawn in the High Church-Champions to *damn the Projects* of their own Party, by running at fuch defperate Extremes as all Men of any Temper muft of courfe abhor, they had been undone; *truly now they began to confider*, and to confult with one another *what was to be done.*

Abundance of Projects were laid before them, fome too Dangerous, fome too Foolifh to be put in practice ; at laft they refolv'd to confult *with my Philofopher.*

He had been but fcurvily treated by them in his Troubles, and fo Univerfally abandon'd by the *Crolians*, that even the *Solunarians* themfelves infulted them on that Head, and laugh'd at them for expecting any Body fhould

ven-

venture for them again. ----- But he forgetting their unkindnefs, ask'd them
what it was they. defir'd of him ?

They told him, they had heard that
he had reported he could put the *Cro-*
lians in a way to fecure themfelves from
any poffibility of being infulted again
by the Solunarians, and yet not difturb
the publlck Tranquility, *nor break the*
Laws ; and they defir'd him, if he knew
fuch a Secret, he would communicate it
to them, and they would be fure to *re-*
member to forget him for it as long as he
liv'd.

He frankly told them *he had faid fo,*
and it was true, he could put them in a
way to do all this if they would follow
his Directions. *What's that, fays one* of the
moft earneft Enquirers ? ----- 'Tis inclu-
ded in one Word, fays he, U n i t e.

This moft fignificant Word, deeply
and folidly reflected upon, put them upon ftrange and various Conjectures, and
many long Debates they had with themfelves about it ; at laft they came again
to him, and ask'd him *what he mean't by it ?*

R 4   He

He told them he knew they were *Strangers to the meaning* of the thing, and therefore if they would meet him the next Day he would come prepar'd to explain himself; accordingly they meet, when inſtead of a long Speech they expected from him what ſort of Union he mean't, *and with who*, he brings them a *Thinking Preſs*, or *Cogitator*, and ſetting it down, goes away without ſpeaking one Word.

This *Hyerogliphical* Admonition was too plain not *to let them all into his meaning*; but ſtill as they are an obſtinate People, and not a little valuing themſelves upon their own Knowledge and Penetration, they ſlighted the Engine and fell to off-hand-*Surmiſes*, *Gueſſes* and *Suppoſes*.

1. Some concluded he mean't *Unite with the Solunarian Church*, and they reflected upon his Underſtanding, that not being the Queſtion in Hand, and ſomething remote from their Intention, or the High *Solunarians* Deſire.

2. Some mean't *Unite* to the moderate Par-

Party *of the Solunarians*, and this they said they had done already.

At laſt ſome *being very Cunning*, found it it out, that it muſt be his meaning *Unite one among another* ; and even there again they miſunderſtood him too; and ſome imagin'd he mean't down right Rebellion, Uniting Power, and Mobbing the whole Moon, *but he ſoon convinc'd them of that too.*

At laſt they took the Hint, that his Advice directed them *to Unite their ſub-divided Parties* into one general Intereſt, and to act in Concert upon one bottom, to lay aſide the *Selfiſh, Narrow, Suſpicious Spirit* ; three Qualifications *the Crolians* were but too juſtly charg'd with, and begin to act with Courage, Unanimity and Largeneſs of Soul, to open their Eyes to their own Intereſt, maintain a regular and conſtant Correſpondence with one another in all parts of the Kingdom, and *to bring their civil Intereſt into a Form.*

The Author of this Advice having thus brought them to underſtand, and

approve his Propofal, they demanded his affiftance for making the Effay, and 'tis a moft wonderful thing to confider what a ftrange effect the alteration of their Meafures had upon the whole *Solunarian* Nation.

As foon as ever they had fettled the Methods they refolv'd to act in, they form'd *a general Council* of the Heads of their Party, to be always fitting, to reconcile Differences, to unite Parties, to fupprefs Feuds in their beginning.

They appointed 3 *general Meetings* in 3 of the moft remote Parts of the Kingdom, to be half yearly, and *one univerfal Meeting* of Perfons deputed to concert matters among them in General.

By that time thefe Meetings had fat but once, and the Conduct of the Council of 12 began to appear, 'twas a wonder to fee the prodigious alteration it made all over the Country.

Immediately *a Crolian* would *never buy any thing* but of a *Crolian*; would hire no Servants, employ neither Porter nor Carman, but what were *Crolians*.

The

The *Crolians* in the Country that wrought and manag'd the Manufactures, would employ no body but *Crolian Spinners*, *Crolian Weavers*, and the like.

In their capital City the Merchandizing *Crolians* would freight no Ships but of which the Owners and Commanders were *Crolians*.

They call'd all their Cash out of the *Solunarian Bank*; and as the Act of the *Cortez* confirming the Bank then in being feem'd to be their Support, they made it plain that Cash and Credit will make a Bank without a publick Settlement of Law; *and without thefe* all the Laws in the *Moon* will never be able to fupport it.

They brought all their running Cash into one Bank, and fettled a fub-Cash depending upon the Grand-Bank in every Province of the Kingdom; in which, by a ftrict Correfpondence and crediting their Bills, they might be able to fettle a Paper Credit over the whole Nation.

They

They went on to settle themselves in all sorts of Trade in open Companies, and sold off their Interests in the publick Stocks then in Trade.

If the Government wanted a Million of Mony upon any Emergency, they were ready to lend it as a Body, not by different Sums and private Hands blended together with their Enemies, but as will appear at large presently, *it was only Crolian Mony*, and pass'd as such.

Nor were the Consequences of this *New Model* less considerable than the Proposer expected, for the *Crolians* being generally of the Trading Manufacturing part of the World, and *very Rich*; the influence this method had upon the common People, upon Trade, and upon the Publick was very considerable every way.

1. All the *Solunarian Trades-Men* and *Shop-keepers* were at their Wits end, they sat in their Shops and had little or nothing to do, while the Shops of the *Crolians* were full of Customers, and their People over Head and Ears in Business; this turn'd

turn'd many of the *Solunarian* Trades-Men quite off *of the hooks*, and they began to break and decay ſtrangely, till at laſt a great many of them to prevent their utter Ruin, turn'd *Crolians* on purpoſe to get a Trade; and what forwarded that part of it was, that when *a Solunarian*, who had little or no Trade beſore, came but over to *the Crolians*, immediately every Body come to Trade with him, and his Shop would be full of Cuſtomers, ſo that this preſently encreas'd the number of the *Crolians*.

2. The poor People in the Countries, *Carders*, *Spinners*, *Weavers*, *Knitters*, and all ſorts of *Manufaƈturers*, run in Crowds to the *Crolian Temples* for fear of being ſtarv'd, for the *Crolians* were two thirds of the Maſters or Employers in the Manufaƈtures all over the Country, and the Poor would ha' been ſtarv'd and undone if they had caſt them out of Work. Thus inſenſibly the *Crolians* encreas'd their number.

3. The *Crolians* being Men of *vaſt Caſh*, they no ſooner withdrew *their Mony* from the *General Bank* but the *Bank languiſht,*
Credit

Credit *funk*, and in a short time they had little to do, but *diffolv'd of Courfe.*

One thing remain'd which People expected would ha' put a Check to this Undertaking, and that was a way of Trading in Claffes, *or Societies*, much like our *Eaft-India Companies* in *England*; and thefe depending upon publick Privileges granted by the Queen of the Country, or her Predeceffors, no Body could Trade to thofe Parts but the Perfons who had thofe Priviledges: The cunning *Crolians*, who had great Stocks in thofe Trades, and forefaw they could not Trade by themfelves without the public *Grant or Charter*, contriv'd a way to get almoft all that Capital Trade into their Hands as follows.

They concerted Matters, and all at once fell to *felling off their Stock*, giving out daily Reports that they would be *no longer concern'd*, that it was a lofing Trade, that the *Fund at bottom was good for nothing*, and that of two Societies *the Old one* had not 20 *per Cont. to divide*, all their Debts being paid; that the *New Society* had Traded feveral Years, but if
they

they were diſſolv'd *could not ſay they had got any thing*; and that this muſt be a Cheat at laſt, and ſo they reſolv'd to ſell.

By this Artifice, they daily offering to Sale, and yet in all their Diſcourſe *diſcouraging the thing they were to ſell*, no Body could be found to buy.

The offering a thing to Sale and no Bidders, is a certain never-failing proſpeĉt of *a lowring the Price*; from this Method therefore the value of all the Banks, Companies, Societies and Stocks in the Country fell to be little or nothing worth; and that was to be bought for 40 or 45 *Lunarians* that was formerly ſold at 150, and ſo in proportion of all the reſt.

All this while the *Crolians* employ'd their Emiſſaries to buy up privately all the Intereſt or Shares in theſe Things that any of the *Solunarian* Party would ſell.

This Plot took readily, for theſe Gentlemen expoſing the weakneſs of
theſe

thefe Societies, and running down the value of *their Stocks*, and at the fame time warily buying at the loweft Prices, not only *in time got Poffeffion of the whole Trade*, with their Grants, Privileges and Stocks, but got into them at a prodigioufly low and defpicable Price.

They had no fooner thus worm'd them out of the Trade, and got the greateft part of the Effects in their own Hands, and confequently the whole Management, but they run up the Price of the Funds again as high as ever, and laught at the folly of thofe that fold out.

Nor could the other People make any Reflections upon the honefty of the practife, for it was *no Original*, but had its birth among the *Solunarians themfelves*, of whom 3 or 4 had frequently made a Trade of raifing and lowring the Funds of the Societies by all the Clandeftine Contrivances in the World, and had ruin'd abundance of Families to raife their own Fortunes and Eftates.

One of the greateft Merchants *in the Moon* rais'd himfelf by this Method to
fuch

such a heighth of Wealth, that he left all his Children married to Grandees, Dukes, and Great Folks ; and from a *Mechanick Original*, they are now rankt among the *Lunarian* Nobility, while multitudes of ruin'd Families helpt to *build his Fortune*, by finking under the Knavery of his Contrivance.

His Brother in the fame Iniquity, being at this time *a Man of the Feather*, has carry'd on the fame intrieguing Trade with all the *Face* and *Front* imaginable ; it has been nothing with him to perfuade his moft intimate Friends to *Sell*, or *Buy*, juft as he had occafion for his own Intereft to have it *rife*, or *fall*, and fo to make his own Market of their Misfortune. Thus he has *twice rais'd his Fortunes*, for the *Houfe of Feathers* demolifht him *once*, and yet he has by the fame clandeftine Management work'd himfelf up again.

This *civil way of Robbing Houfes*, for I can efteem it no better, was carry'd on by a middle fort of People, call'd in the Moon BLOUTEGONDEGOURS,

S   which

which signifies *Men with two Tongues,* or
in English, *Stock-Jobbing Brokers.*

These had formerly such an unlimit-
ed Power and were *so numerous,* that indeed they govern'd the whole Trade of
the Country; no Man knew when he
Bought or *Sold,* for tho' they pretended
to Buy and Sell, and Manage *for other
Men* whose Stocks they had very much
at Command, yet nothing was more
frequent than *when they bought a thing
cheap,* to buy it for *themselves*; if *dear,*
for their *Employer*; if they were to Sell,
if the Price rise, it was *Sold,* if it *Fell,*
it was *Unsold*; and by this Art no body
got any Mony but themselves, that at
last, excepting the two *capital Men* we
spoke of before, these govern'd the
Prizes of all things, and nothing could
be Bought or Sold to Advantage *but
thro' their Hands*; and as the Profit
was prodigious, their number encreas'd
accordingly, so that Business seem'd en-
gross'd by these Men, and they govern'd
the main Articles of Trade.

This Success, and the *Imprudence of their
Conduct,* brought great Complaints a-
gainst

gainſt them to the Government, and a Law was made to *reſtrain them*, both in Practice and *Number*.

This Law has in ſome meaſure had its Effect, the number is not only leſſen'd, but *by chance* ſome honeſter Men *than uſual* are got in among them, but they are ſo *very, very, very* Few, hardly e-nough to ſave a Man's Credit that ſhall vouch for them.

Nay, ſome People that pretend to un-derſtand their Buſineſs better than I do, having been of their Number, have af-firm'd, it is impoſſible to be honeſt in the employment.

I confeſs when I began to ſearch into the Conduct of theſe Men, at leaſt of ſome of them, I found there were abun-dance of black Stories to be told of them, a great deal known, and a great deal more unknown; for they were from the beginning continually Encroaching into all ſorts of People and Societies, and in Conjunction with ſome that were not qualify'd by Law, but meerly Volun-tarily, call'd in the Moon by a hard long

Word

Word, in *Englifh* fignifying PROJECTORS
thefe erected Stocks *in Shadows*, Societies *in Nubibus*, and Bought and Sold
meer Vapour, Wind, Emptinefs and
Blufter for Mony, till they drew People
in to lay out their Cafh, and then
laught at them.

Thus they erected Paper Societies,
Linnen Socities, Sulphur Societies, Cop-
per Societies, Glafs Societies, Sham
Banks, and a thoufand mock Whimfies
to hook unwary People in; at laft
fold themfelves *out*, left the Bubble
to float a little in the Air, and then van-
ifh of it felf.

The other fort of People *go on* after
all this; and tho' thefe Projectors began
to be out of Fafhion, they always found
one thing or other to amufe and deceive
the Ignorant, and went *Jobbing on* into
all manner of things, Publick as well as
Private, whether the Revenue, the Publick Funds, Loans, Annuities, *Bear-Skins*,
or any thing.

Nay they were once grown to that
extravagant highth, that they began to
Stock-

Stock-Job the very Feathers of the Confolidator, and in time the King's employing thofe People might have had
what Feathers they had occafion for,
without concerning the Proprietors of the
Lands much about them.

'Tis true this began to be notorious,
and receiv'd fome check in a former
meeting *of the Feathers*; but even *now*,
when I came away, the three Years
expiring, and by Courfe a new Confolidator being to be built, they were as
bufie as ever. Bidding, Offering, Procuring, Buying, Selling, and Jobbing of
Feathers to who bid moft; and notwithftanding feveral late wholefome and
ftrict Laws againft all manner of Collu-
fion, Bribery and clandeftine Methods,
in the Countries procuring thefe Feathers; never was the Moon in fuch an
uproar about picking and culling the
Feathers, fuch Bribery, fuch Drunkennefs, fuch Caballing, efpecially among
the High *Solunarian* Clergy and the *Lazognians*, fuch Feafting, Fighting and
Diftraction, as the like has never been
known.

And

And that which is very Remarkable, all this not only before the Old Confolidator was broke up, but even while it was actually whole and in use.

Had this hurry been to send up good Feathers, there had been the less to say, but that which made it very strange to me was, that where the very worst of all the Feathers were to be found, there was the most of this wicked Work; and tho' it was bad enough every where, yet the greatest bustle and contrivance was in order to send up the worst Feathers they could get.

And indeed some Places such Sorry, Scoundrel, Empty, Husky, Wither'd, Decay'd Feathers were offer'd to the Proprietors, that I have sometimes wonder'd any one could have the Impudence to send up such ridiculous Feathers to make a Confolidator, which, as is before obferv'd, is an Engine of such Beauty, Ufefulness and Neceffity.

And still in all my Obfervation, this Note came in my way, there was always the most bustle and disturbance about the worst Feathers.   It

It was really a melancholly Thing to
confider, and had this Lunar World
been my Native Country, I fhould ha' been
full of concern to fee that one thing, on
which the welfare of the whole Nation
fo much depended, put in fo ill a Method, and gotten into the management
of fuch Men, who for Mony would certainly ha' fet up fuch Feathers, that wher-
ever the Confolidator fhould be form'd,
it would certainly *over-fet* the firft
Voyage; and if the whole Nation fhould
happen to be Embarkt in it, *on the dangerous Voyage to the Moon,* the fall would
certainly give them fuch a Shock, as
would put them all into Confufion, and
open the Door to the *Gallunarian,* or any
Foreign Enemy to deftroy them.

It was really ftrange that this fhould
be the Cafe, after fo many Laws, and fo
lately made, againft it; but in this, thofe
People are too like our People in *England,*
who have the beft Laws the worft executed of any Nation under Heaven.

For in the Moon this hurry about
choofing of Feathers was grown to
the greateft heighth imaginable,

as

as if it encreaſt by the very Laws that
were made to ſupprefs it; for now at a
certain publick Place where the *Blloute-
gondegours* us'd to meet every Day, any
Body that had but Mony enough might
buy a Feather at a reaſonable Rate, and
never go down into the Country to
fetch it; nay, the Trade grew ſo
hot, that of a ſudden as if no other Buſineſs was in Hand, all People were upon it, and the whole Market was chang'd
from Selling of Bear-Skins, to Buying of
Feathers.

Some gave this for a Reaſon why all
the Stocks of the Societies fell ſo faſt,
but there were other Reaſons to be given for that, ſuch as Clubs, Cabals,
Stock-Jobbers, Knights, Merchants and
Thie---s. I mean *a private Sort*, not ſuch
as are frequently Hang'd there, but *of a
worſe Sort*, by how much they *merit that
Puniſhment more*, but are out of the
reach of the Law, can Rob and pick
Pockets in the Face of the Sun, and
laugh at the Families they Ruin, bidding Defiance to all legal Reſentment.

To

To this height things were come under the growing Evil of this fort of
People.

And yet in the *very Moon* where, as I
have noted the, People are fo exceeding
clear Sighted, and have fuch vaft helps
to their *perceptive Faculties,* fuch Mifts
are fometimes caft before the publick
Underftanding, that they cannot fee the
general Intereft.

This was manifeft, in that juft as I
came away from that Country, the
great Council of their Wife Men, *the
Men of the Feather,* were a going to repeal the old Law of Reftraining the
Number of thefe People ; and tho' *as it
was,* there was not Employment for half
of them, there being 100 in all, and not
above 5 honeft ones ; yet when I came
away they were going to encreafe their
Number. I have nothing to fay to this
here, only that all Wife Men that *underftand Trade* were very much concern'd at
it, and lookt upon it as a moft *deftru-
ctive Thing to the Publick,* and forboding
the fame mifchiefs that Trade fuffer'd
before.

It

It was the particular Misfortune to thefe Lunar People that this Country had a better Stock of Governors in all Articles of their Well-fare, than in their Trade; their Law Affairs had good Judges, their Church good Patriarchs, *except*, *as might be excepted*; their *State* good *Minifters*, their *Army* good *Generals*, and their *Confolidator* good *Feathers*; but in Matters relating to Trade, they had this particular Misfortune, that thofe Cafes always came before People *that did not underfland them*.

Even the Judges themfelves were often found at a Lofs to determine Caufes of Negoce, fuch as *Protefts*, *Charter-Parties*, *Avarages*, *Baratry*, *Demorage* of Ships, Right of *detaining Veffels* on Demorage, and the like; nay, the very Laws themfelves are fain to be filent and yield in many things a Superiority to *the Cuftom of Merchants*.

And here I began to *Congratulate my Native Country*, where the Prudence of the Government has provided for thefe things, by Eftablifhing in *a Commiffion of Trade* fome of the *moft experienc'd Gentlemen*

tlemen in the Nation, to Regulate, Settle, Improve, and revive Trade in General, by their unwearyed Labours, and *moſt conſummate Underſtanding*; and this made me pity theſe Countries, and think it would be an Action worthy of this Nation, and be ſpoken of *for Ages to come* to their Glory, if in *meer Charity* they would appoint or depute *theſe Gentlemen* to go a Voyage to thoſe Countries *of the Moon*, and bleſs thoſe Regions with the Schemes of their ſublime Undertakings, *and aiſtoveries in Trade.*

But when I was expreſſing my ſelf thus, my Philoſopher interrupted me, and told me I ſhould ſee they were already furniſht for that purpoſe, when I came to examine the publick Libraries, *of which by it ſelf.*

But I was farther confirm'd in my Obſervation of the weakneſs of the *publick Heads* of that Country, *as to Trade,* when I ſaw another moſt prepoſterous Law going forward among them, the Title of which was ſpecious, and contain'd ſomething relating *to employing the Poor,* but the ſubſtance of it *abſolutely deſtructive*

to

to the very Nature of their Trade, tended to Tranfpofing, *Confounding* and De-
ftroying their Manufactures, and to the
Ruin of all their *Home-Commerce* ; never
was Nation fo blind to their own Intereft as thefe *Lunarian Law Makers*, and
the People who were the Contrivers of
this Law were fo *vainly Conceited,* fo fond
of *the guilded Title*, and fo *pofitively Dog-
matick,* that they would not hear the frequent Applications of Perfons better acquainted with thofe things than themfelves, but pufht it on meerly *by the
ftrength of their Party,* for the Vanity of
being Authors of fuch a Contrivance.

But to return to the new Model of
the *Crolians*. The advice of the *Lunarian* Philofopher run now thro' all their
Affairs, U N I T E *was the Word* thro'
all the Nation, in Trade, in Cafh, in
Stocks, as I noted before.

If a *Solunarian* Ship was bound to a-
ny *Out Port,* no *Crolian* would load any
Goods aboard ; if any Ship came to feek
Freight abroad, none of the *Crolians*
Correfpondents would Ship any thing
unlefs they knew the Owners *were Crolians* ;

lians ; the *Crolian Merchants* turn'd out
all their *Solunarian Mafter's*, *Sailors* and
Captains from their Ships ; and thus, as
the *Solunarians* would have them be fe-
parated in refpect of the Government,
Profits, *Honours* and *Offices*, they refolv'd
to feparate in *every thing elfe* too , and
to ftand by themfelves.

At laft, upon fome publick Occafion,
the publick *Treafurers* of the Land fent
to the capital City, to borrow 500000
Lunarians upon very good Security of
eftablifht Funds ; *truly no Body would lend
any Mony*, or at leaft they could not raife
above a 5th part of that Sum, enquiring
at the Bank, at their general *Societies Cafh*,
and other Places, all was *languid* and
dull, and *no Mony to be had* ; but being
inform'd that the *Crolians* had erected a
Bank of their own, they *fent thither*,
and were anfwered *readily*, that whatever Sum the Government wanted, was at
their Service, only it was to be lent not
by particular Perfons, but *fuch a Grandee*
being one of the prime Nobility, and
who *the Crolians* now call'd their Protector, was to be *Treated with about it*.

The

The Government faw no harm in all this here was no Law broken, here was nothing but Oppreffion anfwered with Policy, and Mifchief fenc'd againſt with Reafon.

The Government therefore took no Notice of it, *nor made any Scruple when they wanted any Mony* to Treat with this Nobleman, and borrow any Sum *of the Crolians,* as *Crolians*; on the contrary in the Name of the *Crolians*; their *Head or Protector* prefented their *Addreffes* and *Petitions*, procur'd Favours on one Hand, and Affiſtance on the other; and thus *by degrees* and *infenfibly* the *Crolians* became *a Politick Body,* fettled and eſtablifh'd by Orders and Rules among themfelves; and while *a Spirit of Unanimity* thus run thro' all their Proceedings, *their Enemies could never hurt them,* their Princes always faw it was *their Intereſt* to keep Meafures with them, and they were fure to have Juſtice upon any Complaint whatfoever.

When I faw this, it forc'd me to reflect upon Affairs in our own Country; *Well, faid I,* 'tis happy for *England* that our
Dif-

Diſſenters have not this Spirit of *Union*, and Largeneſs of Heart among them ; for if they were not a *Narrow*, mean-*Spirited*, ſhort-*Sighted*, *ſelf-Preſerving*, *friend-Betraying*, *poor-Neglecting People*, they might ha' been every way as Safe, as Conſiderable, as Regarded and as Numerous as the *Crolians* in the *Moon* ; but it is not in their Souls to do themſelves Good, nor to Eſpouſe, or Stand by thoſe that would do it for them ; and 'tis well for the Church-Men that it is ſo, for many Attempts have been made to ſave them, but their own narrowneſs of Soul, and dividedneſs in Intereſt has always prevented its being effectual, and diſcoutag'd all the Inſtruments that ever attempted to ſerve them.

'Tis confeſt the Caſe was thus at firſt among the *Crolians*, they were full of Diviſions among themſelves, as I have noted already of the *Solunarians*, and the unhappy Feuds among them, had always not only expos'd them to the Cenſure, Reproach and Banter of their *Solunarian* Enemies, but it had ſerv'd to keep them under, prevent their being valued in the Government, and

given

given the other Party vaſt Advantages againſt.

But the *Solunarians* driving thus furj-ouſly *at their Deſtruction* and entire Ru-in, open'd their Eyes to the following Meaſures for their preſervation: And here again *the high Solunarians* may ſee, and doubtleſs whenever they made uſe of the Lunar-Glaſſes they muſt ſee it, that nothing could ha' driven the *Cro-lians* to make uſe of ſuch Methods for their Defence, but the raſh Proceedings of their own warm Men, in order to ſuppreſſing the whole *Crolian* Intereſt. And this might inform our Country-men of the Church of *England*, that it cannot but be their Intereſt to Treat their Brethren with Moderation and Temper, leaſt their Extravagances ſhould one time or other drive the other as it were by Force into their Senſes, and open their Eyes to do only all thoſe Things which by Law they may do, and which they are laught at by all the World for not doing.

This was the very Caſe in the Moon : The Philoſopher, *or pretended-ſuch as be-fore, before* had often publifh'd, that *it was their Intereft to* UNITE ; but their Eyes not being open to the true Caufes and Neceffity of it, their Ears were fhut a-gainft the Council, *till Oppreffion and Neceffities drove them to it.*

Accordingly they entred into a ferious Debate, of the State of their own Affairs, and finding the Advice given, very reafonable; they fet about it, and the Author gave them a Model, Entitl'd *An enquiry into what the Crolians may lawfully do, to prevent the certain Ruin of their Intereft, and bring their Enemies to Peace.*

I will not pretend to examine the Contents of this fublime Tract ; but from this very Day, we found the *Crolians* in the Moon, acting quite on a different Foot from all their former Conduct, putting on a new Temper, and a new Face, as you have hear'd.

All this while the hot *Solunarians* cried out *Plots, Affociations, Confederacies* and *Rebellions,* when indeed here was nothing done but what the *Laws jufti-*

T   *fy'd,*

fy'd, what *Reafon directed*, and what *had the Crolians but made ufe of the Cogitator*, they would ha' done 40 Year before.

The Truth is, the other People had no Remedy, but *to cry Murther*, and make *a* Noife ; for the *Crolians* went on with their Affairs, and Eftablifht themfelves fo, that when I came away, they were become a moft Solid, and well United Body, made a confiderable Figure in the Nation, and yet the Government was eafy ; for the *Solunarians* found when they had attain'd the utmoft end of their Wifhes, her *Solunarian Majefty* was as fafe as before, and the *Crolians* Property being fecur'd, they were as Loyal Subjects as the *Solunarians*, as confiftent with Monarchy, as ufeful to it, and *as pleas'd with it.*

I cannot but Remark here, that this *Union of the Crolians* among themfelves had another Confequence, which made it appear it was not only to their own Advantage, but to the general Good of all the Natien.

For,

For, *by little, and little,* the Feuds of
the Parties cool'd, and the *Solunarians*
began to be better reconcil'd to them;
the Government was *eafy and fafe,* and
the private Quarrels,as I have been told
fince, begin to be quite forgot.

What Blindnefs, *faid I to my felf,* has
poffeft the Diffenters in our unhappy
Country of *England,* where by eternal
Difcords, Feuds, Diftrufts and *Difgufts* a-
mong themfelves, they always fill their
Enemies with Hopes, that by pufhing
at them, they may one time or other
compleat their Ruin; which Expectation has always ferv'd as a means to
keep open the Quarrel; whereas had
the Diffenters been United in *Intereft,*
Affection and *Mannagement* among themfelves, all this Heat had long ago *been*
over, and the Nation, tho' there had
been *two Opinions* had retain'd but *one*
Intereft, been joyn'd in Affection, and
Peace at Home been rais'd up to that Degree that all Wife Men wifh, as it is
now among the Inhabitants of the
World in the Moon.

Tis

Tis true, in all the Obfervations I
made in this Lunar Country, the vaft
deference paid to the Perfons of Princes
began to leffen, and whatever Refpect
they had for the *Office*, they found it neceffary frequently to tell the World that
on occafion, they could Treat them with
lefs Refpect than *they pretended to owe
them.*

For about this time, the *Divine Right*
of Kings, and the Inheritances of Princes *in the Moon*, met with a terrible
Shock, and that by the *Solunarian Party
themfelves*; and infomuch that even my
Philofopher, and he was none of the *Jure
Divino Men*, neither declar'd, againft it.

They made *Crowns perfect Foot-balls*,
fet up what Kings' they would, and
pull'd down fuch as they did not like, *Rati-
tione Voluntas*, right or wrong, as they
thought beft, of which fome Examples
fhall be given by and by.

After I had thus enquir'd into the Hiftorical Affairs of this Lunar Nation,
which for its Similitude to my Native
Country, I could not but be inquifitive
in ;

in; I wav'd a great many material Things, which at leaft I cannot enter upon the Relation of here, and began to enquire into their Affairs abroad.

I think I took notice in the beginning of my Account of thefe Parts, that I found them engag'd in a tedious and bloody War, with one of the moft mighty Monarchs of all the Moon.

I muft therefore hint, that among the multitude of things, which for brevity fake I omit, the Reader may obferve thefe were fome.

1. That this was the fame Monarch who harbour'd and entertain'd the *Abrogratzian* Prince, who was fled as before, and who we are to call the King of *Gallunaria*.

2. I have omitted the Account of a long and bloody War, which lafted a great many Years, and which the prefent Queens Predeceffor, mannag'd with a great deal of Bravery and Conduct, and finifht very much to his own Glory, and the Nations Advantage.

3. I

3. I have too much omitted to Note, how *Barbarously* the *High Solunarian Church Men* treated him for all his Services, upbraided him with the Expence of the War; and tho' he fav'd them all from Ruin and *Abrogratzianifm*, yet had not one good Word for him, and indeed 'tis with fome difficulty that I pafs this over, becaufe it might be neceffary to obferve, befides what is faid before, that Ingratitude is a Vice in Nature, and practis'd every where, as well as in *England*.So that we need not upbraid the*Party* among us with their ill Treatment of the late King, for thefe People us'd their good King every Jot as bad, till their unkindnefs perfectly broke his Heart.

Here alfo I am oblig'd to omit the Hiftorical Part of the War, and of the Peace that follow'd ; only I muft obferve that this Peace was very *Precarious*, Short and *Unhappy*, and in a few Months the War broke out again, with as much Fury as ever.

In thisWar happen'd one of theftrangeft, unaccountable and moft prepofterous

rous Actions, that ever a People in their
National Capacity could be guilty of.

Certainly if our People in *England*,
who pretend that Kingſhip is *Jure Divino*, did but know the Story of which
I ſpeak, they would be quite of another
Mind ; wherefore I crave leave to re-
late part of the Hiſtory, or Original of
this laſt War, as a neceſſary Introduction to the proper Obſervations I ſhall
make upon it.

There was a King of a certain Country
in the Moon, call'd in their Language,
Ebronia, who was formerly a Confederate with the *Solunarians*. This Prince
dying without Iſſue, the great Monarch
we ſpeak of, ſeiz'd upon all his Dominions as his Right.----- Tho' if I remember right, he had formerly Sworn never
to lay Claim to it, and after that by a
ſubſequent Treaty had agreed with the
Solunarian Prince, that another Monarch
who claim'd a Right as well as he,
ſhould divide it between them.

The breach of this Agreement, and
ſeizing this Kingdom, put almoſt all the

T 4   Lunar

Lunar World into a Flame, and War hung over the Heads of all the Northern Nations of the Moon, for several Claims were made to the Succession by other Princes, and particularly by a certain Potent Prince call'd the *Eagle*, of an Ancient Family, whose *Lunar* Name I cannot well express, but in *English*, it signifies *the Men of the great Lip*; whether it was Originally a fort of a Nick Name, or whether they had any such thing as a great Lip Hereditary to the Family, by which they were distinguisht, is not worth my while to Examine.

'Tis without question that the successive Right, *if their Lunar Successions, are Govern'd as ours are in this World*, devolv'd upon this Man *with the Lip* and his Families; but the *Gallunarian* Monarch brought things so to pass, by his extraordinary Conduct, that the *Ebronian* King was drawn in by some of his Nobility, *who this Prince had Bought* and Brib'd to betray their Country to his Interest, and particularly a certain *High Priest* of that Country, to make an Assignment, or *deed of Gift* of all his Dominions to the Grand-

Grandfon of this *Gallunarian* Monarch.

By Vertue of this Gift, or Legacy, as
foon as the King dyed, who was then
languifhing, and as the other Party alledg'd, not in *a very good capacity to make
a Will*; the *Gallunarian* King fent his
Grandfon to feize upon the Crown, and
backing him with fuitable Forces, took
Poffeffion of all his ftrong Fortifications
and Frontiers.

Nor was this all, *the Man with the Lip*
indeed talkt big, and threatned War
immediately, but the *Solunarians* were
fo unfettl'd at Home, fo unprepar'd for
War, having but juft difmift their Auxi-
liar Troops, and disbanded their own,
and the Prince was fo ill ferv'd by his
Subjects, that both he and a Powerful
Neighbour, Nations in the fame Intereft, were meerly Bullyed by this *Gallunarian*; and as he threatned immediately to Invade them, which they were
then in no Condition to prevent, he
forc'd them both to fubmit to his Demand, *tacitely allow* what he had done
in breaking the Treaty with him, and
at laft openly *acknowledge* his new King.
This

This was indeed a moſt unaccountable Step,
but there was a neceſſity to plead, for
he was at their very Doors with his Forces; and this Neighbouring People, who
they call *Mogenites,* could not reſiſt him
without help from the *Solunarians ,*
which they were very backward in,
notwithſtanding the *earneſt Sollicitations
of their Prince,* and notwithſtanding they
were oblig'd to do it *by a ſolemn Treaty.*

Theſe delays oblig'd them to this ſtrange
Step of *acknowledging* the Invaſion of
their Enemy, and *pulling off the Hat* to
the New King he had ſet up.

*'Tis true,*the Policy of theſe Lunar Nations was very Remarkable in this Caſe,
and they out-witted the *Gallunarian* Monarch in it; for by the owning this
Prince, whom they immediately after
Declar'd a Uſurper, and made War a-
gainſt; they ſtopt the Mouth of the
Gallunarian his Grandfather, took from
him all pretence of Invading them,
and *making him believe they were Sincere,*
Wheedl'd him to reſtore ſeveral Thou-
ſands of their Men who he had taken
Pri-

Prisoners in the Frontier Towns of the *Ebronians.*

Had the *Gallunarian* Prince had but the forecast to ha' seen, that this was but a fore'd pretence to gain Time, and that as soon as they had *their Troops clear* and Time to raise more, they would certainly turn upon him again, he would never ha' been put by with so weak a Trifle as the *Ceremony of Congratulation*; whereas had he immediately pusht at them with all his Forces, they must ha' been Ruin'd, and he had carry'd his Point without much Interruption.

But here he lost his Opportunity, which he never retriev'd ; *for 'tis in the Moon, just as 'tis here,* when an Occasion is lost, it is not easy to be recover'd, for both the *Solunarians* and the *Mogenites* quickly threw off the Mask, and declaring this new Prince an *Usurper,* and his Grandfather an *Unjust breaker of Treaties,* they prepar'd for War against them both.

As to the Honesty of this matter, my Philosopher and I differ'd extremely, he

ex-

exclaim'd againſt the Honour of acknowledging a King, with a deſign to Depoſe
him, and pretending Peace when War
is deſign'd ; tho' 'tis true, they are too
cuſtomary in our World ; but however,
as to him I inſiſted upon the lawfulneſs
of it, from the univerſal Cuſtom of Nations, who generally do things ten times
more Prepoſterous and Inconſiſtent,
when they ſuit their Occaſions. Yet I
hope no Body will think I am recom-
mending them by this Relation to the
Practice of our own Nations, but rather
expoſing them as unaccountable things
never to be put in Practice, without
quitting all pretences to Juſtice and national Honeſty.

The Caſe was this.

As upon the Progreſs of Matters before related, the *Solunarians* and *Mogenites* had made a formal acknowledg-
ment of this new Monarch, the Grandſon of the *Gallunarian* King, ſo as I have
hinted already, they had no other deſign than to Depoſe him, and pull him
down.

Accord-

Accordingly, as foon as *by the aforefaid Wile* they had gain'd Breath, and
furnifht themfelves with Forces, they
declar'd *War* againft both the *Gallunarian* King, and his Grandfon, and entred
into ftrict Confederacy with *the Man of
the great Lip*, who was the Monarch of
the *Eagle*, and who by right of Succeffion, had the true Claim to the *Ebronian* Crowns.

In thefe Declarations they alledge that
Crowns do not *defcend by Gift*, nor are
Kingdoms given away *by Legacy*, like a
Gold *Ring at a Funeral*, and therefore this
young Prince could have no Right, the
former deceas'd King having *no Right to
difpofe it by Gift.*

I muft allow, 'that judging by our
Reafon, and the Practice in our Coun-
tries here, *on this fide the Moon*; this
feem'd plain, and I faw no difference in
matters of Truth there, or here, but
Right and Liberty both of Princes and
People feems to be the fame in that
World, as it is in this, and upon this
account I thought the Reafons of this
War very Juft, and that the Claim of
Right

Right to the Succeffion of the *Ebronian*
Crown, was undoubtedly *in the Man
with the Lip*, and his Heirs, and fo far
the War was moft Juft, and the Defign
reafonable.

And thus far my Lunar Companion
agreed with me, and had they gone on fo,
fays he, they had my good Wifhes, and
my Judgment had been Witnefs to my
Pretences, that they were in the right.

But in the profecution of this War,
fays he, they went on to one of the
moft Impolitick, Ridiculous, Difhoneft,
and Inconfiftent Actions, that ever any
Nation in the Moon was guilty of; the
Fact was thus.

Having agreed among themfelves that
the *Ebronian* Crown fhould not be poffeft by the *Gallunarian* King's Grandfon,
they in the next Place began to confider
who fhould have it.

The Man with the Lip had the Title, but
he had a great Government of his own,
Powerful, Happy and Remote, being as
is noted, the Lord of the great *Eagle*,
and

and he told them he could not pretend *to come to Ebronia to be a King there* ; his eldeft Son truly was not only declar'd Heir apparent to his Father, but had another *Lunarian Kingdom* of his own ftill more remote than that, and he would not quit all this for the Crown of *Ebronia*, fo it was concerted by all the Confederated Parties, that the *fecond Son* of this Prince, *the Man with the Lip*, fhould be declar'd King, and here lay the Injuftice of all the Cafe.

I confefs at my firft examining this Matter, I did not fee far into it, nor could I reach the Difhonefty of it, and perhaps the Reader of thefe Sheets may be in the fame Cafe ; but my old *Lunarian Friend* being continually exclaiming againft the Matter, and blaming his Country-men the *Solunarians* for the Difhonefty of it, but efpecially the *Mogenites*, he began to be fomething peevifh with me that I fhould be fo dull as not to reach it, and askt me if he fhould fcrew me into the *Thinking-Prefs* for the Clearing up my Underftanding.

At laft he told me he would write his

par-

particular Sentiments of this whole Affair in a Letter to me, which he would
fo order as it fhould *effectually open mine
Eyes*; which indeed it did, and fo I believe it will the Eyes of all that read it;
to which purpofe I have obtain'd of the
Author *to affift me in the Tranflation* of it,
he having fome Knowledge alfo in our
Sublunar Languages.

*The Suftance if a Letter, wrote to the Au-
thor of thefe Sheets, while he was in the
Regions of the Moon.*

'*Friend from the Moon,*
' A Ccording to my promife, I hereby
' give you a Scheme of *Solunarian*
' Honefty, join'd with *Mogenite* Policy,
' and my Opinion of the Action of my
' Country-men and their Confederates,
' in declaring their new made *Ebronian*
' King.

' The *Mogenites* and *Solunarians* are
' look'd upon here to be the Original
' Contrivers of this ridiculous piece of
' Pageantry, and tho' fome of their
' Neighbours are fuppos'd to have a
' Hand in it, yet we all lay it at the
' door

' door of their Politicks, and for the Ho-
' nesty of it let them answer it if they
' can.

' 'Tis observ'd here, that as soon as
' the King of *Gallunaria* had declar'd
' that he accepted the Will and Dispoſi-
' tion of the Crown of *Ebronia*, in fa-
' vour of his Grandſon, and that ac-
' cording to the said Dispoſition, he
' had own'd him for King; and in or-
' der to make it effectual, had put him
' into immediate Poſſeſſion of the King-
' dom. The *Mogenites* and their Confede-
' rates made wonderful Clamours at the
' Injuſtice of his Proceedings, and par-
' ticularly on account of his breaking
' the Treaty then lately entred into
' with the King of the *Solunarians* and the
' *Mogenites*, for the settling the Matter of
' Right and Poſſeſſion, in caſe of the De-
' miſe of the *Ebronian* King.

' However, the King of *Gallunaria* had
' no sooner plac'd his Grandſon on the
' Throne, but the *Mogenites* and other
' Nations, and *to all our Wonder*, the
' King of *Solunaria* himſelf acknowledg'd
' him, own'd him, ſent their Minſters,

'and

‘ and Compliments of Congratulation,
‘ and the like, giving him the Title of
‘ King of *Ebronia.*

‘ Tho’ this proceeding had fomething
‘ of Surprize in it, and all Men expect-
‘ ed to fee fomething more than ordina-
‘ ry Politick in the effect of it, yet it
‘ did not give half the aftonifhment to
‘ the Lunar World, as this unaccounta-
‘ ble Monfter of Politicks begins to
‘ do.

‘ We have here two unlucky Fellows,
‘ call’d *Pafquin* and *Marforio,* thefe had a
‘ long Dialogue about this very Matter,
‘ and *Pafquin* as he always lov’d Mifchief,
‘ told a very unlucky Story to his Com-
‘ rade, of a high *Mogenite* Skipper, as fol-
‘ lows.

‘ A *Mogenite* Ship coming from a far
‘ Country, the Cuftom Houfe Officers
‘ found fome Goods on Board, which
‘ were Controband, and for which they
‘ pretended the Ship and Goods were
‘ all Confifcated; the Skipper, or *Cap-*
‘ *tain* in a great Fright, comes up to the
‘ Cuftom-Houfe, and being told he muft
‘ Swear

'Swear to something relating to his
'taking in those Goods, reply'd in his
'Country Jargon, *Ya, dat sall Ick doen*
'*Myn Heer;* or in *English,* Ay, Ay, I'll
'Swear. ----- But finding they did not af-
'sure him that it would clear his Ship
'he scruples the Oath again, at which
'they told him it would clear his Ship
'immediately. *Hael, well Myn Heer,*
'says the *Mogen* Man, *vat mot Ick sagen,*
'*Ick sall all Swear myn Skip to salvare,* i. e.
'I shall Swear any thing to save my
'Skip.

'We apply this Story thus.

'If the *Mogenites* did acknowledge the
'King of *Ebronia,* we did believe it was
'done *to save the Skip*; and when they
'reproacht the *Gallunarian* King, with
'breaking the Treaty of Division, we
'us'd to say we would all break thro'
'twice as many Engagements for half as
'much Advantage.

'This setting up a new King, a-
'gainst a King on the Throne, Acknow-
'ledg'd and Congratulated by them, is
'not only look'd on in the Lunar World,
U 2   'as

' as a thing Ridiculous, but particularly
' Infamous, that they fhould firft acknow-
' ledge a King, and then fet up the Ti-
' tle of another. If the Title of the
' firft *Ebronian* King be good, this muft
' be an Impoftor, an Ufurper of another
' Man's Right ; if it was not good, why
' did they acknowledge him, and give
' him the full Title of all the *Ebronian*
' Dominions? Carefs and Congratulate
' him, and make a publick Action of
' it to his Ambaffador.

' Will they tell us they were Bully'd,
' and Frighted into it ? that is to own
' they may be hufft into an ill Action ; for
' owning a Man in the Poffeffion of what
' is none of his own, is an ill thing, and he
' that may be hufft into one ill Action,
' may by Confequence be hufft into ano-
' ther, and fo into any thing.

' What will they fay for doing it ? we
' have heard there has been in the
' World you came from, a way found
' out to own Kings *de Facto*, but not *de*
' *Jure*; if they will fly to that ridiculous
' Shift, let them tell the World fo, that
' we may know what they mean, for
' thofe

[293]

' thofe foolifh things are not known
' here.

' If they own'd the King of *Ebronia*
' voluntarily, and acknowledg'd his Right
' as we thought they had ; how then
' can this young Gentleman have a Ti-
' tle, unlefs they have found out a new
' Divifion, and fo will have two Kings
' of *Ebronia*, make them Partners, and
' have a *Gallunarian* King of *Ebronia*, and
' a *Mogenite* King of *Ebronia*, both toge-
' ther ?

' Our Lunar Nations, Princes and
' States, whatever they may do in your
' World, always feek for fome Pretences
' at leaft to make their Actions feem
' Honeft, whither they are fo or no ;
' and therefore they generally publifh
' Memorials, Manifefto's and Decla-
' rations, of their Reafons why, and
' on what account they do fo, or fo ;
' that thofe who have any Grounds to
' charge them with Unjuftice, may be
' anfwer'd, and filenc'd ; 'tis for the
' People in your Country, to fall upon
' their Neighbours, only becaufe they
' will do it, and make probability of

U 3   ' Con-

' Conqueſt, a ſufficient Reaſon of Con-
' queſt ; the *Lunarian* Nations are
' ſeldom ſo deſtitute of Modeſty, but
' that they will make a ſhew of Juſtice,
' and make out the Reaſons of their Pro-
' ceedings ; and tho' ſometimes we find
' even the Reaſons given for ſome A-
' ctions are weak enough ; yet it is a
' bad Cauſe indeed, that can neither
' have a true Reaſon, nor a pretended
' one. The cuſtom of the Moon has o-
' blig'd us to ſhow ſo much reſpect to
' Honeſty, that when our Actions
' have the leaſt colour of Honeſty, yet
' we will make Reaſons to look like a
' Defence, whether it be ſo or no.

' But here is an Action that has nei-
' ther reality, nor pretence, here is not
' Face enough upon it to bear an Apolo-
' gy. Firſt, they acknowledge one King,
' and then ſet up another King againſt
' him ; either they firſt acknowledg'd a
' wrong King, and thereby became Par-
' ties to a Uſurper, or they act now a-
' gainſt all the Rules of common Juſtice
' in the World, to ſet up a ſham King,
' to pull down a true one, only becauſe
' 'tis their Intereſt to have it ſo.
                              ' This

' This makes the very Name of a *So-*
' *lunarian* ſcandalous to all the Moon,
' and Mankind look upon them with the
' utmoſt Prejudice, as if they were a
' Nation who had ſold all their Honeſty
' to their Intereſt; and who could act
' this way to Day, and that way to Mor-
' row, without any regard to Truth, or
' the Rule of Honour, Equity or Con-
' ſcience; *This is Swearing any thing to*
' *ſave the Skip*; and never let any Man
' Reproach the *Gallunarian* King with
' breaking the Treaty of Diviſion, and
' diſregarding the Faith and Stipulations
' of Leagues; for this is an Action ſo in-
' conſiſtent with it ſelf, ſo incongruous
' to common Juſtice, to the Reaſon and
' Nature of things, that no Hiſtory of
' any of theſe latter Times can parallel
' it, and 'tis paſt the Power of Art, to
' make any reaſonable Defence for it.

' Indeed ſome lame Reaſons are gi-
' ven for it by our Polititians. Firſt,
' they ſay the Prince with the great
' Lip was extremely preſt by the *Gal-*
' *lunarians* at Home in his own Coun-
' try, and not without apprehenſions
' of

' of feeing them e'er long, under the
' Walls of his capital City.

'From this circumftance of the Man
' with the Lip, 'twas not irrational to
' expect that he might be induc'd to make
' a feparate Peace with the *Gallunarians*,
' and ferve them as he did once the Prince
' of *Berlindia* at the Treaty of Peace in a
' former War, where he deferted him after
' the folemneft Engagements never to
' make Peace without him; but his
' preffing Occafions requiring it, con-
' cluded a Peace without him, and left
' him to come out of the War, as well
' as he could, tho' he had come into it
' only for his Affiftance. Now find-
' ing him in danger of being ruin'd by
' the *Gallunarian* Power, and judging
' from former Practice in like Cafes,
' that he might be hurry'd into a Peace,
' and leave them in the Lurch; they
' have drawn him into this Labrinth, as
' into a Step, which can never be re-
' ceded from without the utmoft Affront
' and Difgrace, either to the Family of
' the *Gallunarian*, or of the Lip; an A-
' ction which in its own Nature, is a
' Defiance of the whole *Gallunarian*
'Pow-

' Power, and without any other Mani-
' festo, may be taken as a Declaration
' from the House of the *Lip*, to the *Gal-*
' *lunarian*, that this War shall never
' end, till one of those two Families are
' ruin'd and reduc'd.

   ' What Condition the Prince with
' the Lip's Power is in, to make such a
' huff at this Time, shall come under
' Examination by and by ; in the mean
' time the *Solunarians* have clench'd the
' Nail, and secur'd the War to last as
' long as they think convenient.

   ' If the *Gallunarians* should get the
' better, and reduce the *Man with the*
' *Lip* to Terms never so disadvantageous,
' he cannot now make a Peace without
' leave from the *Solunarians* and the
' *Mogenites*, least his Son should be ruin'd
' also.----- Or if he should make Articles
' for himself, it must be with ten times
' the Dishonour that he might have
' done before.

   ' Politicians say, 'tis never good for a
' Prince to put himself into a case of
' Desperation. This is drawing the
                      ' Sword,

'Sword, and throwing away the Scab-
'bard; if a Difafter fhould befal him,
'his Retreat is impoffible, and this
'muft have been done only to fecure
'the *Man with the Lip* from being hufft,
'or frighted into a feparate Peace.

'The fecond Reafon People here give,
'why the *Solunarians* are concerning
'themfelves in this Matter, is drawn
'from Trade.

'The continuing of *Ebronia* in the
'Hands of the *Gallunarians*, will moft
'certainly be the Deftruction of the
'*Solunarian* and *Mogenites* Trade, both
'to that Kingdom, and the whole Seas
'on that fide of the Moon; as this Ar-
'ticle includes a fifth Part of all the
'Trade of the Moon, and would in
'Conjunction with the *Gallunarians* at
'laft bring the Mafterfhip of the Sea,
'out of the Hands of the other, fo it
'would in effect be more detriment to
'thofe two Nations, than ten Kingdoms
'loft, if they had them to part with.

'This

'This the *Solunarians* forefeeing, and
'being extremely fenfible of the entire
'Ruin of their Trade, have left no
'Stone unturn'd to bring this piece of
'Pageantry on the Stage, by which they
'have hook'd in the Old Black *Eagle* to
'plunge himfelf over Head and Ears in
'the Quarrel, in fuch a manner, as he
'can never go back with any tolerable
'Honour; he can never quit his Son and
'the Crown of *Ebronia*, without the
'greateft Reproach and Difgrace of all
'the World in the Moon.

'Now whether one, or both of thefe
'Reafons are true in this Cafe, as moft
'believe both of them to be true; the
'Policy of my Country-men, the *Solu-*
'*narians* is vifible indeed, but as for their
'Honefty, it is paft finding out.

'But it is objected here, this Son *of*
'*the Lip* has an undoubted Right to the
'Crown of *Ebronia*. We do not Fight
'now to fet up an Ufurper, but to pull
'down an Ufurper, and it has been made
'plain by the Manifefto, that the giv-
'ing a Kingdom by Will, is no convey-
'ance of Right; the Prince of the *Ea-*
'*gle*

‘ *gle* has an undoubted Right, and they
‘ Fight to maintain it.

‘ If this be true, then we muſt ask
‘ theſe High and Mighty Gentlemen
‘ how came they to recognize and ac-
‘ knowledge the preſent King on the
‘ Throne? why did they own a Uſurper
‘ if he be ſuch? either one or other muſt
‘ be an act of Cowardize and Injuſtice,
‘ and all the Politicks of the Moon can-
‘ not clear them of one of theſe two
‘ Charges ; either they were Cowardly
‘ Knaves before, or elſe they muſt be
‘ Cunning Knaves now.

‘ If the Young *Eagle* has an undoubted
‘ Title now, ſo he had before, and they
‘ knew it as well before, as they do
‘ now ; what can they ſay for them-
‘ ſelves, why they ſhould own a King,
‘ who they knew had no Title, or what
‘ can they ſay for going to pull down one
‘ that has a Title ?

‘ I muſt be allow’d to diſtinguiſh be-
‘ tween Fighting with a Nation, and
‘ Fighting with the King. For Example.
‘ Our Quarrel with the *Gallunarians* is
‘ with

‘ with the whole Nation, as they are
‘ grown too ftrong for their Neighbours.
‘ But ourQuarrel with *Ebronia* is not with
‘ the Nation, but with their King, and
‘ this Quarrel feems to be unjuft in this
‘ particular, at leaft in them who own’d
‘ him to be King, for that put an end
‘ to the Controverfy.

‘ ’Tis true, the Juftice of publick A-
‘ ctions, either in Princes, or in States,
‘ is no fuch nice Thing, that any Body
‘ fhould be furpriz’d, to fee the Govern-
‘ ment forfeit their Faith, and it feems
‘ the *Solunarians* are no more careful
‘ this way, than their Neighbours. But
‘ then thofe People fhould in efpecial
‘ manner forbear to reproach other Na-
‘ tions and Princes, with the breaches
‘ which they themfelves are fubject
‘ too

‘ As to the *Eagle*, we have nothing to
‘ fay to the Honefty of his declaring his
‘ Son King of *Ebronia*, for as is hinted be-
‘ fore, he never acknowledg’d the Title of
‘ the Ufurper, but always declar’d, and
‘ infifted on his own undoubted Right,
‘ and

'and that he would recover it if he
' could.

' Without doubt the *Eagle* has a Title
' by Proximity of Blood, founded on the
' renunciation of the King of *Galluna-*
' *ria* formerly mention'd, and if the
' Will of the late King be Invalid, or
' he had no Right to give the Soveraign-
' ty of his Kingdoms away, then the
' *Eagle* is next Heir.

' But as we quit his Morals, and ju-
' ftify the Honefty of his Proceedings in
' the War, againft the prefent King of
' *Ebronia*, fo in this Action of declaring
' his fecond Son. We muft begin to
' queftion his Underftanding, and fav-
' ing a refpect of decency, it looks as if
' his Mufical Head was out of Tune,
' to *Illus tratellus.* I crave leave to
' tell you a Story out of your own
' Country, which we have heard of hi-
' ther. A *French* Man that could fpeak
' but broken *Englifh*, was at the Court
' of *England*, when on fome occafion he
' happen'd to hear the Title of the King of
' *England* read thus, *Charles the* II. *King*
' *of England, Scotland France and Ireland.*
' Vat

' Vat is dat you fay ? fays Monfieur, be-
' ing a little affronted, the Man reads
' it again, as before. *Charles the Second,*
' *King of England, Scotland, France and*
' *Ireland.* ----- *Charles the Second, King of*
' *France ! Ma Foy,* fays the *French* Man,
' *you can no read, Charles the Second, King*
' *of France,* ha! ha! ha! *Charles the Se-*
' *cond, King of France, when he can catch.*
' Any one may apply the Story, whether
' it was a true one or no.

 ' All the Lunar World looks on it,
' therefore, as a moft Ridiculous, Senfe-
' lefs Thing, to make a Man a King of
' a Country he has not one Foot
' of Land in, nor can have a Foot there,
' but what he muft Fight for. As to the
' probability of gaining it, I have no-
' thing to fay to it, but if we may guefs
' at his Succefs there, by what has been
' done in other Parts of the Moon, we
' find he has Fought three Campaigns,
' to lofe every Foot he had got.

 ' It had been much more to the Ho-
' nour of the *Eagle*'s Conduct, and of
' the young Hero himfelf, firft to ha'
' let him ha' fac'd his Enemy in the Field,
         ' and

' and as foon as he had beaten him, the
' *Ebronians* would have acknowledg'd
' him faft enough; or his own Victorious
' Troops might have Proclaim'd him at
' the Gate of their Capital City; and if
' after all, rhe Succefs of the War had
' deny'd him the Crown he had fought
' for, he had the Honour to have fhown
' his Bravery, and he had been where he
' was, a Prince of the Great Lip. A Son
' of the *Eagle* is a Title much more Ho-
' nourable than a King without a Crown,
' without Subjects, without a Kingdom,
' and another Man upon his Throne;
' but by this declaring him King, the
' *old Eagle* has put him under a neceffity
' of gaining the Kingdom of *Ebronia,*
' which at beft is a great hazard, or if
' he fails to be miferably defpicable, and
' to bear all his Life the conftant Cha-
' grin of a great Title and no Poffef-
' fion.

' How ridiculous will this poor Young
' Gentleman look, if at laft he fhould
' be forc'd to come Home again with-
' out his Kingdom?. what a King of
' Clouts will he pafs for, and what will
' this *King-making old Gentlemen, his Fa-*
' *ther,*

' *ther fay,* when the young Hero fhall
' tell him, your Majefty has made me a
' Mock King for all the World to laugh
' at.

' 'Twas certainly the weakeft Thing
' that could be, for the *Eagle* thus to make
' him a King of that, which, were the pro-
' bability greater than it is, he may eafily,
' without the help of a Miracle, be difap-
' pointed of.

' 'Tis true, the Confederates talk
' big, and have lately had a great Victo-
' ry, and if Talk will beat the King
' of *Ebronia* out of his Kingdom, he is
' certainly undone, but we do not find
' the *Gallunarians* part with any thing
' they can keep, nor that they quit any
' thing without Blows; It muft coft a
' great deal of Blood and Treafure be-
' fore this War can be ended; if abfolute
' Conqueft on one fide muft be the Mat-
' ter, and if the Defign on *Ebronia*
' fhould mifcarry, as one Voyage thither
' has done already, where are we then?
' Let any Man but look back, and con-
' fider what a forry Figure your Confe-
' derate Fleet in your World had made,

' af-

‘ after their *Andalufian Expedition* , if
‘ they had not more by Fate than Con-
‘ duct, chopt upon a Booty at *Vigo* as
‘ they came back.

‘ In the like condition, will this new
‘ King come back, if he fhould go for a
‘ Kingdom and fhould not *Catch*, as the
‘ *French* Man call'd it. 'Tis in the Senfe
‘ of the probability of this mifcarriage,
‘ that moft Men wonder at thefe unac-
‘ countable Meafures , and think the
‘ *Eagles* Councils look a little Wildifh,
‘ as if fome of his great Men were grown
‘ Dilirious and Whymfical, that fancy'd
‘ Crowns and Kingdoms were to come
‘ and go, juft as the great Divan at their
‘ Court fhould direct. This confufion
‘ of Circumftances has occafion'd a cer-
‘ tain Copy of Verfes to appear about
‘ the Moon, which in our Characters
‘ may be read as follws.

Wondelis Idulafin na Perixola Metartos,
  Strigunia Crolias Xerin Hytale fylos ;
Farnicos Galvare Orpto fonamel Egonsberch,
  Sih lona Sipos Gullia Ropta Tylos.

‘ Which

' Which may be Englifh'd thus.

Cæfar you Trifle with the World in vain,
Think rather now of Germany *than* Spain ;
He's hardly fit to fill th' Eagle's Throne,
Who gives new Crowns, and can't protect his
(own.

' But after all to come clofer to the Point,
' if I can now make it out that whate-
' ver it was before, this very Practice of
' declaring a fecond Son to be King of
' *Ebronia,* has publickly own'd the Pro-
' ceedings of the King of *Gallunaria* to
' be Juft, and the Title of his Grandfon
' to be much better than the Title of the
' now declar'd King, what fhall we call
' it then ?

' In order to this, 'tis firft neceffary to
' examine the Title of the prefent King,
' and to enter into the Hiftory of his
' coming to the Crown, in which I fhall
' be very Brief.

' The laft King of *Ebronia* dying with-
' out Iffue, and a former Renunciation
' taking Place, the Succeffion de-
X 2   ' volves

' volves on the House of the *Eagle* as be-
' fore, of whom the present *Eagle* is the
' eldest Branch.

' But the late King of *Ebronia*, to pre-
' vent the Succession of the *Eagle*'s Line,
' makes a Will, and supplies the Proviso
' of Renunciation by Devising, Giving, or
' Bequeathing the Crown to the Grand-
' son of his Sister.

' The King of *Gallunaria* insists that
' this 'is a lawful Title to the Crown,
' and seizes it accordingly, instating his
' Grandson in the Possession.

' The *Eagle* alledges the Renunciati-
' on to confirm his Title as Heir; and
' as to the Will of the late King, he
' says Crowns cannot descend by Gift,
' and tho' the late King had an undoubt-
' ed Right to enjoy it himself, he had
' none to give it away.

' To make the application of this Hi-
' story as short as may be, I demand
' then what Right has the *Eagle* to give
' it to his second Son? If Crowns are
' not to descend by Gift, he may have a
' Right

'Right to enjoy it, but can have none
' to give it away, but if he has a Right
' to give it away ; so had the former
' King, and then the present King has a
' better Title to it than the new one,
' because his Gift was Prior to this of
' the *Eagle*.

' I would be glad to see this answer'd ;
' and if it can't, then I Query whether
' the *Eagle's* Senses ought not to be que-
' stion'd, for setting up a Title on the
' very Foundation for which he quarrels
' at him that is in Possession, and so con-
' firm the honesty of the Possessor's Ti-
' tle by his own Practice. ?

' From the whole, I make no Scruple
' to say that either the *Eagle's* second
' Son has no Title to the Kingdom of E-
' *bronia*, or else giving of Crowns is a
' legal Practice; and if Crowns may def-
' cend by Gift, then has the other King
' a better Title than he, because it was
' given him first, and the *Eagle* has on-
' ly given away what he had no Right
' to, because 'twas given away before
' he had any Title to it himself.

X 3   ' Fur-

' Further, the Posterity of the *Eagle*'s
' eldest Son are manifestly injur'd in this
' Action, for Kings can no more give a-
' way their Crowns from their Posterity,
' than from themselves ; if the Right be
' in the *Eagle*, 'tis his, as he's the eldest
' Male Branch of the House of *the great*
' *Lip*, not as he is *Eagle*, and from him
' the Crown of *Ebronia* by the same
' Right of Devolution descends to his
' Posterity, and rests on the Male Line
' of every eldest Branch. If so, no Act
' of Renunciation can alter this Succes-
' sion, for that is a Gift, and the Gift is
' exploded, or else the whole House of
' *the great Lip* is excluded ; so that let
' the Argument be turn'd and twisted
' never so many ways, it all Centers in
' this, that the present Person can have
' no Title to the Crown of *Ebronia.*

' If he has any Title, 'tis from the
' Gift of his Father and elder Brother ;
' if the Gift of a Crown is no good Title,
' then his Title cannot be good ; If the
' Gift of a Crown is a good Title, then the
' Crown was given away before, and so
' neither he nor his Father has any Ti-
' tle.

Let

' Let him that can anfwer thefe Pa-
' radoxes defend his Title if he can; and
' what fhall we now fay to the War in
Ebronia, only this, that they are going
to fight for the Crown of *Ebronia*? and
to take it away from one that has no
Right to it, to give it to one that
has a lefs Right than he, and 'tis to be
' fear'd that if Heaven be Righteous,
' 'twill fucceed accordingly.

' The Gentlemen of Letters who have
' wrote of this in our Lunar World, on
' the Subject of the *Gallunarians* Title,
' have took a great deal of Liberty in
' the *Eagle*'s behalf, to Banter and Ri-
' dicule the *Gallunarian* fham of a Title,
' as if it were a pretence too weak for a-
' ny Prince to make ufe of, to talk of
' Kings giving their Crowns by Will.

Kingdoms and Governments, *fays a
Learned Lunar Author, are not things of fuch
indifferent Value to be given away, like a
Token left for a Legacy. If any Prince has
ever given or transferr'd his Government,
it has been done by folemn Act, and the People have been call'd to affent and confirm fuch
Conceffions.*

X 4   ' Then

'Then the fame Author goes on, to
'Treat the King of *Gallunaria* with a
'great deal of Severity, and expofes his
'Politicks, that he fhould think to put
'upon the Moon with fo empty, fo weak,
'fo ridiculous a Pretence, as the Will of
'a weak Headed Prince, who neither
'had a Right to give his Crown, nor a
'Brain to know what he was doing,
'and he laughs to think what the
'King of *Gallunaria* would have faid
'to have fuch a dull Trick as that, put
'upon him in any fuch Cafe.

'Now when we have been fo Witty
'upon this very Article, of giving away
'the Crown to the King of *Gallunaria*'s
'Grandfon, as an incongruous and ri-
'diculous Thing, fhall we come to make
'the fame Incongruity be the Founda-
'tion of a War?

'With what Juftice can we make a
'War for a Prince who has only a good
'Title, by Vertue of the felf fame Acti-
'on which makes the Grandfon of his
'Enemy have a bad Title.

'I al-

' I always thought we had a
' Juſt Ground to make War on *Ebronia*,
' as we were bound by former Alliances
' to aſſiſt the *Eagle* in the recovery of
' it in caſe of the death of the late King
' of that Country.

' But now the *Eagle* has refus'd the
' Succeſſion, and his Eldeſt Son has re-
' fus'd it, I would be glad to ſee it
' prov'd how the ſecond Son can have a
' Title, and yet the other King have no
' Title.

' What a ſtrange ſort of a Thing is
' the Crown of *Ebronia*, that two of the
' greateſt Princes of the Lunar World
' ſhould Fight, not who ſhall have it,
' for neither of them will accept of it,
' but who ſhall have the Power of giving
' it away.

' Here are four Princes refuſe it ; the
' King of *Gallunaria*'s Sons had a Title
' in Right of their Mother, and 'twas
' not the former Renunciations that
' would have barr'd them, if this ſofter
' way had not been found out ; for
' time was it has been pleaded on behalf
'   ' of

' of the eldeſt Son of the *Gallunarian*
' King, that his Mother could not give
' away his Right before he was born.

' Then the *Eagle* has a Right, and
' under him his eldeſt Son ; and none of
' all theſe four will accept of the Crown ;
' I believe all the Moon can't find four
' more that would refuſe it.

' Now, tho' none of theſe think it
' worth accepting themſelves, yet they
' fall out about the Right of giving it
' away. The King of *Gallunaria* will
' not accept of it himſelf, but he gets a
' Gift from the laſt Incumbent. This,
' ſays the *Eagle*, can't be a good Title,
' for the late King had no Right to make
' a Deed of Gift of the Crown, ſince a
' King is only Tennant for Life, and
' Succeſſion of Crowns either muſt de
' ſcend by a Lineal Progreſſion in the
' Right of Primogeniture, or elſe they
' loſe the Tenure, and devolve on the
' People.

' Now as this Argument holds good
' the *Eagle* has an undoubted Title to
' the Crown of *Ebronia* : But then, ſays
' his

' his *English Majesty*, I cannot accept of the
' Crown my self for I am the *Eagle*, and
' my eldeft Son has two Kingdoms al-
' ready, and is in a fair way to be *Eagle*
' after me, and 'tis not worth while for
' him, but I have a fecond Son, and we
' will give it him.

' Now may the King of *Gallunaria* fay,
' if one Gift is good, another is good, and
' ours is the firft Gift, and therefore we
' will keep it ; and tho' I folemnly de-
' clare I fhould be very forry to fee the
' Crown of *Ebronia* reft in the Houfe of
' the *Gallunarian*, becaufe our Trade
' will fuffer exceedingly ; yet if never fo
' much damage were to come of it, we
' ought to do Juftice in the World ; if
' neither the *Eagle* nor his eldeft Son will
' be King of *Ebronia*, but a Deed of Gift
' fhall be made, the firft Gift has the
' Right, for nothing can be given away
' to two People at once, and 'tis appa-
' rent that the late King had as much
' Right to give it away as any Body.

' The poor *Ebronians* are in a fine Con-
' dition all this while, that no Body con-
' cerns them in the Matter ; neither
                                        ' Par-

' Party has fo much as thought it worth
' while to ask them who they would
' have to Reign over them, here has
' been no Affembly, *no Cortez*, no Meet-
' ing of the People of *Ebronia*, neither
' Colleftively or Reprefentatively, no
' general Convention of the Nobility,
' no Houfe of Feathers, but *Ebronia* lies
' as the fpoil of the Viftor wholly paffive,
' and her People and Princes, as if they
' were wholly unconcern'd, lie by and
' look on, whoever is like to be King,
' they are like to fuffer deeply by the
' Strife, and yet neither fide has thought
' fit to confult them about it.

   ' The conclufion of the whole Mat-
' ter is in fhort this, here is certainly a
' a falfe Step taken, how it fhall be refti-
' fy'd is not the prefent Bufinefs, nor am I
' Wife enough to Prefcribe. One Man
' may do in a Moment what all the Lu-
' nar World cannot undo in an Age.
' 'Tis not be thought the *Eagle* will be
' prevail'd on to undo it, nay he has
' Sworn not to alter it.

   ' I am not concern'd to prove the Ti-
' tle of the prefent King of *Ebronia*, no,
           ' nor

' nor of the *Eagles* neither; but I think
' I can never be anfwer'd in this, that
' this Gift of the *Eagles* to his fecond
' Son is prepofterous, inconfiftent with
' all his Claim to the Crown, and the
' greateft confirmation of the Title of
' his Enemy that it was poffible to give,
' and no doubt the *Gallunarians* will lay
' hold of the Argument.

' If this Prince was the *Eagle's* eldeft
' Son, he might have a Juft Right from
' the conceffion of his Father; becaufe
' the Right being inherent, he only re-
' ceiv'd from him an Inveftiture of Time,
' but as this young Gentleman is a fe-
' cond Son he has no more Right, his
' elder Brother being alive, than your
' *Grand Seignior*, or *Czar* of *Mufcovy* in
' your World.

' Let them Fight then for fuch a Caufe,
' who valuing only the Pay, make War
' a Trade, and Fight for any thing they
' are bid to Fight for, and as fuch value
' not the Juftice of the War, nor trou-
' ble their Heads about Caufes and Con-
' fequences, fo they have their Pay, 'tis
' well enough for them.

' But

'But were the Justice of the War ex-
'amin'd, I can see none, this Declar-
'ing a new King who has no Right but
'by a Gift, and pulling down one that
'had it by a Gift before, has so much
'Contradiction in it, that I am afraid
'no Wise Man, or Honest Man will em-
'bark in it.

Your

Humble Servant,

The Man in the Moon.

I wou'd have no Body now pretend to scandalize the Writer of this
Letter, which being for the *Gallunarians*, for no *Man in the Moon* had more
Aversion for them than he, but he would
have had the War carry'd on upon a
right Bottom, Justice and Honesty regarded in it, and as he said often, they
had no need to go out of the Road of Justice, for had they made War *in the
great Eagle's Name* all had been well.

Nor

Nor was he a false Prophet, for as this
was ill grounded, so it was as ill carry'd
on, met with *Shocks*, *Rubs* and *Disappoint-
ments* every way. The very first Voyage the new King made, he had like to
ha' been drown'd by a very violent Tem-
pest, things not very usual in those Countries; and all the Progress that had been
made in his behalf when I came away from
that Lunar World, had not brought him
so much as to be able to set his Foot upon his new Kingdom of *Ebronia*, but his
Adversary by wonderful Dexterity, and
the Assistance of his old Grandfather
the *Gallunarian* Monarch, beat his Troops
upon all Occasions, invaded his Ally
that pretended to assist him, and kept
a quiet Possession of all the vast *Ebronian
Monarchy*; and but at last by the powerful Diversion of the *Solunarian* Fleet, a
Shock was given them on another Side,
which if it had not happen'd, it was
thought the new King had been sent
home again *Re Infecta*.

Being very much Shockt in my Judgment of this Affair, by these unanswerable Reasons; I enquir'd of my Author
who were the Directors of this Matter?

he

he told me plainly it was done by thofe great States Men, which the *Solunarian* Queen had lately very Juftly turn'd out, whofe Politicks were very unaccountable in a great many other things, as well as in that.

'Tis true, the War was carry'd on under the new Miniftry, and no War in the World can be Jufter, on account of the Injuftice and Encroachment of the *Gallunarian* Monarch.

The Queen therefore and her prefent Minifters, go on with the War on Principles of Confederacy; 'tis the bufinefs of the *Solunarians* to beat the Invader out, and then let the People come and make a fair Decifion who they will have to Reign over them.

This indeed juftifies the War in *Ebronia* to be Right, but for the Perfonal Proceedure as before, 'tis all Contradiction and can never be anfwer'd.

I hope no Man will be fo malicious, as to fay I am hereby refleding on our War with *Spain*. I am very forward to fay,
it

it is a moft Juft and Reafonable War, as
to paralels between the Cafe of the Princes, in defending the Matter of Perfonal Right, *Hic labor*, *Hoc opus*.

Thus however you fee *Humanum eft
Errare*, whether in this World or in the
Moon, 'tis all one, Infallibility of Coun-
cels any more than of Doctrine, is not
in Man.

The Reader may obferve, I have formerly noted there was a new Confolidator to be Built, and obferv'd what ftrug-
gle there was in the Moon about choofing the Feathers.

I cannot omit fome further Remarks
here, as

1. It is to be obferv'd, that this laft
Confolidator was in a manner quite
worn out.----- It had indeed continu'd
but 3 Year, which was the ftated Time
by Law, but it had been fo *Hurry'd*, fo
Party Rid, fo often had been up in *the
Moon*, and made *fo many* fuch *extravagant Flights*, and unneceffary *Voyages thither*, that it began to be exceedingly
worn and defective.   Y   2. This

2. This occasion'd that the light fluttering Feathers, and the fermented Feathers *made strange Work of it* ; nay, sometimes they were so hot, they were like to ha' ruin'd the whole Fabrick, and had it not been for the *great Feather* in the Center, and a few *Negative* Feathers who were Wiser than the rest, all the *Machines* had been broke to pieces, and the whole Nation put into a most strange Confusion.

Sometimes their Motion was *so violent and precipitant,* that there was great apprehensions of its being *set on Fire by its own Velocity,* for swiftness of Motion is allow'd by the Sages and *so so's* to produce *Fire,* as in *Wheels, Mills* and several forts of *Mechanick Engines* which are frequently Fir'd, and so in *Thoughts, Brains, Assemblies, Consolidators,* and all such combustible Things.

Indeed these things were of great Consequence, and therefore require some more nice Examination than ordinary, and the following Story will in part explain it.

Among

Among the rest of the Broils they had
with the *Grandees*, one happen'd on this
occasion.

One of the Tacking *Feathers* being ac-
cidentally met by a *Grandee*'s Footman,
whom it feems wanted fome Manners,
the Slave began to haloo him in the
Street, with a Tacker, a Tacker, a *Feather*-Fool, a Tacker, &c. and fo brought
the Mob about him, and had not the
Grandee himfelf come in the very inte-
rim, and refcu'd the *Feather*, the Mob
had demolifht him, they were fo enrag'd.

As this Gentleman-*Feather* was refcu'd
with great Courtefie by the *Grandee*, taken into his Coach and carry'd home to
his Houfe, he defir'd to fpeak with the
Footman.

The Fellow being call'd in, was ask't
by him who employ'd him, or fet him
on to offer him this Infult? the Footman
being a ready bold Fellow, told him no
Body Sir, but you are all grown fo ridiculous to the whole Nation, that if
the 134 of you were left but to us Foot-

men

men, and it was not in more refpect to
our Mafters, than you, we fhould Cure
you of ever coming into the *Confolidator*
again, and all the People in the Moon
are of our Mind.

But fays the *Feather*, why do you call
me Fool too? why Sir, fays he, becaufe
no Body could ever tell us what it was
you drove at, and we ha' been told you
never knew your felves; now if one of
you Tacking *Feathers* would but tell the
World what your real Defign was, they
would be fatisfy'd, but to be leaders
in the *Confolidator*, and to Act without
Meaning, without Thought or Defign,
muft argue your' Fools, or worfe,
and you will find all the Moon of my
Mind.

But what if we had a meaning, fays
the *Feather*-Man? why then, fays the
Footman, we fhall leave calling you Fools,
and call you Knaves, for it could never
be an Honeft one, fo that you had better ftand as you do : and I make it out
thus.

You knew, that upon your Tacking
the

the *Crolians* to the Tribute Bill, the *Grandees* muſt reject both, they having declar'd againſt reading any Bills Tackt together, as being againſt their Priviledges. Now if you had any Deſign, it muſt be to have the Bill of Tribute loſt, and that muſt be to diſappoint all the publick Affairs, expoſe the Queen, break all Meaſures, diſcourage the Confederates, and putting all things backward, bring the *Gallunarian* Forces upon them, and put all *Solunaria* into Confuſion. Now Sir, ſays he, we cannot have ſuch courſe Thoughts of you, as to believe you could deſign ſuch dark, miſchievous things as theſe, and therefore we choſe to believe you all Fools, and not fit to be put into a *Conſolidator* again ; than Knaves and Traytors to your Country, and conſequently fit for a worſe Place.

The plainneſs of the Footman was ſuch, and ſo unanſwerable, that his Maſter was fain to check him, and ſo the Diſcourſe broke off, and we ſhall leave it there, and proceed to the Story.

The Men of the Feather as I have noted, who are repreſented here by the

Y 3   *Con-*

Confolidator, fell all together by the Ears, and *all the Moon* was in a combuftion. The Cafe was as follows.

They had three times loft *their quallifying Law*, and particularly they obferv'd the *Grandees* were the Men that threw it out, and notwithftanding *the Plot of the Tackers*, as they call'd them, who were *as I noted*, obferv'd to be in Conjunction *with the Crolians*, yet the Law always paft *the Feathers*, but ftill the *Grandees* quafht it.

To fhow their Refentment *at the Grandees*, they had often made *attempts to mortify them*, fometimes Arraigning them in general, fometimes *Impeaching private Members* of their Houfe, but ftill all wou'd not do, *the Grandees* had the better of them, and going on with Regularity and Temper, the *Confolidators* or Feather-Men always had the worft, *the Grandees had the applaufe of all the Moon*, had *the laft Blow* on every Occafion, and the other funk in their Reputation exceedingly.

It

It is neceffary to underftand here, that the Men of the Feather ferve in feveral Capacities, and under feveral Denominations, and *act by themfelves*, fingly confider'd, they are call'd *the Confolidator*, and the Feathers we mention'd abftracted from their Perfons, make the glorious Engine we fpeak of, and in which, when any fuddain Motion takes them, they can all fhut themfelves up, and away for the Moon.

But when thefe are *joyn'd with the Grandees, and the Queen,* fo United, they make a great *Cortez,* or general Collection of all the Governing Authority of the Nation.

When this laft Fraction happen'd, the *Men of the Feather* were under an exceeding Ferment, they had in fome Paffion taken into their Cuftody, fome good Honeft *Lunar Country-Men,* for an Offence, which indeed few but themfelves ever immagin'd was a Crime, for the poor Men did nothing but purfue their own Right by the Law.

'Tis

'Tis thought the Men of the Feather soon saw they were in the Wrong, but acted like some Men in our World, that when they make a miftake, being too Proud to own themselves in the wrong, run themselves into worfe Errors to mend it.

So *thefe Lunar Gentlemen* difdaining to have it faid they *could be miftaken*, committed two Errors to conceal one, 'till at laft they came to be laught at by *all the Moon.*

Thefe poor Men having lain a long while in Prifon, for little or no Crime, at laft were advis'd to apply themfelves *to the Law for Difcharge*; the Law would fairly have Difcharg'd them ; for *in that Country*, no Man may be Imprifon'd, but he muft in a certain Time be Tryed, or let go upon Pledges of his Friends, *much like our giving Bail on a Writ of Habeas Corpus* ; but the Judges, whether over-aw'd by the Feathers, or what was the Caufe, Authors have not determin'd, did not care to venture Difcharging them.

The

The poor Men thus remanded, apply'd themselves *to the Grandees* who were then Sitting, and who are *the Soveraign Judicature* of the Country, and before whom Appeals lie from all Courts of Juſtice. *The Grandees* as in Duty bound, appear'd ready to do them Juſtice, but the Queen was to be apply'd to, firſt to grant a Writ, or a Warrant for a Writ, call'd in their Country *a Writ of Follies,* which is as much as to ſay Miſtakes.

The *Confolidators* foreſeeing the Conſequence, immediately apply'd themſelves to the Queen with an Addreſs, the Terms of which were ſo *Undu----l and Unman--ly,* that had ſhe not been a Queen of unuſual Candor and Goodneſs, ſhe would have Treated them as they deſerv'd, for they upbraided her with their Freedom and Readineſs in granting her Supplies, and therefore as good as told her they expected ſhe ſhould do as they deſir'd.

Theſe People that knew the Supplies given, were from *neceffity, Legal,* and for their *own Defence,* while the granting their Requeſt, muſt have been *Illegal, Arbi-*

Arbitrary, a *Difpenfing* with the Laws, and *denying Juftice* to her Subjects, *the very thing they ruin'd her Father for*, were juftly provok'd to fee their good Queen fo barbaroufly Treated.

The Queen full of Goodnefs and Calmnefs, gave them a gentle kind Anfwer, but told them fhe muft be careful to Act with due Regard to the Laws, and could not interrupt the courfe of Judicial Proceedings; and at the fame time granted the Writ, having firft confulted with her Council, and receiv'd the Opinion of all the Judges, that it was not only Safe, but Juft and Reafonable, and a Right to her People which fhe could not deny.

This Proceeding gall'd the Feathers to the quick, and finding the *Grandees* refolv'd to proceed Judicially upon the faid *Writ of Follies*, which if they did, the Prifoners would be deliver'd and the Follies fixt upon the Feathers, they fent their Pourfuivants took them out of the Common Prifon, and convey'd them feparately and privately into Prifons of their own.

This

This rafh and unprecedented Proceedings, pufht them farther into a Labrinth, from whence it was impoffible they could ever find their way out, but with infinite Lofs to their Reputation, like a Sheep in a thick Wood, that at every Briar pulls fome of the Wool from her Back, till fhe comes out in a moft fcandalous Pickle of Nakednefs and Scratches.

The *Grandees* immediately publifht fix Articles in Vindication of the Peoples Right, againft the affum'd Priviledges of the *Feathers*, the Abftract of which is as follows.

1. That the *Feathers* had no Right to Claim, or make any new Priviledges for themfelves, other than they had before.

2. That every Freeman of the Moon had a Right to repel Injury with Law.

3. That Imprifoning the 5 Countrymen by the *Feathers*, was affuming a new Priviledge they had no Right to, and a fubjecting the Subjects Right to their Arbitrary Votes.

4. That

4. That a *Writ of Deliverance*, or re-
moving the Body, is the legal Right of
every Subject in the Moon, in order to
his Liberty, in case of Imprisonment.

5. That to punish any Person for af-
sifting the Subject, in procuring or pro-
secuting the said *Writ of Deliverance*, is
a breach of the Laws, and a thing of
dangerous Consequence.

6. That a *Writ of Follies* is not a Grace,
but a Right, and ought not to be deny'd
to the Subject.

These Resolves struck the languish-
ing Reputation of the *Feathers* with
the dead Palsie, and they began to stink
in the Nostrils of all the Nations in the
Moon.

But besides. this, they had one strange
effect, which was a prodigious disap-
pointment to the Men of the *Feather*.

I had observ'd before, that there was
to be a new Set of *Feathers*, provided
in order to Building another *Consolidator*, according to a late Law for a new
Engine

Engine every three Years. Now feveral of thefe Men of the *Feather*, who
thought their *Feathers* capable of ferving again, had made great Intereft, and
been at great Coft to have their old
Feathers chofen again, but the People
had entertain'd fuch fcoundrel Opinions
of thefe Proceedings, fuch as Tacking,
Confolidating, Imprifoning Electors, Impeaching without Tryal, *Writs of
Follies* and the like, that if any one was
known to be concern'd in any of thefe
things, no Body would Vote for him.

The Gentlemen were fo mortify'd at
this, that even the hotteft High-Church
Solunarian of them all, if he put in any
where to be re-chofen, the firft thing he
had to do, was to affure the People he
was no Tacker, none of the 134, and a
vaft deal of difficulty they had to Purge
themfelves of this bleffed Action, which
they us'd to value themfelves on before,
as their Glory and Merit.

Thus they grew afham'd of it as a
Crime, got Men to go about to vouch
for them to the Country People, that
they were no Tackers, nay, one of them
to clear himfelf loudly forfwore it, and
tak-

taking a Glafs of Wine wifht it might never pafs thro' him, if he was a Tacker, tho' all Men fufpected him to be of that Number too, he having been one of the forwardeft that way on all Occafions, of any Perfon among the *South Folk of the Moon.*

In like manner, one of the *Feathers* for the *middle Province* of the Country, who us'd to think it his Honour to be for the qualifying Law, feeing which way the humour of the Country ran, took as much Pains now to tell the People he was no Tacker, as he did before, to promife them that he would do his utmoft to have the *Crolians* reduc'd, and that Bill to pafs, the Reafon of which was plain, that he faw if it fhould be known he was a Tacker, he fhould never have his *Feather* return'd to be put into the *Confolidator.*

The Heats and Feuds that the *Feathers* and the *Grandees* were now run into, began to make the latter very uneafie, and they fent to the *Grandees* to haften them, and put them in mind of paffing fome Laws they had fent up to them for raifing Mony, and which lay before

fore them, knowing that as foon as thofe Laws were paft, the Queen would break 'em up, and they being very willing to be gone, before thefe things came too far upon the Stage, urg'd them to difpatch.

But the *Grandees* refolving to go thoro' with the Matter, fent to them to come to a Treaty on the foot of the fix Articles, and to bring any Reafons they could, to prove the Power they had to Act as they had done with the Countrymen, and with the Lawyers they had put in Prifon for affifting them.

The *Feathers* were very backward and ftiff about this Conference, or Treaty, 'till at laft the *Grandees* having fufficiently expos'd them to all the Nation, the Bills were paft, the *Grandees* caus'd the particulars to be Printed, and a Reprefentation of their Proceedings, and the *Feathers* foul Dealings to the Queen of the Country, and fo her Majefty fent them Home.

But if they were afham'd of being call'd Tackers before, they were doubly mortify'd at this now, nay the Country refent-
ed

ed it fo exceedingly, that fome of them
began to confider whether they fhould
venture to go Home or no; Printed Lifts
of their Names were Publifh'd, tho' we
do not fay they were true Lifts, for it
was a hard thing to know which were
true Lifts, and which were not, nor indeed could a true Lift be made, no Man
being able to retain the exact Account of
who were the Men in his Memory.

For as there were 134 Tackers, fo
there were 141 of thefe, who by a Name
of Diftinction, were call'd *Lebufyraneim*,
in *Englifh Ailesbury-men*.

The People were fo exafperated a-
gainft thefe, that they exprefs'd their
Refentment upon all Occafions, and leaft
the Queen fhould think that the Nation
approv'd the Proceedings, they drew
up a Reprefentation or Complaint, full of
moft dutiful Expreffions to their Queen,
and full of Refentment againft the *Feathers*, the Copy of which being hand-
ed about the Moon the laft time I was
there, I fhall take the Pains to put it
into *Englifh* in the beft manner I can,
keeping as near the Original as poffible.

An

If any Man shall now wickedly suggest, that this Relation has any retrospect to the Affairs of *England*, the Author declares them malitious Misconstruers of his honest Relation of Matters from this remote Country, and offers his positive Oath for their Satisfaction, that the very last Journy he made into those Lunar Regions, this Matter was upon the Stage, of which, if this Treatise was not so near its conclusion, the Reader might expect a more particular Account.

If there is any Analogy or Similitude between the Transactions of either World, he cannot account for that, 'tis application makes the Ass.

And yet sometimes he has thought, as some People Fable of the Platonick Year, that after such a certain Revolution of Time, all Things are Transacted over again, and the same People live again, are the same Fools, Knaves, Philosophers and Mad-men they were before, tho' without any Knowledge of, or Retrospect to what they acted before; so why should it be impossible, that as the

Z   Moon

Moon and this World are noted before to be Twins and Sifters, equal in Motion and in Influence, and perhaps in Qualities, the fame fecret Power fhould fo act them, as that *like* Actions and Circumftances fhould happen in all Parts of both Worlds at the fame time.

I leave this Thought to the improvement of our Royal Learned Societies of the *Anticacofanums*, *Oppofotians*, *Periodicarians*, *Antepredeftinarians*, Univerfal *Soulians*, and fuch like unfathomable People, who, without queftion, upon mature Enquiry will find out the Truth of this Matter.

But if any one fhall fcruple the Matter of Fact as I have here related it, I freely give him leave to do as I did, and go up to the Moon for a Demonftration ; and if upon his return he does not give ample Teftimony to the Cafe in every part of it, as here related, I am content to pafs for the Contriver of it my felf, and be punifh'd as the Law fhall fay I deferve.

Nor

Nor was this all, the publick Matters in which this Nation of *Solunarians* took wrong Measures, for about this time, the Misunderstandings between the Southern and Northern Men began again, and the *Solunarians* made several Laws, as they call'd them, to secure themselves against the Dangers they pretended might accrue from the new Measures the *Nolunarians* had taken; but so unhappily were they blinded by the mong themselves, and by-set by Opinion and Interest, that every Law they made, or so much as attempted to make, was really to the Advantage, and to the Interest of the Northern-Men, and to their own loss; so Ignorantly and Weak-headed was these *High Solunarian* Church-Men in the true Interest of their Country, led by their implacable Malice at *Crolianism*, which as is before noted, was the Establisht Religion of that Country.

But as this Matter was but Transacting when I took the other Remarks, and that I did not obtain a full Understanding of it, 'till my second Voyage, I refer it to a more full Relation of my far-

Z 2   ther

ther Travels that way, when I shall not fail to give a clear State of the Debate of the two Kingdoms, in which the Southern Men had the least Reason, and the worst Success that ever they had in any Affair of that Nature for many Years before.

It was always my Opinion in Affairs *on this side the Moon,* that tho' sometimes a foolish Bolt may hit the Point, and a random Shot kill the Enemy, yet that generally Discretion and Prudence of Mannagement, had the Advantage, and met with a proportion'd Success, and things were, or were not happy, in their Conclusion as they were, more or less wisely Contriv'd and Directed.

And tho' it may not be allow'd to be so here, yet I found it more constantly so there, Effects were true to their Causes, and confusion of Councils never fail'd *in the Moon* to be follow'd by distracted and destructive Consequences.

This appear'd more eminently in the Dispute between these two Lunar Nations we are speaking of ; never were
People

People in the Moon, *whatever they might be in other Places*, so divided in their Opinions about a matter of such Consequence. Some were ʃfor declaring War immediately upon the Northern Men, tho' they cou'd show no Reason at all why, only becauʃe they would not do as they would have 'em ; *a parcel of poor Scoundrel, Scabby Rogues*, they ought to be made ʃubmit, *what !* won't they declare the ʃame King as we do ! *hang them Rogues ! a pack of Crolian Preʃtarian Devils*, we muʃt make them do it, *down with them the ʃhorteʃt Way*, declare War immediately, and *down with them.* ------ Nay ʃome were for falling on them directly, without the formality of declaring War.

Others, more afraid than hurt, cry'd out Invaʃions, Depredation, Fire and Sword, the Northern Men would be upon them immediately, and propos'd to Fortify their Frontiers, and file off their Forces to the Borders ; nay, ʃo apprehenʃive did thoʃe Men of Prudence pretend to be, that they order'd Towns to be Fortify'd 100 *Mile off of the Place*, when all this while the poor Northern

Men

Men did nothing but tell them, that unlefs they would come to Terms, they would not have the fame King as they, and then took fome Meafures to let them fee they did not purpofe to be forc'd to it.

Another fort of Wifer Men than thefe, propos'd to Unite with them, hear their Reafons, and do them Right. Thefe indeed were the only Men that were in the right Method of concluding this unhappy Broil, and for that Reafon, were the moft unlikely to fucceed.

But the Wildeft Notion of all, was, when fome of the *Grandees* made a grave Addrefs to the Queen of the Country, to defire the Northern Men to fettle Matters firft, and to tell them, that when that was done, *they fhould fee what thefe would do for them.* This was a home Stroke, if it had but hit, and the Misfortune only lay in this, *That the Northern Men were not Fools enough;* the clearnefs of the Air in thofe cold Climates generally clearing the Head fo early, that thofe People fee much farther into a Mill-ftone, than *any Blind Man*

*Man in all the Southern Nations of the
Moon.*

There was an another unhappinefs in
this Cafe, which made the Matter yet
more confus'd, and that was, that the
Souldiers had generally no guft to this
War.--- This was an odd Cafe; for thofe
fort of Gentlemen, efpecially *in the
World in the Moon,* don't ufe to enquire
into the Juftice of the Cafe they Fight
for, but they reckon 'tis their Bufinefs
to go where they are fent, and kill any
Body they are order'd to kill, leaving
their Governors to anfwer for the Juftice of it; but there was another Reafon
to be given why *the Men of the Sword*
were fo averfe, and always talk't cold-
ly of the fighting Part, and tho' the
Northern Men call'd it fear, yet I cannot joyn with them in that, for *to fear*
requires Thinking; and fome of our *Solunarians* are abfolutely protected from
the firft, becaufe they never meddle
with the laft, *except when they come to the
Engine,* and therefore 'tis plain it could
not proceed from Fear.

It

It has puzzl'd the moſt diſcerning Heads of the Age, to give a Reaſon from whence this Averſion proceeded, and various Judgments have been given of it.

The *Nolunarians* jeſted with them, and when they talk't of Fighting, bad them look back into Hiſtory, and examine what they ever made of a *Nolunarian War*, and whether they had not been often well beaten, and ſent ſhort home, bid them have a care *of catching a Tartar*, as we call it, and always made themſelves merry with it.

They banter'd the *Solunarians* too, about the Fears and Terrors they were under, from their Arming themſelves, and putting themſelves in a poſture of Defence,-----When it was eaſy to ſee by the nature of the thing, that their Deſign was *not a War, but a Union* upon juſt Conditions, that it was a plain Token that they deſign'd either to put ſome affront upon *the Nolunarians*, to deny them ſome juſt Claims, or to impoſe ſomething very Provoking upon them more than they had yet done, that
they

they were fo exceeding fearful of an Invafion from them.

Tho' thefe were fufficient to pafs for
Reafons in other Cafes, yet it could not
be fo here, but I faw there mutt be fomething elfe in it. As I was thus wondering
at this unufual backwardnefs of the Souldiers, I enquir'd a little farther into the
meaning of it, and quickly found the Reafon was plain, *there was nothing to be got
by it*, that People were *Brave*, *Defperate*
and *Poor*, the Country *Barren*, Moun-
tainous and *Empty*, fo that in fhort there
would be nothing but Blows, and *Souldiers Fellows* to be had, and I always obferv'd that Souldiers never care to be
knockt on the Head, and get nothing by
the Bargain.

In fhort, I faw plainly the Reafons
that prompted the *Solunarians* to Infult
their Neighbours of the North, were
more deriv'd from the regret at their
Eftablifhing *Crolianifm*, than at any
real Caufes they had given, or indeed
were in a condition to give them.

Thefe, and abundance more particular

lar Obfervations I made, but as I left
the thing ftill in agitation, and unde-
termin'd, I fhall refer it to another Voyage which I purpofe to make thither,
and at my return, may perhaps fet that
Cafe in a clearer Light than our Sight
can yet bear to look at it in.

If in my fecond Voyage I fhould undeceive People in the Notions they entertain'd of thofe Northern People, and
convince them that the *Solunarians*
were really the Aggreffors, and had put
great hardfhips upon them, I might
poffibly do a Work, that if it met with
Encouragement, might bring the *Solunarians* to do them Juftice, and that
would fet all to Rights, the two Nations
might eafily become one, and Unite for
ever, or at leaft become Friends, and
give mutual Affiftance to each other;
and I cannot but own fuch an Agreement
would make them both very formida-
ble, but this I refer to another time. -----

At the fame time I cannot leave it without a Remark that this Jealoufy between
the two Nations, may perhaps in future A-
ges be neceffary to be maintain'd, in order
to

to find fome better Reafons for *Fortifi-cations*, *Standing Armies*, *Guards* and *Garifons* than could be given in the Reign of the great Prince I fpeak of, the Queen's Predeceffor, tho' his was againft a Forreign infulting Enemy.

But the Temper of the *Solunarian High Party* was always fuch, that they would with much more eafe give thanks for a Standing Army againft the *Nolunarians and Crolians*, than agree to one Legion againft the *Abrogratzians* and *Galluna-rians*.

But of thefe Things I am alfo promis'd a more particular Account upon my Journy into that Country.

I cannot however conclude this Matter, without giving fome Account of my private Obfervations, upon what was farther to be feen in this Country.

And had not my Remarks on their State Matters taken up more of my Thoughts than I expected, I might have entred a little upon their other Affairs, fuch as their *Companies*, their *Commerce*,

their

their *Publick Offices*, their *Stock-Jobbers*,
their *Temper*, their *Converfation*, their
Women, their *Stages*, *Univerfities*, their
Courtiers, their *Clergy*, and the Characters of *the feverals* under all thefe Denominations, but thefe muft be referr'd
to time, and my more perfect Obfervations.

But I cannot omit, that tho' I have
very little Knowledge of Books, and
had obtain'd lefs upon their Language,
yet I could not but be very inquifitive
after their Libraries and Men of Letters.

Among their Libraries I found not
abundance of their own Books, their
Learning having fo much of . Demonftration, and being very Hieroglyphical, but I found to my great Admi-
ration vaft quantities of Tranflated
Books out. of all Languages of our
World.

As I thought my felf one of the firft,
at leaft of our Nation, that ever came
thus far; it was, you may be fure no fmall
furprize to me, to find all the moft valluable

luable parts of Modern Learning, efpecially of Politicks, Tranflated from
our Tongue, into the Lunar Dialect,
and ftor'd up in their Libraries with the
Remarks, Notes and Obfervations of
the Learned Men of that Climate upon
the Subject.

Here, among a vaft croud of *French*
Authors condemn'd in this polite World
for trifling, came a huge Volume containing, *Les Oevres de fcavans*, which
has 19 fmall Bells painted upon the
Book of feveral difproportion'd fizes.

I enquir'd the meaning of that Hiero-
glyphick, which the Mafter of the Books
told me, was to fignify that the fubftance was all Jingle and Noife, and
that of 30 Volumes which that one
Book contains, 29 of them have neither
Subftance, Mufick, Harmony nor value
in them.

The Hiftory of the Fulfoms, or a Collection of 300 fine Speeches made in
the *French* Accademy at *Paris*, and 1500
gay Flourifhes out of Monfieur *Boileau*,
all in Praife of the invincible Monarch
of *France*.   The

The Duke of *Bavaria*'s Manifefto, fhewing the Right of making War againft our Sovereigns, from whence the People of that Lunar World have noted that the fame Reafons which made it lawful to him to attempt the Imperial Power, entitle him to lofe his own, *viz.* Conqueft, and the longeft Sword.

Jack a both Sides, or a Dialogue between *Pafquin* and *Marforio*, upon the Subjeƈt Matter of the Pope's fincerity in Cafe of the War in *Italy.* Written by a Citizen of *Ferrara.* One fide arguing upon the occafion of the Pope's General wheedling the Imperialifts to quit that Country. The other bantering Imperial Policy, or the *Germains* pretending they were Trickt out of *Italy*, when they could ftay there no longer.

Lewis the Invincible, by Monfieur *Boileau.* A Poem, on the Glory of his moft Chriftian Majefties Arms at *Hochftedt*, and *Verue.*

All thefe Tranflations have innumerable Hyerogliphical Notes, and Emblems painted on them, which pafs as
Com-

Comments, and are readily underftood in that Climate. For Example, on the Vol. of Dialogues are two Cardinals wafhing the Pope's Hands under a Cloud that often befpatters them with Blood, fignifying that in fpight of all his Pretenfions he has a Hand in the Broils of *Italy*. And before him the Sun fetting in a Cloud, and a Blind Baliad-Singer making Sonnets upon the brightnefs of its Luftre.

The three Kings of *Brentford*, being fome Hiftorical Obfervations on three mighty Monarchs in our World, whofe Heroick Actions may be the Subject of future Ages, being like to do little in this, the King of *England*, King of *Poland*, and King of *Spain*. Thefe are defcrib'd by a Figure, reprefenting a Caftle in the Air, and three Knights pointing at it, but they *could not catch*.

I omit abundance of very excellent pieces, becaufe remote, as three great Volumes of *European* Mifteries, among the vaft varieties of which, and very entertaining, I obferv'd but a few, fuch as thefe:

1. Why

1. Why Prince *Ragotski* will make no Peace with the Emperor.--- But more particularly why the Emperor won't make Peace with him.

2. Where the Policy of the King of *Sweden* lies, to perfue the King of *Poland*, and let the *Mufcovites* ravage and deftroy his own Subjects.

3. What the Duke of *Bavaria* propos'd to himfelf in declaring for *France*.

4. Why the Proteftants of the Confederacy never reliev'd the *Camifars*.

5. Why there are no Cowards found in the *Englifh* Service, but among their Sea Captains.

6. Why the King of *Portugal* did not take *Madrid*, why the *Englifh* did not take *Cadiz*, and why the *Spaniards* did not take *Gibraltar*, viz. becaufe the firft were Fools, the fecond Knaves, and the laft *Spaniards*.

7. What became of all the Silver taken at *Vigo*.   8. Who

8. Who will be the next King of *Scotland.*

9. If *England* fhould ever want a King, who would think it worth while to accept of it.

10. What fpecifick difference can be produc'd between a Knave, a Coward, and a Traytor.

Abundance of thefe Myfteries are Hieroglyphically defcrib'd in this ample Collection, and without doubt our great Collection of Annals, and Hiftorical Obfervations, particularly the Learned Mr. *Walker,*would make great Improvements there.

But to come nearer home, *There,* to *my great Amafement,* I found feveral new Tracts out of our own Language, which I could hardly have imagin'd it poffible fhould have reacht fo far.

As firft, fundry Tranfactions of our Royal Society about Winds, and a valuable Defertation of Dr. *B* . . . . .'s about Wind in the Brain.

A Difcourfe of Poifons, by the Learned Dr. *M* ..... with *Lunar* Notes upon
it, wherein it appears that Dr. *C* .... *d*
had more Poifon in his Tongue, than
all the Adders the Moon have in their
Teeth.

Nec Non, or Lawyers *Latin* turn'd
into *Lunar Burlefque*. The Hyerogli-
phick was the *Queens Mony toft in a
Blanket*, Dedicated to the Attorney
General, and five falfe *Latin* Councellors.

Mandamus, as it was Acted at *Abb* ...
ton Affizes, by Mr. So....r General,
where the Qu..n had her own So...r
againft her for a bad Caufe, and never a
Counfel for her in a good one.

Lunar Reflections, being a Lift of a-
bout 2000 ridiculous Errors in Hiftory,
palpable Falfities, and fcandalous Omiffi-
ons in Mr. *Collier's* Geographical Diction-
ary; with a fubfequent Enquiry by way
of Appendix, into which are his own,
and which he has ignorantly deduc'd
from ancient Authors.

Affaf-

Affaſſination and Killing of Kings,
prov'd to be a Church of *England* Doctrin ; humbly Dedicated to the Prince
of *Wales,* by Mr. *Collier* and Mr. *Snat* ;
wherein their Abſolving Sir *John Friend*
and Sir *William Parkins* without Repentance, and while they both own'd and
juſtify'd the Fact, is Vindicated and De-
fended.

Les Bagatelles, or *Brom* . . *ys* Travels
into *Italy,* a choice Book, and by great
Accident pieſerv'd from the malitious
Deſign of the Author, who diligently
Bought up the whole Impreſſion , for
fear they ſhould be ſeen, as a thing of
which this ungrateful Age was not
worthy.

Killing no Murther, being an Account
of the ſevere Juſtice deſign'd to be in-
flicted on the barbarous Murtherers of
the honeſt Conſtable at *Bow,* but unhappily prevented by my Lord *N* . . . . . *m*
being turn'd out of his Office.

De modo Belli, or an Account of the
beſt Method of making Conqueſts and
Invaſion *a la Mode de Port St. Mary,* 3

Vo-

Volumes in 8o. Dedicated to Sir *Hen. Bell...s.*

King *Charles* the firſt prov'd a T...t. By *Edward* Earl of *Clarendon,* 3 Vol. in Fol. Dedicated to the Univerſity of *Ox-ford.*

The Bawdy Poets, or new and accurate Editions of *Catullus, Propertius,* and *Tibullus,* being the Maiden-head of the new Printing Preſs at *Cambridge,* Dedicated by the Editor Mr. *Ann...y* to the Univerſity, and in conſideration of which, and ſome Diſorders near *Ca-ſterton,* the Univerſity thought him fit to repreſent them in P......t.

Alms no Charity, or the Skeleton of Sir *Humphry Mackworth's* Bill for relief of the Poor : Being an excellent new Contrivance to find Employment for all the Poor in the Nation, *viz.* By ſetting them at Work, to make all the reſt of the People as Poor as themſelves.

Synodicum Superlativum, being ſixteen large Volumes of the vigorous Proceedings

ceedings of the *Englijh* Convocation, digefted *into Years*, one Volume to every Year. -- Wherein are feveral large Lifts of the Heretical, Atheiftical, Deiftical and other pernitious Errors which have been Condemn'd in that Venerable Affembly, the various Services done, and weighty Matters difpatcht, for the Honour of the *Englijh* Church, for fixteen Years laft paft, with their formal Proceedings againft *Afgil*, *Coward*, *Toland* and others, for reviving old Antiquated Errors in Doctrine, and Publifhing them to the World as their own.

New Worlds in Trade, being a vaft Collection out of the Journals of the Proceedings of the Right Honourable the *Commiffioners of Trade*, with feveral Eminent Improvements in *general Negoce*, vaft Schemes of Bufinefs, and new Difcoveries of Settlements and Correfpondences in Forreign Parts, for the Honour and Advantage of the *Englijh* Merchants, being 12 Volumes in Fol. and very fcarce and valluable Books.

Legal

Legal Rebellion, or an Argument proving that all forts of Infurrections of Subjects againft their Princes, are lawful, and to be fupported whenever they fuit with our Occafions, made good from the Practice of *France* with the *Hungarians*, the *Englifh* with the *Cami-fars*, the *Swede* with the *Poles*, the Emperor with the Subjects of *Naples*, and all the Princes of the World as they find occafion, a large Volume in Folio, with a Poem upon the Sacred Right of King-ly Power.

Ignis Fatuus, or the Occafional Bill in Minature, a Farce, as it was acted by his Excellency the Lord Gr... *il's* Ser-vants in *Carolina.*

Running away the fhorteft way to Victory, being a large Differtation, fhew-ing to fave the Queens Ships, is the beft way to beat the *French.*

The Tookites, a Poem upon the 134.

A

A new Tract upon Trade, being a
Demonstration that to be always putting the People upon customary Mourning, and wearing Black upon every
State Occasion, is an excellent Encouragement to Trade, and a means to employ the Poor.

City Gratitude, being a Poem on the
Statue erected by the Court of Alder-
men at the upper end of *Cheapside*, to
the Immortal Memory of King *William*.

There were many more Tracts to be
found in this place ; but these may suf-
fice for a Specimen, and to excite all
Men that would encrease their Under-
standings in humane Mysteries, to take
a Voyage to this enlightned Country. Where their Memories, thinking Faculties and Penetration, will no question
be so Tackt and Consolidated, that
when they return, they all Write Memoirs of the Place, and communicate
to their Country the Advantages they
have

have reapt by their Voyage, according to the laudable Example of their

Moſt Humble Servant,

The Man in the Moon.

F I N I S.

Juſt Publiſh'd,

THE *Double Welcome:* A Poem, to the Duke of *Marlborough,* by the Author of the *True-born Engliſh Man.* Sold by *Ben. Bragg* in *Ave Mary-Lane.*

In a Day or two will be Publiſh'd,

The Experiment, or the ſhorteſt way with the Diſſenters exemplify'd ; being the Caſe of Mr. *Abraham Gill,* a Diſſenting Miniſter in the Iſle of *Ely :* And a full Account of his being ſent for a Soldier by Mr. *Fern* an Eccleſiaſtical Juſtice of Peace, and other Conſpirators; to the Eternal Honour of the Temper and Moderation of High Church-Principles.